All I Want For Christmas

Gina Johnson ~ Stacie Lee ~ Keleigh Hadley ~ Sonia
Johnston ~ Princess F.L. Gooden ~ Patricia Woodside ~
Jamantha Williams Watson ~ Jeida K. Storey ~ Cryssy
Dee ~ Candy Jackson ~ Yvette Danielle ~ A. Rozelle ~
KP Holley ~ Terri Johnson ~ Sonya Visor ~ Tomeka
Farley Daugherty ~ Joyce A. Brown ~ Dwon D. Moss ~
Venita Alderman Sadler

BROWN GIRLS BOOKS

Houston, Texas * Washington, D.C. * Raleigh/Durham, NC

Letter from the Publishers

Dear Reader,

Brown Girls Books is excited to present *All I Want For Christmas,* a compilation of short stories written by nineteen talented authors who walk you through nineteen different reasons to celebrate the reason for the season.

Love, sacrifice, suffering, death, and birth are just a few of the themes that unfold through the pages of *All I Want For Christmas*, but the one consistent desire is peace.

As our country changes guard and our climate changes, Brown Girls Books will remain vigilant in our continued effort to afford our authors an unabridged voice of freedom of expression. *All I Want For Christmas* is a complete characterization of what was, what is, and what could be for many of these authors and many of you. We pray the future is bright and this book is a shining light.

Enjoy this awesome collection of short stories written from the heart!

ReShonda Tate Billingsley & Victoria Christopher Murray
Brown Girls Books

Table of Contents

My Merry Christmas
By Gina Johnson

This is the story of how I killed my entire family on Christmas. I kid. This is actually the story of how I finally got what I had been needing and wanting for Christmas, and it came at just the right time. What is it that I wanted, you ask? A Christmas for me. Now before you accuse me of sounding selfish, let me explain. I'm a people pleaser and I have been for as long as I can remember. Every year I go above and beyond assuring that everyone else has their merry Christmas, but this year I finally found my voice and had *my* merry Christmas.

Now I've heard the phrase that God never sleeps or never slumbers, but I'm pretty sure that dealing with my mother made God take naps on the regular. Mama had that effect on people. My father took regular naps and I'm sure it's because her regular panicking and drama tired him beyond measure. As for me, I had purchased a special flask that I kept filled to the brim with my drink of choice to help me get through visits with my mother. Or conversations with my mother. Or even thoughts of my mother. The woman was a walking anxiety attack and I couldn't deal.

I looked at the caller id and cringed. "Yes, Mama," I answered.

"Zaundra!" my mother hollered.

"Mama, why are you—"

"Zaundra, the Lord woke me up this morning and told me to call you! Are you listening, Zaundra? Are you listening because God is speaking and I just had to call you!"

I sat up in my queen sized bed and reached for my flask on the nightstand. I knew it was too early to be drinking, but this was an emergency. I took a swig and responded, "I'm listening, Mama. What is it?"

"Zaundra! Are you listening? Zaundra!"

Playing kickball barefoot with a brick, running in the middle of the Dan Ryan Expressway, or playing fetch with a saber-toothed tiger. Those were just a few of the activities that I would've rather been involved in instead of talking to my mother at that moment. Whenever God "spoke" to her, it got real, and there wasn't enough liquor in my flask to deal with it. Heck, there wasn't enough liquor on the earth for me to deal with it.

"I'm listening, Mama. What did God say this time?"

"It's time for you to get married, Zaundra!"

Lord Help. I need to leave the earth.

"Did you hear me, Zaundra? It's time! Last night I had a dream about you, and when I woke up I heard the Lord tell me to call you and tell you about it!"

I got out of the bed and put on my plush leopard print slippers. I walked from my bedroom to the kitchen with my phone in one hand and my flask in the other.

"Tell me about the dream, Mama. I'm listening."

Mama cleared her throat so loud that I jumped. "There was this little brown bunny rabbit in a huge field, and she was being chased! You want to know what she was being chased by?"

"No, but that won't stop you from telling me."

"Carrots! Carrots, Zaundra!"

Silence.

"Don't you see what the Lord was saying?" Mama yelled.

More silence.

"Zaundra! Don't you see what the Lord was saying?"

"I guess I'm not as spiritual as you, Mama," I said, rolling my eyes. "Go ahead and make it plain."

I could hear the smile in my mother's voice. "Zaundra, that little brown rabbit is you, baby! She was running around in that field because she was lost. And you know what those carrots represent?"

"Mama, I have no idea."

"Sperm!"

I spit my drink all over the floor.

"Zaundra, those carrots were something that that bunny wanted, but she was afraid to get. The Lord told me that that's you! You want a man, but you're afraid to get one, so you're running from him!"

"Then maybe the carrots represent men. I mean sperm, Mama? That escalated quickly, don't you think?"

"Zaundra, you're a virgin! I know you want some sex! Those sperm are chasing you and you're afraid!"

"Mama, I'm not a virgin, but I *am* celibate, and I'm not afraid of anything. I just think that a physical relationship alters my judgment in making an intelligent decision when choosing a mate. Not to mention the fact that the Bible kind of mentions a few things about fornication."

"Zaundra, you're forty years old! Those fornication verses don't apply to you!"

"Bye, Mama."

"Don't you hang up!"

"I've got to go."

"But I need to talk to you about Christmas!"

I was just about to hang up the phone until my mother mentioned Christmas. As much as she drove me crazy, Christmas was her favorite holiday and I loved seeing her happy. All three of my mother's sisters would come to town, along with their children and grandchildren, and we'd all cram into my parent's house to eat soul food and play games. By the end of the day, I'd be ready to throw myself off of a balcony, but somehow that didn't stop me from looking forward to seeing that beautiful smile on my mother's face each year.

"What about Christmas? Have plans changed?"

Mama hesitated. "Well not entirely, but I wanted to talk to you about one of the guests."

I raised an eyebrow as Mama explained.

"See in light of my dream, I felt that I needed to act on it, ya know? I mean faith without works is dead, Zaundra."

"What did you do?"

"Mother Pearline's son is a fine man and I think he's sweet on you, Zaundra!"

"Mama, what did you do?"

"Mother Pearline told me that Percy hasn't given up on looking for a wife, so I invited him to Christmas dinner. I invited Mother Pearline, too, so she wouldn't be left out."

"You're trying to fix me up with Percy? Bye Mama. Bye!"

I hung up the phone and drank every drop left in my flask.

Chapter 2

Brian was laughing so hard that he almost choked on his chicken wings.

"Sperm chasing you? Zaundra, that is the funniest thing I've heard all week!"

Brian's six-foot-three inch frame shook with laughter. The white Polo shirt he had on seemed to make his ebony skin look even more velvety smooth than it already was. God, he was fine.

I shook that thought out of my head and said, "Brian, she was so serious, too!" I chomped on a mozzarella stick. "I love my mama, but that was crazy even for her."

Our chipper waitress appeared, asking if we wanted our lemonades refilled. She had a figure that would make even the Queen Bey green with envy and she was eyeing Brian the whole time. I couldn't wait to tease Brian when she left.

"I think our waitress wants to take a bite out of you." I laughed.

Brian pulled his locs into a ponytail and took a sip of his lemonade. "Zaundra, you play too much."

"Whatever, Brian. You should ask her out." My heart stopped beating for two seconds when it seemed like Brian was considering my advice.

We had been best friends for fifteen years, but it always made me crazy when Brian was in a relationship. Maybe I was in denial about my feelings for him, but I didn't want to risk ruining our friendship by coming clean that I was attracted to him and starting to ever-so-slightly fall for him.

"Ask her out? Nah, she's not my type. But the real question is, is Percy your type?" Brian started laughing all over again.

I didn't want to laugh, but I couldn't deny the comedy of the situation.

"I guess Percy would be my type if I was a seventy-year-old blind woman."

More laughter.

I took a quick peek at myself in my handheld mirror. Twist out was perfect, MAC Ruby Woo lipstick was perfect, and my black sweater dress fit me in all the right places.

You're just friends, remember? Stop trying to impress him.

I ignored my conscience's voice and continued laughing with my best friend.

I knew that all I wanted was to truly enjoy myself for Christmas, but I sure wouldn't have minded having Brian on the side.

Chapter 3

It was Christmas Eve and Mama was, well, being Mama.

"Bob, have you seen that box of icicle lights in the basement? Doreen is bringing Jovan and he said he'd hang my icicle lights since you wouldn't do it!"

"Helen, I'm too darn old to be outside risking my life to hang some darn lights!"

"Bob, we are in our early seventies! We aren't that old, you're just that lazy! Now will you please bring those icicle lights up from the basement? I don't want to have to be fishing for them when Jovan gets here!"

I sat at the Oakwood table in my parent's dining room chuckling to myself as I peeled the potatoes for the potato salad. Sometimes I wished that I had siblings, but with my parents always going back and forth, every day was as lively as fireworks.

Mama walked in the kitchen and checked the chitterlings that were cooking on the stove.

"So Zaundra…"

Uh-Oh.

The smile on my mother's face, coupled with the hesitation in her voice, assured me that some foolishness would follow.

"I talked to Percy today."

"Mama. Why?"

"Because onions give Mother Pearline gas, and Percy wanted to make sure that we made a small portion of food with no onions for his mother. Isn't that nice? He's looking out for his mother. Any man that will look out for his mother is a good man in my book."

"Percy isn't my type."

"Oh and that rope-haired boy is?"

"They're locs, Mama, and I've told you before. Brian and I are just friends."

"Mmm-hmm. Well I don't trust him and you know why."

"Not that again."

"Zaundra, anyone who would allow their mother to be buried in someone else's dress is someone who cannot be trusted!"

I picked up the pot of cubed potatoes and made my way toward the stove.

"Don't forget to turn the chitterlings down."

"I'm not talking about those chit'lins, Zaundra. I'm talking about what Earlene did."

When Brian's mother passed away three years ago, my mother insisted that the dress she was wearing in the casket was hers. She said that she had let Earlene wear the dress on Easter and that Earlene had never returned the dress. I couldn't understand why it bothered Mama so much. It wasn't like Earlene dressed herself for her funeral.

My tone was sarcastic. "Mama, I'm sure Brian felt really bad about the fact that you didn't approve of his mother's wardrobe selection for her funeral, but there was nothing he could do."

"If that was Percy, he would've made sure the dress was returned to me."

"Helen, quit talking about that poor woman and that Easter dress!" Daddy walked into the kitchen holding a box of Christmas lights. He walked up to me and gave me a kiss on the cheek.

"How ya doing, babygirl?" he said with a wink.

"I'm doing fine, Daddy."

"And what is Santa bringing you for Christmas?" Daddy chuckled.

"He needs to bring her a man!" Mama hollered.

"And he needs to bring you some business, so you can mind it!" Daddy clapped back.

I was laughing so hard, I snorted. My parents really needed their own reality show. But my laughter came to a screeching halt at the sound of something exploding. Turns out Mama had turned the chitterlings up instead of down.

Mama and Daddy argued a lot, but their love always shined during moments of crisis. I looked up to see them holding hands while scurrying out of the kitchen.

Mama kept yelling, "Hit the deck!"

I joined them in their frantic exit, but not before I got hit by the flying debris of burnt chitterlings, and for the record, that's the most putrid odor on earth.

Chapter 4

Four hours later and I couldn't get the smell of burnt chitterlings out of my nostrils. Mama was so upset, she cried. Daddy and I worked tirelessly to help her get everything cleaned up, but there was nothing we could do to get the stench out of the air.

"We're gonna have to have Christmas at your place, Zaundra!" Mama cried.

I could feel myself becoming lightheaded. "I'm sure we can get it smelling good in here. I'll buy some air freshener and candles and potpourri...shoot I'll even buy some incense!"

"I don't think any of that will work," Mama sobbed. "Please, Zaundra. It's gonna have to be at your place."

Where was my flask when I needed it?

Because I love my mama, I reluctantly agreed to have Christmas at my house. Even though my cousin, Nadine, would be judging me for owning anything expensive. My Aunt Iris would tell me that I needed to lose about ten pounds, and my Uncle Tommie would tell me that if I didn't get a man soon, I'd die alone. Yep, I was looking forward to hosting Christmas at my house.

I caught a whiff of myself on my way home and gagged. I needed to bathe to rid myself of the chitterling stench. I was headed to the shower when my cell phone rang.

"Hey, Brian."

"Hey, Zaundra. You home? I was gonna stop by for a minute."

"Sure. Is everything all right?"

"It is. I just really need to talk to you. It's um…urgent."

"Wow. All right. Can you give me about thirty minutes?"

"Sure. I'll see you then."

I hung up with Brian and jumped in the shower. I scrubbed my body and washed my hair like I was going to be on display at the State Fair.

Thirty minutes later, I had showered, deep conditioned my hair, and changed into a pair of yoga pants with an oversized sweatshirt from my alma mater, Alcorn State University. I swooped my hair up into a bun and put on a subtle amount of sheer lip gloss. I wanted to be cute, but not overdo it. I tried not to be nervous, but I had no idea what Brian wanted to talk about. Had he noticed that I was developing feelings for him? Maybe he wanted to take a step back in our friendship because my feelings were becoming obvious.

The doorbell rang and my stomach did a somersault into my chest. I took a deep breath and opened the door.

Brian looked amazing as usual. He had on a charcoal grey pea coat with a baggy pair of blue jeans. He stomped his black Timberland boots off on my welcome mat to rid his shoes of all of the freshly fallen snow. If this conversation didn't end well, at least I'd still have a white Christmas and that was something that I always hoped for, year after year.

Brian looked so nervous. "You mind if I have a seat?"

"Of course not," I replied, pointing to the sofa. "Go ahead."

I took a seat next to Brian and looked at him with concern in my eyes.

"Everything all right?" I asked as calmly as I knew how.

"It is," Brian said. "I just wanted to be up front with you on something." Brian took a deep breath. "Zaundra, you're one of my closest and dearest friends, but over the last couple of months my feelings for you have started to change and I just wanted…no, I just *needed* to tell you about it."

I swallowed so hard, I thought my throat would collapse.

"Zaundra, I think you're a beautiful, intelligent, and overall an amazing woman. I've been feeling this way about you for a while now, but why keep it to myself? I want to be with you. I don't want to ruin our friendship, but I know you like the back of my hand, and if I'm not mistaken, you want to be with me, too."

On the inside, I was turning cartwheels, but on the outside I just smiled and said, "You know me well, Brian."

Brian took my hands and kissed them. It was a moment that I'll always cherish. After that we talked about what we both wanted in a relationship, and reminisced about the past. When Brian left my house that night he gave me a simple kiss on my lips and I thought I'd float right up to Heaven.

Chapter 5

The next day, my house was filled to the brim with aunts, uncles, and cousins. Cousin Nadine had criticized my black art, and Aunt Iris had criticized my figure. Uncle Tommie was about to start in on me not having a man when my doorbell rang and I let Brian in. Everything came to a screeching halt, and silence filled my home as everyone watched me greet Brian with a hug and a kiss on the cheek.

"Well, looks like Zaundra finally got a man, but I need to check him out," said Uncle Tommie.

"I don't know, Zaundra. His clothes look awfully expensive," said Cousin Nadine.

"At least he's in shape," Aunt Iris said. "Now when you lose all that extra weight, the two of you will make a cute couple."

But Mama's comments were what sent me over the edge. "Zaundra, Percy is on his way! Don't you think it will be awkward when he gets here?"

"Mama, the only thing that's awkward is you trying to control my love life. Let it go. And when Percy gets here, I'll tell him the same thing."

I surprised myself by how effortlessly I had put Mama in check. I had finally found my voice and it was time to put *everyone* in their place.

Next was Nadine's turn. "Cousin Nadine, I am a hard-working woman and I will buy what I darn well please. Stop criticizing me for my expensive taste. I didn't spend all those years in law school for nothing. I earned the right to spend a pretty penny on whatever I want, and if it bothers you, then you don't have to come around me anymore. Guess what? My life will go on just fine."

Aunt Iris looked amused until I started on her. "Aunt Iris, leave me alone about my figure. I look fine, all right? Could I stand to lose a few pounds? Yes. But you could stand to lose about fifty and you don't hear me going on and on about that. Now please, let me live."

"I guess she told y'all!" Uncle Tommie said, with a laugh.

"And I'm about to tell you, too, Uncle Tommie," I snapped. "I'm so sick and tired of you making me feel bad for not having a man. Choosing a mate is a serious process that I don't take lightly, and maybe if you understood that you wouldn't have so many ex-wives."

I saw Daddy in my peripheral vision, smiling. He always had my back.

I looked around the room and addressed my entire family.

"Now, I love you all with all my heart, but I will no longer allow you to say and do whatever you want around me. I'm a grown woman and you all will treat me as such. Understood?"

There was a collective hum of "Sures," "I'm sorry's," and "Dang, Zaundra!"

Just as everyone was starting to resume the Christmas festivities, there was a knock on the door. I opened it and there stood Percy. It looked like he was wearing a brand new lace front wig, and his gold tooth was glimmering. He looked me up and down like I was a chicken dinner.

"Well, hello there, Miss Lady," he said. "My apologies for not bringing Mother, but she was feeling a bit under the weather."

I turned and looked at Mama. "Mama, your guest is here."

Before I walked away, Percy said, "You shole is looking mighty fine on this here Christmas day."

"Thanks, Percy," I replied, as I took Brian's hand and walked away.

Before Mama met Percy at the door, she walked up to me, gripped my hand, and whispered in my ear, "I just want you to be happy, baby."

I gave Mama the biggest and most genuine smile. "I *am* happy, Mama. Happier than I've ever been."

As I uttered those words, Brian whispered in my ear. "Let's get out of here. Let's enjoy Christmas *your* way."

Brian and I left, and the only person I told was Daddy who couldn't stop smiling. Everyone else didn't even notice we were gone.

When we got to Brian's condo we sat in front of the warmth of his marble fireplace while enjoying a spread of prosciutto, black olives, crackers, and assorted cheeses.

Brian handed me a glass of moscato and said, "I'd like to propose a toast."

I raised my glass.

"To my beautiful Zaundra. May the rest of your Christmas and every Christmas hereafter be as merry as my heart is right now. To your merry Christmas."

I clinked my glass with Brian's and smiled. "To my merry Christmas."

I had gotten my wish and my Christmas was merry indeed.

Gina Johnson is a content editor and budding author who has been published in multiple anthologies, including the best-selling, award-winning Motherhood Diaries and The Dating Game. When she's not working on literary projects, she keeps people laughing with her hilarious Facebook page, Johnson Family Cirus, where she recounts the precocious antics of her children. She resides in Southwest Michigan with her husband of sixteen years and their four children.

Two Wise Men
By Stacie Lee

I pulled up to 32 Carmichael Way, turned the ignition off, and sat in my car staring at the house. The two-story Craftsman still bore the same mint green and white chipped paint, the same four concrete steps to the front porch, and the same white iron screen door we used to run in and out of as kids. Everything about the house was exactly the same with the exception of the array of Christmas lights aligned along the roof, the poinsettias sitting in the windowsills, and nativity scene displayed on the lawn.

Through the drawn curtains, I could already make out a few familiar faces. I could hear the music, the laughter, and the slamming of dominoes pieces all the way from my car. As joyful as the atmosphere appeared, every ounce of sense I had begged me to turn around and drive away as fast as I could. After several years away, I couldn't find my interest in this holiday reunion if I had a map and a flashlight. Still, I promised to at least make an appearance and in spite of how I felt, I was a man of my word.

With that, I sighed and reached for the door handle. A moment later, I stepped out of my car, smoothed my hands over my new Armani suit, and with a deep breath, made my way up the driveway.

I'd never known the lady of the house to lock her front door so I did what I always had and walked right in. The familiar layout of the living room down to the narrow hallway decorated with dozens of family photos filled me with nostalgia. The few cousins who were in the room paused mid-conversation upon seeing me. I nodded and kept it pushing down the hall. When I reached the dining room, again I was greeted with awkward silence. It was clear from the raised eyebrows, pursed lips, and hostile glares that I was the last person anyone expected to see. I started to turn around and leave when Meredith walked in from the kitchen.

"Oh Marcus!" she squealed. "You're here!"

She set the tray of cornbread she'd been holding onto the dining room table and spread her arms wide.

"Hey Mom, how are you?" I embraced her.

"Oh, better now that you're here. I was beginning to think you wouldn't show. Hey everyone, you remember Marcus! Don't be rude, say hello!"

Collective but monotone greetings floated through the room, none bearing an ounce of sincerity. That was fine with me. The less that was said, the better.

"Come with me into the kitchen. I'm almost finished," she said.

Grateful to get out the lion's den, I followed.

"You look good, Son. Thinner than I remember, but good." She grabbed an oven mitt and headed for the stove.

"And you look even more beautiful than I remember. Do you need any help in here?" I asked.

"Oh no, I'm fine. You just take a seat and tell me what's been going on. How have you been?" She pulled another casserole dish of cornbread from the oven.

"I'm good." I took a seat at a small, fold out table against the wall. "The label is doing well, we've signed two more artists this year, and I was promoted to head of Creative last month."

"Sounds like you've been working hard. Congratulations." she replied.

"Thank you. It took years of long hours with little pay, but things are finally starting to turn around. I'm surviving...I'm good, really." I answered.

"I see...and are you still seeing that grief counselor I emailed you about?"

"No, not anymore. Helen was a nice lady but I don't think she really knew how to handle my situation. Most of the folks in that group therapy class didn't have the same experience I did."

After a few moments of silence she asked, "Marcus, what does Psalms 30:5 say?"

I smiled and lowered my head. It was a scripture she made certain I knew just as well as I knew my own name.

"For His anger lasts only a moment, but His favor lasts a lifetime; weeping may endure for the night, but joy comes in the morning."

"That's right," she replied. "Being rich and successful is a wonderful situation to find yourself in, but as long you keep holding onto that guilt you feel about Robyn's passing, you will spend the rest of your life just surviving instead of living the way God intended...joyously."

It always amazed me how intuitive she was. I suspected most mothers, if not all of them, had the same gift, but I couldn't be too sure as my own birth mother passed away while I was still an infant. I was raised by my father in a house just one block away from where Meredith and her husband, Alan, lived with their two sons, Alan Jr., Calvin, and their only daughter, Robyn.

At eight years old, I was a rather shy kid and rarely had any real friends to call my own. I was younger than Alan Jr. and Calvin, who were both in middle school and wanted nothing to do with me. As a result, I was often left to my own devices for entertainment and companionship as my father spent seven days a week working two jobs just to keep a termite-ridden roof over our heads to make ends meet.

On a warm September day like any other, I was playing a game of marbles along the sidewalk when I first laid eyes on Robyn. Dressed in a marigold knee-length dress and bearing the warmest brown eyes I'd ever seen, she reminded me of a sunflower in the springtime, bright and beautiful.

"What are you doing?" she asked as she approached.

I swallowed, my throat suddenly drier than before.

"Shooting marbles."

She stared a moment, hands stuffed in the pockets of her dress. Twirling back and forth, she finally asked, "Can I play?"

"Girls can't play marbles."

"Why not?" She frowned.

"Because they just can't." I shrugged.

"Chicken."

Taken aback, I made eye contact with her for the first time. "What did just you call me?"

"The only reason you don't want to play with me is because you're chicken, not because I'm a girl."

"I'm not chicken!" I snapped.

She kneeled down beside me and to my surprise, pulled out a large bag of marbles.

"Prove it! If I win, you have to give me your favorite marble. If you win, I'll give you all of my marbles."

"Really?" I eyed the bulging bag beside her.

"What? Are you scared?" She smiled.

I frowned and grabbed her marbles.

"No...let's play."

Ten pitiful minutes later, I gave up my most prized cat's eye marble. She held it in her palm, flashed that megawatt smile I'd soon come to adore and asked, "Best two out of three?"

It didn't take long for us to become friends and by the time we were in high school, we had fallen madly in love. Her father didn't believe she should have boyfriends as long as she lived under his roof, so we dated in secret.

Not long after, my father lost his brief battle with leukemia. With no relatives living within close range, it wouldn't take long, only a matter of time before I would become a ward of the state. Fortunately for me, Meredith would hear none of it. My father hadn't been cold in the ground before she was moving my belongings into Alan Jr.'s bedroom a year after he'd left for Morehouse. Just like that, I not only had another roof over my head, I had another family. I'd only lived with them for three short years, but as far as I was concerned, Meredith was the only mother I'd ever known.

I let out a breath that was only audible to me and said, "I hear you."

Meredith smiled.

"Mmmhmm, I hope you do. After all, Robyn would want more for you. We all do."

"I don't know about *all*." I chuckled.

"I know it may not look that way, but we all love you just as we loved Robyn."

She walked over and gave me a quick peck on the forehead, one that made the growing lump in my throat quiver. I gave her a watery smile.

"Thanks, Mama."

Before she could respond, a loud voice boomed through the hallway and into the kitchen.

"How about we start putting some food on the table, Woman!"

Meredith whipped her head around and faced the hallway, but I didn't have to look to know who was coming. I just braced myself for the inevitable. Alan Sr. walked into the kitchen, pulled his wife of forty years into his arms, and planted a tender kiss on her lips. Meredith stepped out of the embrace, pointed toward me and said, "Look, Honey, look who's here."

The temperature in the room dropped. I cleared my throat, stood to my feet, and forced a smile.

"Merry Christmas, Alan."

"What the hell are you doing here?" he growled. "It's been years and now you decide to show your face? Was my daughter's contribution to your sorry existence not enough motivation?"

"Alan!" Meredith hissed.

"No, it's all right." I stood my ground, refusing to wither under his icy glare. "I expected this."

"As you should," Alan snarled. "I don't even know why you're here. You're certainly not welcomed."

"Alan, stop it! Marcus, you most certainly are welcome in our home. You know that."

"No, Meredith, he's not. I'll have no man grace my doorstep who had a hand in my daughter's death."

The sting of his words tightened my jaw.

"She wasn't just your daughter, Alan. She was my wife, too."

"Your wife?" he snapped. "She was just eighteen years old when you snatched her away from me! Eighteen! What could she have possibly known about being a wife! She was barely a woman!"

"That's enough, Alan!" Meredith yelled.

"Snatched her away?" I laughed. "Whose idea do you think it was to run off and elope in the first place?"

"Marcus, I said enough!" Meredith warned.

Unfortunately, I had already reached my limit. Too far gone. For years, Alan blamed me for turning his little girl against him. There was no way I was going to live with being blamed for her death, too.

"You wouldn't let her date, go out with friends, and you forced her into activities she had zero interest in. You wouldn't even let her decide which college she should attend. You all but strong-armed her into becoming the kind of woman you thought she should be instead of letting her grow into the woman she actually was. You made her a prisoner of your will in her own home. I wasn't going to make her a prisoner of her own body!"

Without warning, he suddenly stood within an inch of me and stuck his finger in my face.

"You will not stand there and tell that lie! I loved my daughter more than I loved myself. I did the best I could for her. While she was with me, she was safe and now because of you and that damned brain tumor, she's gone!"

By now, the rest of the guests had gathered in the doorway of the kitchen, silently watching the tense exchange. I looked from them back to Alan and what I saw unnerved me. Angry tears filled his eyes and the palpable rage I felt moments ago fizzled. I'd always thought of Alan as an overbearing, controlling tyrant, but as he stood there in my face, all I saw was a man in pain and deep grief...no different than me.

Pulling Robyn's life support after several months in the hospital was unequivocally the hardest decision I ever made in my life, but even that hadn't been as painful an experience as watching her deteriorate right before my eyes and being unable to do anything about it. The only comfort I ever enjoyed was the fact that I was at her side when she finally went on to Glory. Unfortunately, Alan could not say the same. I sighed and looked him in the eye.

"You're right. She was safe with you, but she was also unhappy. Life is not about how safe you can be, especially when all the safety in the world will not keep us from standing at death's door anyway. Life is about living the best way we can, whatever that may mean to each of us.

"After we eloped, that's exactly what your daughter did. She traveled to places she had only dreamed about. She did the work she always wanted to do and she spent her time the way she wanted to. After Robyn was diagnosed with brain cancer, she made it clear that she did not want or need to be saved. She wanted to be free...and now, she is."

He glared at me a few moments longer before he finally broke down, his thick tears falling like raindrops.

"My baby girl. My precious baby girl," his voice cracked.

The room fell pin drop silent, but there wasn't a dry eye anywhere. Standing at 6'4, an easy two hundred and fifty pounds, Alan Knight had always been a pillar of strength, but the man before me was just a shell of the former. In all the time I'd known him, Alan had never looked so pitiful.

It was then that an overwhelming urge came over me and I did the unthinkable. I wrapped my arms around Alan and held him tight. When he finally hugged me back, the rock hard lump in my throat exploded and the dam of tears I'd been holding onto for a year flowed.

It wasn't long before we were joined by Meredith, then another pair of arms, and another after that. Soon, the entire family was gathered in the tiny kitchen, weeping and holding one another as tightly as we ever had. For awhile, we all just stood there until the sudden scent of smoke filled the room. Meredith popped her head up and yelled, "Oh, my turkey!"

She ran over to the stove and pulled out a partially burnt turkey. I'm not sure what was so funny about a half-edible bird on the biggest holiday of the year, but as soon as I met Alan's gaze, we broke out into peals of laughter. Tears still streaming down her face, Meredith shook her head and giggled along with everyone else.

"All right everybody! Enough with the tears, it's time to eat...what little we can," she said.

With that, everyone disappeared into the dining room. I wiped my tears and started after them when Alan stopped me.

"Hold up," he said as he headed for a drawer in the corner of the kitchen. When he pulled out a large butcher knife, I held my breath. After the moment we just had, was he really going to cut me down in the middle of his wife's kitchen? He stood before me and for the first time, smiled.

"I don't know if you recall, but in this house, it's tradition to have one of our sons carve the bird after saying grace."

Before I could respond, he turned the handle of the blade toward me.

"Better late than never, right, Son?"

Tears welled up in my eyes as I gazed at the knife, took it, and looked back up at him.

"Yes, Sir."

Stacie Lee is a millennial introvert from Sacramento, CA and an old soul with a baby face. When she's not editing her first full-length novel, she is busy finding ways to please her mischievous, yet lovable two and a half year old tabby named Tigger.

A Christmas Karol
By Keleigh Hadley

Robert hoped against hope that Karol would let him spend the night this time. But she rolled off of him, and instead of wanting to cuddle, her feet hit the floor. She sauntered her 'good-god-almighty' body toward the bathroom for a shower. "See you tomorrow, Rob." She turned to blow him a kiss goodbye, swinging her perfectly messy hair over her shoulder, and dismissed him with a wave.

"Karol, wait...you never answered my question."

She paused in the bathroom doorway, allowing him to get a good look at what he was not sleeping next to that night. "Oh, right. You don't have to get me anything for Christmas." She rubbed her foot against her long, lean leg. "I mean, we aren't that type of couple anymore, right?"

"But you used to love the gifts I made for you in college."

"Love?" She rolled her eyes and laughed. "That was fine when we were broke college kids." She picked up a crystal vase from the nightstand. "As you can see, I have acquired more expensive taste, but you're still..."

"Broke?" Robert flexed his biceps. He could show off his fit physique, too. "I'm doing fine."

"Fine is a relative term, counselor..."

Robert knew he'd lost this argument already, especially when his college sweetheart began to use legal terms.

"...but you lost focus and became a public defender, instead of staying on track like me."

"On track? You're a legal surrogate for Ronald Trumpet." He threw up his hands. "Which was fine when he was just a billionaire reality TV host. But now he wants to run this country! How do you look yourself in the mirror?"

Karol's cell phone chirped. She had a special ring for anything Trumpet related. Lately, it had been ringing around the clock because he was constantly saying things that inspired people to sue him.

It was exhausting, but Karol had made more money working one of Trumpet's lawsuits than Robert made in five years. The downside of working so much was the amount of one-on-one time with Robert had been reduced to nothing.

"Watch it, Robert. Let's not start judging." She glanced at the text and grimaced, but then smiled, more billable hours for her. "We both believe that everyone deserves the right to an attorney. You defended that activist from Black Lives Matter and I didn't hound you about that."

"She was being illegally harassed-"

"I'm not doing this with you again." Karol walked over to him and placed her toned arms around his waist.

"Well, what about what I want? Did you want to know what I want for Christmas?" Robert asked.

Karol gave him a deep, long kiss that made Robert forget all about the argument.

"I know what you want, babe, don't worry." She smiled and Robert saw the young woman he fell in love with five years ago. "I don't expect you to get me anything for Christmas, my birthday or Valentine's Day. Doesn't every man want an easy, low-maintenance woman like that?" She smiled and walked back toward the bathroom. "Lock up on your way out."

Robert sighed and shook his head. "Not this man. All I want for Christmas is the old Karol back."

***

The next evening, after a long day working on one of four thousand lawsuits against her bombastic boss, Karol stopped at the security booth for the gated community where she lived. While waiting to punch in her passcode, she checked her phone. Still no message from Robert. He usually called to make up with her after one of their spats. She frowned. He'll call. He always did.

As usual, the female security guard at the gate could barely contain her jealousy and issued a bitter, "Have a good evening, Ms. Scrooge." "How many times do I have to tell you that my last name is pronounced, 'Scrow-jay,'" Karol said.

The guard smiled, but Karol took it as a smirk. She made a note to call the security company in the morning and have the uppity guard fired. In fact, she'd call the Home Owners' Association and have the entire company canned. A bleeding heart on the HOA committee had hired this all-female security company because they were Somali refugees or something. Karol shook her head. You'd think a refugee would act grateful.

As she approached her mini-mansion, Karol replayed the argument with Robert. Something he said stuck with her.

"Working for Trumpet has changed you, Karol. You were never this cold-blooded before. I don't know if I love you anymore."

Karol was so consumed with the thought that she could lose the only man who'd never betrayed her that she didn't notice the iron knocker on her door had transformed into the spectral image of her deceased father —a man who betrayed her over and over again.

"Karolezza Jean," the image said.

Karol dropped her keys and her head spun back and forth. Where was that coming from? No one called her by that back-country name. No one except…

"Oh, my gosh!" Karol stepped back from her door as her father's face came into clear view.

"Calm down, Karolezza. It's your ol' pops."

Immediately, anger replaced the fear that had shot through Karol's body. "No!" She pointed a finger at him. "You aren't really here!"

She rushed toward the door. Jacob Scrooge was not going to stand in her way again.

Once she was safely on the other side of her door, Karol caught her breath. She scanned the foyer for any signs of breaking and entering. That man had done his share of B&E in his lifetime. She reached for her cell phone, but hesitated. How could she call the police on a figment of her imagination? She took a deep breath. *Get a hold of yourself, Karol. This is the anniversary of that man's death and it always shakes you up. That's all.*

After a long bath and an extra-large glass of Chardonnay, Karol lounged on her massive bed and watched the Yule Log channel on TV… Her head nodded a bit and her eyelids were growing heavier when she heard a long, low moan. And not the good kind that she elicited from Robert. This one sounded hollow and almost painful. She switched the Yule Log channel off and brought all her security cameras on screen. Nothing. But, she could hear the moaning getting closer, and now she heard something scraping against the floor. Not her black mamba bamboo wood floors! Karol pulled a pearl-handled revolver from underneath her pillow.

As the youngest attorney on the "Trumpet Train," Karol knew the laws of the land like the back of her manicured hand. She knew she had the right to use deadly force within her own home. Karol was prepared to blow the head off whoever stepped through her double doors. She was going to shoot first and ask questions later.

"Karolezza Jean I'm coming in..."

BAM! The wood splintered around the first shot and the bullet blew a head-sized hole in her bedroom door.

"A-all right, now. As you can see, I am armed and dangerous." Karol held tightly to the gun. "If you are still alive, take this opportunity to get the hell out of my house." Karol held her breath, and after a long pause, the sight she dreaded stuck its head in the hole.

"Karolezza Jean, I'm actually here to help you get the hell out of your house."

***

"Tonight you will be visited by three spirits..."

Karol tossed and turned as the words that man spoke tormented her. "Like in the Charles Dickens novel?" Karol had asked.

"Silly girl, no. Ain't nobody got time for that," Jacob replied. "I'm just playing with you. It's just me."

Karol sat up in bed and clutched her sheets. That had to have been a bad dream. Too much Chardonnay. She was about to fling her covers back when she noticed the gaping hole in her bedroom door.

"Hey, KJ."

Karol almost jumped out of the bed. It was not a dream.

Standing in the doorway of her bathroom was her father, still eavily draped in chains.

"In life," his woeful eyes pierced her own. "My spirit never rose beyond the limits of beds of the different women I slept with! Every chain you see on me is a heart that I broke, a promise that I didn't keep, and a spirit that I shredded. Now I am doomed to wander without rest or peace, with incessant torture and remorse!"

"Why are you holding that particular chain link so close?" Karol asked.

"Because this one, my daughter, represents your broken heart."

Karol huffed in disgust. "Oh, so you care about my broken heart now?" She got out of bed. "Only because it's weighing you down. Good."

"I deserve that."

"What about Mama's heart?"

"Your mother was a good woman. Too good for me. But I can tell you this, she'd hate to see who you've become."

Karol paused and her father continued. "One thing I know for sure, KJ, if you continue on this path, making a living defending the words and deeds of a heartless man, and running from the love of a giving, good man, you will find yourself draped in heavier, more painful chains." He lifted the chain that represented Karol's heart. "And the chain that you will clutch the closest represents the purest heart that you broke."

"Robert's?"

"Bingo. Speaking of Robert. Let's see what he's up to right now."

"Are you out of your m…" But before Karol could finish her sentence, her bedroom disappeared and she found herself in Robert's shabby little law office. He was embracing a tearful gray-haired woman. A tinge of jealousy ran through Karol.

"Oh, thank you, Mr. Cratchit," the woman said. "God bless you!"

"It was my pleasure," Robert replied. "You and the other activists are doing amazing work for our community. I'm just doing my part."

"I wish more people thought the way you do. This world would be a much better place." She hugged him again and left his office.

Robert sat back down at his desk, piled high with files. He paused for a moment and then opened a side drawer. He pulled out a picture of Karol from their college years.

"That's a good man right there," Jacob said.

"I know that. That's why I'm with him."

"Are you? Because he needs more than, 'wham, bam, thank you, sir.'"

"Can you please stay out of my love life? I know Robert wants a more traditional relationship, but I'm just not ready to commit to that."

"All right, well, how about I show you a little glimpse of your future then? If you stay on this path, this is going to be your life."

Jacob whisked Karol away.

The sky was smoggy and sooty from all the smoke coming out of the factories that dotted the landscape.

Karol coughed. "Where are we?"

"This is where Robert's office used to be. They turned it into a cemetery. It turns out that death has become big business. This is Trumpet's America."

Karol couldn't believe her eyes. Off in the distance, she saw what she thought was a mountain at first, but it was rectangular and flat on top. It was a wall.

"He certainly lived up to some of his promises. He brought jobs back."

Jacob pointed to a lone man walking toward a tombstone. It was Robert but he was so thin and withdrawn, Karol barely recognized him.

"Why did you take me to a cemetery?" Karol hadn't been to one since her mother's death ten years ago.

Jacob ignored her and walked toward Robert.

Robert held a rose in his hand. He lovingly placed the rose on the dirt in front of the tombstone. "I never wanted this for you. I loved you more than you could have ever known. I'm just sorry that you never realized that you were worthy of my love."

A sense of dread wove its way down Karol's spine. She crept up behind Robert and peered around him to see the name on the tombstone.

Karoleeza Jean Scrooge
Sept. 2 1975- Dec 24 2016

Karol gasped and fell to her knees. "That's the day before Christmas! H-how did I die?"

Jacob grimaced. "You were leaving a press conference for Trumpet and one of his 'Open Carry' supporters' guns accidentally went off."

"I don't believe it."

"Yeah, and what really tears it, is Trumpet didn't even show up to your funeral."

Karol looked over at Robert who began to break down and cry.

"That man loves you, KJ. Why can't you see that?"

"What am I supposed to do? Just quit my job? I'll lose my home, my car, my security."

"You'll figure it out. I know you will."

Karol began to walk away from her tombstone. "No, this can't be my future. I don't want this."

"What do you want?" Jacob asked.

"All I want is…"

When Karol opened her eyes the next morning, she sat straight up and looked toward the door. The hole was still there. But did her father really visit her last night? And was his warning to her true? She cut the TV on. Ronald Trumpet was onscreen at a live press conference. "I could stand in the middle of the highway and shoot somebody and not lose voters…"

Karol's cell phone sprang to life. It was her boss and duty called. She was just about to press Talk, like she normally did, but she stopped herself. "What am I doing?" Karol asked herself. "That man…Pops was right. I am going to end up six feet under if I don't end this." She looked up at her ceiling. "Thank you, Pops. I know what I want now."

The phone had stopped ringing, but before she could redial the number again, it rang. Karol pressed the Talk button and said two words. "I'm fired." She hung up and tossed the phone on her bed. Her phone continued to blow up, but she ignored it. They would get the idea soon enough.

She threw on some clothes and headed out the door. Before she locked up, she sent Robert a text: **I know what you want for Christmas - me.**

Keleigh Crigler Hadley is the award-winning author of the Preacher's Kids series, Revenge Inc., What You Won't Do For Love, and has contributed to two best-selling anthologies, The Motherhood Diaries and The Dating Game. Look for her upcoming novels, The Reluctant Mistress and Believer coming soon!

Home for Christmas
By Sonia Johnston

I rolled my eyes as my husband's name splashed across the caller ID. It was the fourth time in ten minutes that he had called, but I refused to answer. What I really wanted to do was throw the phone across the bedroom and watch it break into a thousand pieces, real dramatic like they do in the movies. But I actually hated dealing with Verizon even more than I hated my husband not being home. So to save myself the inconvenience of having to buy a new phone, I turned off the ringer and slammed it face down on the nightstand.

In a huff, I walked over to the fireplace, crossed my arms, and stared down in disgust. On the floor was a makeshift recreation of our first date. Two wineglasses and Grandma's wicker basket sat on top of the afghan that we wrapped ourselves in eleven years ago.

I wanted to kick myself because even though I was mad, I still got butterflies thinking back to how we cuddled and kissed under the stars as we watched, "An Affair to Remember" at the outdoor theater. It was such a romantic night. We had an instant attraction and I knew then that he'd be the man I'd marry.

To celebrate that first kiss, we promised ourselves that the night before Christmas belonged to us. And even though I knew he had to work and even though I was tired from hosting the family dinner alone, I still held up my end of the deal. I even dressed up as Mrs. Claus—complete with thigh-high stockings and red pumps. The scene was perfect. The only thing missing was Malcolm.

I shook my head as I watched the flames, oblivious to my mood, sway along to Tamar Braxton's, "Have Yourself a Merry Little Christmas", as she chimed out from the iPad on the mantel. I listened to the lyrics and looked back down at the floor.

"Yeah, right," I said. *I ought to punt everything into the fire. But why waste good wine?*

I plopped down on the floor and took a swig of the holiday-fused sangria. Next, I closed my eyes and let the chilled taste of zinfandel and cranberries put me at ease with less fall out than a busted phone and burning baskets. I was about five deep breaths into my Zen zone when I was interrupted by more ringing.

I know I turned off that phone.

With one eye open, I glared at my iPad. My husband was calling via FaceTime. He was a determined fart. I wished he was that determined to bring his behind home. I stomped over to the iPad and swiped across the screen.

"What?" I asked as soon as his face popped up.

"I can explain," he said.

"Shove it, Malcolm," I said, rolling my eyes.

"Simone, Come on now. One of the conveyors went down. I have to get it straight before I leave. You know it has to be something big if I'm not home."

I hated Malcolm's line of work, but he loved it. He'd been a tinkerer all of his life, so the fact that he landed his dream job as a materials engineer at a semiconductor plant actually made him happier than a geek at Comic-Con.

"I think you like being at work more than you like being at home."

He raised an eyebrow. "Really, Simone?"

I knew what I said wasn't true. I just wanted to make him feel bad. "You promised."

"I know. Trust me, I don't want to be here either," he said, looking away.

"Well, how long is it going to take?" I asked, this time taking a gulp of sangria.

He didn't answer right away. I knew that meant it was going to be bad. I plopped down on the edge of the bed and braced for the blow.

"It could take all night. They're flying the part in from the Texas plant," he said, pausing. "It's got to be up and running before I can leave."

Ugh!

I flung myself backward onto the heap of pillows at the top of the bed. There was no telling when Malcolm would make it home.

It was our first Christmas in our new house. We were so excited that we planned a huge Christmas Eve dinner with both of our families. But because of Malcolm and his job, I ended up hosting it alone. I was upset, but I didn't complain. I didn't even complain when his grinch of a mother decided to invite herself to stay in our guest house for the rest of the week. Malcolm owed me big time. The least he could do was make it home for Christmas.

"I know you're disappointed."

"You got that right," I said, climbing from underneath the pillows."

He didn't even try to respond. He knew how much Christmas meant to me.

"And what about Ella and Lena?" I asked, thinking about our two daughters. "What are they going to think when Daddy's not here?"

Sighing, Malcolm took off his glasses, closed his eyes, and rubbed the bridge of his nose. It was the first time I paid attention to him long enough to see his pressures at the plant and his responsibilities as a husband and father were wearing on him.

I hated seeing him like that. Malcolm was a good man, a wonderful husband and father who took his role as provider seriously. I was mad, but it wasn't worth having him bear the cross for a busted conveyor and a witch of a mother. After all, it was Christmas. I took a deep breath, another long gulp of the sangria, and prayed for a miracle.

"Is that the sangria?" he asked.

"It is," I said, nonchalantly.

"Save some for me?"

"Nope," I said. "Your mom went to town on it. I had to steal these two glasses away. I polished mine off an hour ago. This one is yours."

"You all drank two gallons of sangria?

"It was a long night."

I decided to leave out the part of his mother making my mom so mad that Daddy had to walk over and take the sweet potato pie out of Mom's hand.

"That bad, huh?"

I nodded.

"And apparently, I can't cook," I said, thinking back to how Malcolm's mom made a big deal over the turkey being a bit dry. We had gravy. It wasn't like she was going to choke.

"Who said that?"

"You know who said it."

Malcolm looked embarrassed. "I'm sorry, baby. Did you at least get a chance to open my present?"

"No," I said. "Why would I do that? We open our presents and kiss at midnight."

"Go ahead. Just this once. It may make you feel better."

"No. I'll wait," I said, blowing a kiss through the iPad. I really didn't want to be mad anymore. Especially after the day I had. It was too exhausting. "We've broken enough promises. Let's keep one thing intact."

"I love you," he said, lowering his voice in that rich, warm baritone that made me shiver and boil at the same time. The dreamy look on his face confirmed everything he said. I felt all the stress of the day melt away like butter on a warm biscuit. I couldn't wait for him to get home so that I could show him how I felt.

"I had plans with you," I said, feeling seductive. I took the tablet and panned it across my body, stopping just below my thighs. When I looked back at his face, he was smiling like a kid at Santa's workshop.

"Keep that on until I get there."

"I cannot," I said, taking another sip of the sangria. "It disintegrates at sunrise."

He laughed. "Disintegrates at sunrise? Yea, I'm going to need you to put down the wine."

"Don't mock me," I said, burying my face into the pillows. "I'm trying to drown my sorrow."

"Whatever," he said, still smiling. "Just keep that on."

"I really can't, you know. What will the girls think? Besides, your mother would pass out if she had proof that you and I actually had relations."

"Two kids aren't proof enough?" He laughed.

"You know I'm an alien that can't possibly birth babies," I teased.

"Speaking of babies," he said, lowering his voice. "Are you ready for baby number three?"

His words rang between my ears like bells on a sled. I beamed as bright as the Christmas star leading the Magi. That's what I loved about my Malcolm. The engineer in him knew how to fix everything. Even me.

"Malcolm Junior?" I asked, toying with the name. We always wanted three kids. Our girls were six and three. Malcolm loved our girls, and he tried to get them interested in his hobbies. However, if it didn't involve glitter, castles, or Doc McStuffins, they weren't interested. Boy or girl, I knew he hoped our next child would share his passions. I was definitely down for trying.

"I like the sound of that already."

I looked back at the screen. "I love you, Malcolm Christian. And I want you to hurry home to me. To us."

"Baby, I'm doing everything I can," he said, blowing a kiss into the air.

I made like I caught his kiss with my hand and placed it next to my heart.

When the call ended, the iPad returned to Christmas music. This time, "Santa Claus is Coming to Town" rang out. Once again, I listened to the lyrics, but this time I smiled because I knew my Malcolm would be working his way home.

Comforted in his promise, I took the last swallow of wine and propped up the pillows, trying to recreate the feeling of laying on his chest. Worn out from a day of cooking, way too much sangria, and Malcolm's mother, I went right to sleep.

***

I awoke with a start. Something was bumping.

Were the girls up already? Was it Malcolm?

I glanced over at the alarm. It was almost four o'clock. It was still dark outside and the smoldering embers that glowed from the fireplace did little to add to the light. With squinted eyes, I strained to see if anyone was in the room.

I rolled to the other side of the bed to reach the lamp. When I clicked the switch, I practically fell off the bed.

"Fannie?" I yelled. It was Malcolm's mother. "What are you doing in here?"

She didn't say anything. For a second, I wondered if she was sleep walking. Then it slowly dawned on me that I still had on the lingerie.

Jesus, Joseph, and Mary! I told Malcolm she couldn't take seeing me in lingerie.

I couldn't hustle fast enough to our walk-in closet. When I reappeared, I had on a full-length robe. But, she was still standing there, with her mouth open, like she'd just seen Rudolph prancing on the roof.

I didn't know what was wrong with her, but I knew I'd had enough. She was, after all, in our bedroom. "I mean really, Fannie. We are married."

"Huh?" She shook her head and frowned like she'd just tasted a sour pickle.

Rolling my neck, I pointed toward the robe.

"Oh child, hush," she said, walking off toward the armoire. She threw open the doors to the TV. "That's the least of my worries. Have you heard from Malcolm?"

I didn't like the sound of her voice so I hurried back over to the night stand to check the phone. "He called to say he was working late, but I haven't heard from him since. Why? Is everything all right?"

She twisted her fingers together, overlapping them like she was twisting French bread. It was a nervous habit of hers. I knew because she constantly contorted her fingers like that on my wedding day. "I want you to sit down," she said.

Whoa. Fannie never had sympathy for me, not even when I get sick. "What's going on, Fannie? You're scaring me."

"My sister just called me and told me to turn on the news."

"Why?" I asked, still trying to get answers

"Just turn the damn thing on."

There were two things Fannie didn't do: Fannie didn't curse and Fannie didn't scream. She had done both. I didn't know what was on TV, but for the second time in a matter of hours, I braced myself for bad news.

As soon as the TV came on, we both stood there trying to make sense of the flashing blue lights and fire engine sirens blaring through the speakers. At the bottom of the screen, a red ticker scrolled across reading, "Breaking news: Active shooter. Two dead. Eleven hostages."

In the foreground, a reporter was being given the cue to start his coverage, but I tuned him out before he started speaking. I gasped as my eyes zeroed in on the yellow sign that glowed on top of the building in the background: SemCom International. The plant where Malcolm worked.

"Oh, my God," I screamed, covering my mouth. Fannie gasped too and gripped my shoulders as a crutch to steady herself.

"No, no, no," I said, prying myself from her grip to race back to my phone. I tried his cell. No answer. I tried his desk number and floor number, getting more panicked by empty rings. By the time I tried FaceTime, I was near hysterics.

"He's not answering," I said and broke down in tears. I flung the iPad across the room.

"Lord, have mercy," Fannie said and dropped down on the bench at the end of the bed. She slumped her head. I could tell by the way her shoulders shook, she was crying, too.

How could this be happening to us? I'd seen these situations play out a hundred times on times on TV. Never did I think it could happen to us. I shuddered when I thought about the possibility of my man being confronted by a madman or worse. How could I go on if something happened to him? Malcolm was my whole heart. I dropped to my knees and cried when I thought about how silly I treated him earlier.

"Dear God, please let Malcolm be okay."

Just then, the anchor cut in saying that they were getting mixed reports. There was a possibility that the two people who were previously reported as dead were only injured and that negotiations were ongoing for the hostages.

That was all I needed to hear. I sprang into action. "I can't stay here," I said, slipping on a pair of jeans. "I've got to go down there. I need to know firsthand. I can't depend on these news reports."

Fannie turned around to face me. She looked like the news had added fifteen years to the sixty she'd earned on her own. "Simone, you can't go there. It's an active shooter situation." She tried to stand, but she didn't have the strength.

"I can't stay here," I said. I pulled on Malcolm's old MIT hoodie and slipped into a pair of Ugg's.

"Simone, it's not safe," she said. "You need to be here for the girls."

My mind was made up. "Thank God you're here," I said, leaving her in my bedroom. I headed for the garage, hopping down the stairs three at a time.

"Simone," she called out again. Her voice hushed so as not to awaken the girls.

I spun around on my heels, ready to tell her for the last time that nothing but God could keep me from getting to that plant. "What?"

She stood at the top of the stairs, looking down at me like a mother sending her child off to war. "Be careful. I couldn't take it if something happened to the both of you."

Her words made me more determined than ever to get to that plant. I tipped my head to her and headed out the mudroom door.

Fifteen seconds later, I tried to back out of the driveway without ripping off the garage door while I waited for it to open. As soon as it was high enough for the top of the truck to squeeze through, I rolled onto the street.

Snow didn't usually fall in Richmond in December, but the unexpected weather didn't slow me down. My mind went into auto-pilot as my eyes strained against the tears and the snowflakes that bounced off the windshield. My only mission was to get to SemCon, even if I had to slide all the way there.

What was supposed to be a thirty minute drive took less than twenty, even with all the ice. I double parked in front of a car and hurried out of the truck.

A small crowd had gathered just outside the main gate. Police were taping off the area and pushing the onlookers back to their cars.

I ignored them because I made out the frame of one of the crew chiefs who worked in Malcolm's department, Bryan Henderson. He and Malcolm went to college together. Even though he was busy rolling out blueprints and working with the police, I had to get his attention. I knew he'd give me the answers I needed.

"Bryan," I yelled out, moving closer to the tape. "Bryan Henderson."

"Ma'am, we're clearing this area," a heavily armed officer said as he walked toward the tape.

I ignored him. Leaving was not an option.

"Bryan," I yelled out through tears.

"I'm going to have to ask you to leave."

"Please, I need to find out about my husband. He works here. If I could just speak to that man there in the yellow uniform. Please," I begged. "Bryan!"

Finally, Bryan turned around. Spotting me in the crowd, he crossed the yellow tape to reach me. His eyes looked weary. "Simone, what are you doing here?"

"Have you seen Malcolm?" I asked. "The last thing he told me was that he was working late. Do you know anything?" My voice was shaking. It was all I could do to stand up straight and keep my knees from buckling.

He looked down. "I haven't heard from him either."

"No," I said, covering my mouth.

He pulled me close. "I think our guys are going to be okay. They've been talking to the suspect."

"But I need to know," I said, wiping snow and tears from my face.

"I know you want more answers. But this place isn't safe right now. The best place for you is home."

"I can't go home," I said. "Not until I see him walking out of that building."

"Ma'am, you're going to have to leave," the policeman insisted.

"I've got to get back, Simone," Bryan said, hugging me. "We're doing everything we can. You'll be the first person I call. I promise."

I had enough with promises. I needed someone to deliver on their word. I squeezed my eyes shut, trying to fight back more tears. I prayed that Malcolm was going to be okay.

"Last time I'm going to ask," the policeman said.I took a deep breath and nodded in agreement. I had done all I could, but it didn't make me feel better. I felt alone and absolutely helpless.

I need to hug my girls.

Defeated, I spun around to head back to my car. It was then that I noticed a lady standing under the light of a pole lamp. She called out to me as I walked past. She approached me as I got into the truck. "I came here to pray," she said.

"You've got someone here, too?" I asked.

"No. It's just that it's Christmas and these folks belong home with their families. I prayed for everyone in the building, even the shooter."

When she said that, I broke down in tears. "I just want to hold my husband," I sobbed. "I want to tell him how much I love him. How much we need him."

"He's coming home," she said, hugging me. "I believe it in my heart. You've got to believe it, too."

I tried to let her words sink in. I had to believe. I tried to get myself together, if not for me, for our girls. I dried my tears, but my heart was still swimming in pain.

"Everything is going to be okay," she reassured. "Your husband is going to make it home for Christmas," she said, staring directly into my eyes.

Something about the way she said it made me believe. She tapped the truck before walking away. Just as I backed out into the street, the pole light blinked out, and just like that, the lady was gone.

The drive home was nothing like the drive into town. Ice stuck to the roads and I couldn't go further than a mile at a time without spinning my wheels. It took almost an hour to get home. I cursed and prayed all the way home. I felt a tinge of relief when I turned into our neighborhood. That relief quickly changed to dread when I saw the black and white police car parked in front of our house.

"Oh, my God." *Not my Malcolm.*

The SUV jerked from me shifting into park so fast. I bolted up the steps and burst through the kitchen doors.

But what I saw was the exact opposite of anything I had expected.

There, in the kitchen were our two girls, sitting at the table, dipping bacon into a flood of maple syrup. Eddie Kendricks was hitting all the high notes to "Silent Night," in the background, while a policeman sat at the counter sipping on a cup of coffee. Fannie was at the other counter adding cream to hers.

"What the heck is going on here?" I asked.

"Merry Christmas, Mama," the girls yelled out in unison. They ran over to me, nearly knocking me over from their hugs.

"I heard you were looking for me."

45

Malcolm?

But I already knew who it was in my heart. I recognized that baritone anywhere. I turned around and jumped into his arms.

"Malcolm," I cried, kissing him everywhere there was skin. "I was so scared. What are you doing here? What happened?"

"The Texas plant called back. They weren't able to get the part out like they had expected, so I came home."

"You rushed out of here so fast that you forgot your phone. We've been trying to call you," Fannie said, sipping on the coffee. She walked over to hug me.

"So, wait a minute. You weren't there when the plant was on lockdown? What about the people back at the plant?" I asked.

"They all got out safely," the trooper explained. "They just called it in on the radio."

"And the active shooter?" I asked.

"He surrendered," they all replied.

"They're calling it a Christmas miracle on the news," Fannie said.

"So why are you here?" I asked, looking at the trooper.

"My tire blew out and my phone died," Malcolm said. "Officer Cringle was nice enough to drive me home."

This was way too much to process. I sat down on the stool near the counter.

"Your name's not really Cringle?" I asked.

"It really is," he said.

They all laughed and pointed to his badge.

"Well, isn't this a blessing," I said, stumped.

Malcolm wrapped his arms around me. "I told you I'd be home before you'd know it."

"You did say that, didn't you."

"I did. Now did you live up to your end of the bargain?" he asked, whispering in my ear.

I grinned, biting my lip once I remembered I still had on the lingerie. Malcolm bent down and gave me a long, sensuous kiss that made everyone in the room blush. The girls giggled their way out of the kitchen and back out to the Christmas tree to play with their toys.

"Thank you so much for the coffee. Merry Christmas, everyone," Officer Cringle said, heading toward the door.

"Thank you for helping my husband get home," I said.

He nodded his head. Fannie winked at me and walked him to the door.

Malcolm took my hand as he led me down the hallway to our bedroom. "What about the girls?" I asked.

"They are not thinking about us," he said.

I glanced back into the family room. Ella and Lena were entranced with castles and doll babies. I thought back to the lady at the plant and smiled. My heart was filled with gratitude. I couldn't get any happier. It even felt good to hear Fannie laughing in the foyer.

"Do you really know how much I love you, Malcolm Christian?" I asked.

"I do," he whispered, leaning in for another kiss. "I think it's pretty sexy the way you went looking for me."

"I meant what I said. I wanted you home for Christmas." I kissed him back and silently thanked God for bringing our family together. I buried myself into the warmth of his chest. "Merry Christmas, baby."

He took my hand and led me into our bedroom, shutting the door behind him. "Merry Christmas, Mrs. Claus."

Sonia Johnston is a contributing author to the best-selling anthology, Single Mama Dating Drama. A wife, mom, and entrepreneur, she's hard at work on her debut novel, Real Love. You can check her out at www. sonialovestowrite.com to connect with her on social media.

All Wrapped Up
By Princess F.L. Gooden

I remembered the last time I was home for Christmas and I was sure that it would literally be the last time. I was never going back. I promised. And my good old southern Alabama upbringing taught me to always say what I meant and to mean what I said. My exact last words were, "I'll sleep on the streets before I come back to this religious hellhole."

Tears had formed in my mother's eyes as I grabbed the trash bag that held the only clothes my eighteen-year-old self had paid for. The bag wasn't heavy, but my heart was.

It was all my mentally-ill Uncle Levi's fault. He had a problem with keeping his hands to himself and a few other things. My father listened to my cries, but his only reason for wiping my tears was so no one would see them. His fifteen-member congregation trusted that he too patterned his life after his "holier than thou" teaching so he had to maintain the image that his house was without sins, spots, wrinkles, or blemishes.

"How can you lead people to Christ when your family members are standing on the stairways to hell?" he asked almost every Sunday.

My question followed, "How could you preach the wages of sin is death and let my uncle live after what he'd done to me?" I had had enough. So I left…

The streets called my name and before the sun rose, I answered. My first night was under a bridge that had cars riding along side, around, and on top of it. Sadly, it was the safest I'd felt in a long time.

Ten Christmas Eves Later…

I called myself braiding my hair even though it was too matted for that. Then I repinned the holes in my jacket and used bread ties as buttons to close it so no one could see that my shirt was dirty too. The first two fingers of each of my gloves were missing so I could freely open and close things that I needed. I only missed them when it was extremely cold. I put all three of my multi-colored hats on since each one of them covered an area that was missing on the other. My socks were different in color, but the same length, making it look like a style. A style that I was pleased to have since so many of my homeless friends didn't have any socks at all.

Just as I repacked my rusted silver-framed buggy to prepare for my journey to Jones Powell United Methodist Church, PJ turned the corner and headed toward me. PJ had been my "road dog" for the last ten years. We did everything together and looked out for one another like a brother and sister would.

"You know if we don' get there by five, they ain't gone let us in," he said. "I don' wanna spend Christmas Eve out here ta-night."

I looked at PJ, who was fairly handsome despite his rugged beard/mustache combo and discolored skin, and realized that he had on some new black and red Jordans. Well, not new like straight out of the store, but new to me and him. "PJ, you stole somebody's shoes?"

"Naw, girl. The officer that be on graveyard shift at Mr. Ylang Lung's store gave them to me last night. He gave me some other clothes too."

That's when I noticed the hooded all-black jacket with the Nike logo. It was like new, too. "You need to hurry up," he said. "You know it's gone be a long line."

I looked myself over and nodded. I was pleased. So I turned the buggy around and headed out of the alley.

The light poles had a combination of decorations with lights that the city keep on the entire days of Christmas Eve and Christmas, even during daylight hours. All of the stores played Christmas music, some of which we could hear on the streets. The smell of cinnamon, pine, apple or a combination of all three passed under our noses as people exited or entered the stores. It wasn't cold enough for puff clouds to form when we talked, but it was cold.

It only took PJ and I twenty minutes to walk to the church that had promised sixty homeless bodies a warm place to sleep, three meals, and a care package. It was about three-ish when we got in front of the church decorated with the nativity scene and bright white lights. The line already had about thirty straggly and rough looking bodies waiting. PJ held up his hoodie to show me his matching Jordan shirt. "You ain't gone believe me, I know, but I prayed for this." Then he dropped the hoodie and his head.

With his hand on his hip, his head shaking side to side, he whispered, "Thank you, Jesus!"

"PJ, don't you start crying. You know how it is out here on the streets 'cause you taught me. We got to be strong."

He sniffed, then grabbed his nose as if his hand was tissue. "Aww'ight. I'm good. But Muffin…" he called me by the name he'd given me twenty seconds after we met, "I miss home sometimes. You don't."

"I'on know. I guess. I try not to think about it, 'cause every time I do, my mind recollects more of the bad. I told you 'bout my uncle and my daddy. The sun doesn't come out when it's raining. And if it does, it ain't bright enough to make you forget the rain. You feel me?"

"Yeah." Then he looked as if he was forcing himself to laugh. "I shole miss them sweet 'tata pies, collards, and corn bread, though."

"Me too. And that ham and turkey."

Right then, the grumpy old man who stood in front of us turned and snapped, "I shole wish y'all would shut up. Tonight you gone have soup and sandwich. Ain't no need of teasing yourselves." He mumbled the rest of what he had to say and me and PJ looked at each other and laughed. At first softly, then louder. We paused. Then laughed again.

Shortly after that, the doors of the church opened and the Christmas music escaped from the fellowship hall into the streets. "And this Christmas will be a very merry Christmas…" played as we made our way in.

People wearing aprons and Santa hats hugged and welcomed us, while guiding us to empty seats, filling in one row after the other. "Find you a seat and get comfortable," the man with the preacher collar and black shirt shouted.

It took a few minutes, but finally everyone was settled. They locked the doors and then the same man stood in front of us and said he had a few words.

"Tonight we are blessed to have you all celebrate Christmas with us. We are going to have a good time! I am so grateful to the other church that joined in to help us make tonight's festivities possible." He looked around the room. "Where is Pastor Anthony and his wife, April?"

My heart stopped. My breathing followed. It couldn't be. There was no way. Maybe it was just two people with the same names.

A pumpkin-shaped woman with a lot of make-up and what looked like chicken grease on her lips spoke out and said, "Pastor, they still bringing in the gifts from their car. Somebody went to tell them you're looking for them, but it may be a minute."

"All right, then moving right along. I'll introduce them when they come in. " He finished explaining the rules, activities, and prayed over the first meal. It was soup and sandwiches just like the old man said, but it was good. I looked at PJ and we laughed again, except this time my laugh was fake. I was worried. I didn't want Pastor Anthony or his wife to see me. I also didn't know how I would escape just in case they were who I thought they were. The other Pastor had made it clear that we were to stay until Christmas in order to receive all that they had for us. And I needed all that they wanted to give. I looked around the room to see if I saw any more familiar faces. There were none.

If it was them, maybe they wouldn't recognize me. I'd changed a lot. My hair was long, but not as pretty as it was when I was a teenager. I hadn't done real bad by myself, but I didn't have the proper things to do any better either. Just as I was taking the third bite out of my ham, turkey, and salami sub, they walked in.

I thought that I'd never see them again, but there they were. Both my parents. My father's wrinkled forehead and droopy jaws indicated that he'd aged a lot faster than my mother, although they were the same age. He didn't even seem as tall as he once was. My mother on the other hand, was slimmer and her face was radiant. Her hair had turned gray, but the beauty of it embraced my mother's youthfulness.

The Pastor introduced them and asked them to join him at his table.

"Muffin, that lady looks like an older version of you," PJ said, interrupting my thoughts.

I crammed some chips in my mouth and shook my head like "nah". He was right, though. People had always said I was my mother's twin even when I was a little girl. And if it was still obvious, then I needed to make sure I stayed away from the both of them. My first escape would be the bathroom.

"PJ, hold my seat. I got to go pee." I didn't wait on him to answer me because I knew he would hold my seat even if I hadn't asked. I followed the instructions the Pastor had given during his speech. Down the hall and two doors to the left and there it was.

One lady was changing her baby while another was touching up her make-up and putting her hair back into place.

I quickly went into the middle of the three stalls and locked the door.

Once I heard the main door close twice, I figured everybody was gone, so I opened the door and walked out.

Just seconds after, the main door opened and in walked my mother. I dropped my face to pretend I didn't see her and turned on the water. As I washed my hands she walked over to me and stopped at the sink next to mine before saying, "Melissa."

I hesitated then said, "Mama."

She grabbed me and squeezed so tight. "Thank you, God. Thank you, God," she cried. "Oh Lord, I thank you for letting me see my baby again."

Uncontrollable tears fell from my face but I kept my arms and wet hands to the side of me. She released me, then pulled me right back in. This time squeezing me tighter.

When she let me go, we just stood there. Even though her eyes never left my face, I could tell that any parts of my body that was in that visual perimeter was being examined. I wiped my tears quickly.

"I miss you so much," she said as she interrupted the silence. "Where? What?" she started asking, but not knowing how to say all of what she wanted to.

"I'm doing good, Mama. I'm alive."

"I am thankful for that. It's been so long." Then she grabbed me again. "You know you can come back home."

"Mama, please. You know I can't. Daddy and Uncle Levi…" I signed. "I can't."

"Your Uncle Levi died two weeks ago in a car accident and your daddy is sick. He has been praying, just like me, for a second chance. We're sorry." Then she turned toward the sink, braced herself on the edge, and slumped. "We should have listened to you. We should. Have. Done. Something." A different set of tears formed after each word. "It was just hard to believe that your uncle would do something like that to his only niece."

"But not hard for you all to think I was making it up. Mama, I've been out here in the streets ten years now. Not one of you came."

"I did. But I could never find you. When I asked, no one knew you by name. I even showed pictures. A couple of times when I thought I was close, I ended up finding some other girl." She turned back around to me. "I didn't know what to say if I found you or what to do. I just wanted to see and hold you again." This time when she grabbed me, she kissed my face. I didn't have the strength to be tough anymore. I fell into her arms and broke down. We cried for what seemed like an hour. Then there was a knock on the door.

It startled the both of us. It had to be a man since we were in the bathroom and a woman wouldn't have a reason to knock.

My daddy's weak voice called out to my mother, "April, honey, you in there? You alright?"

"Yes. I'm talking to..."

I shook my head.

She mouthed, "It's okay, sweetie. I promise." Then she repeated herself. This time finishing her sentence, "Melissa."

"Our daughter?" You could hear the shock in his voice. "Melissa?"

My mother grabbed my hand and we made our way to the door.

Before I could get all of the way out and into the hallway, my father slowly dropped to his knees and grabbed my legs.

"Oh God! Oh..."

I had never seen my father this way. Never. A tsunami of tears went down his face and chest. His words were unclear, but I could tell they all led to how sorry he was.

PJ's appearance pulled us out of the emotional hurricane that we'd all been in. "Muffin, what the world?"

I reached down to help my daddy up. My mother had at some point grabbed me from behind and was holding me that way. She came around to help me help my daddy. PJ stood there waiting on an answer.

I introduced my parents and before I could say who my mother was, PJ interrupted. "I knew it. I knew it. I told you this lady looked like you." Then he reached out to shake their hands.

The three of us followed PJ to the sanctuary. Everyone had moved from the fellowship hall for the Christmas program.

We found seats in the back, but before my daddy could sit down, the Pastor called him out. "Pastor Anthony, if you don't mind, would you come up here and give us a testimony or words of encouragement, and then we can get to the singing of the Christmas carols."

Slowly my father made his way to the pulpit. He grabbed the microphone, closed his eyes, and lifted his head toward the sky. "Sometimes you ask God for things you don't deserve. You don't deserve them because you didn't appreciate them when you had them."

Amens from the congregation followed my daddy's words.

He continued, "Sometimes we get caught up in materialistic things and/or what people will think or say about us and we forget about the things that are most important. Things that God gives everyday. Like life. Love. Understanding. Peace. Patience. Forgiveness. Family and friends. Those are all gifts that He gives year round. And sometimes we don't know they are gifts until they are gone. Some of us push some of our gifts away."

People began to rise out of their seats. Some nodding. Some waving their hands. And a few of them chanting words that encouraged my daddy to keep going.

"This year as I have been battling cancer, I only asked for one gift. All I wanted for Christmas was to see my daughter again. A gift that I didn't deserve. A gift that had been given to me that I didn't protect. A gift that I didn't appreciate. All of us have been given those kinds of gifts. They can't fit under trees. You won't find a price on them. And only God can restore them if you lose them. Tonight as we celebrate Christmas, I'm asking you to think about those gifts. The ones sitting next to you. The ones that are year round. The ones that you need to keep wrapped up in love and close to your heart so you will always be reminded that they are gifts. Look at your neighbor and say, "All wrapped up! I have you all wrapped up!"

Eye to eye and side to side, the people did exactly as my father had asked.

Then he looked at me and said, "Melissa, please forgive me. I promise to spend the rest of my life 'wrapping you up' in my love."

The water in my eyes formed while he was speaking, making it hard for me to see anything clearly. All I could do was nod.

PJ threw his arms around my shoulders and pulled me into his embrace. My mother looped her arm through my other arm and leaned in whispering for me to forgive her also.

At that moment something came over me and I knew I could no longer be mad at my parents. I knew I'd have to heal, but I would be in the best arms to do it. In my parents arms, "all wrapped up."

Princess F. L. Gooden is a novelist, dramatist, poet, motivational speaker, educator, producer/ director of stageplays, actor, dancer, singer and radio show personality, but her favorite titles are wife and mother. She is married to Reginald R. Gooden. They collectively have six children. In 2014 her very first novel, with the very talented and gifted Best Selling Author, co-founder of Brown Girls Books, and NAACP Author of the Year, Victoria Christopher Murray, was published. Their book "Touched By An Angel" won "Christian Fiction of the Year Award" and is still floating around in the TOP 20. "The Dating Game", "Bigmama Quotes", "Single Mama Dating Drama", are among her other titles and they are all bestsellers.

Basketful of Miracles
By Patricia Woodside

Chapter One

Giselle jetted into her reserved space right in front of Gigi's Gifts Galore. Gift cards, gift wrap, gift supplies, gift baskets, and personal gift consultations or shopping for all occasions—what better business to be in at Christmas?

Except G3 probably wouldn't make it past the holidays.

The cheery bell over the front door tinkled when she pushed in the door, but one glance and her heart sank. Less than two weeks before Christmas and only one customer, who was doing more browsing than buying based on the two small items in her basket. A gift business that couldn't make money during the biggest gift-giving season of the year was no business at all.

"Good morning," Gigi called out, then winced, lifting a hand to her cheek. Sales associate Kaley waved and returned to straightening shelves. Gigi continued back to the work area where she set her product-laden bag on the table.

Renata, her assistant, said, "Good morning, boss lady. Today will be a good day. I can feel it."

Only Renata knew what Gigi had planned. She strode down the narrow hallway between the storefront and work area and turned into her office. She tucked her purse into the desk drawer, then powered up her laptop to tap out a calendar reminder. A list of G3's steady customers would receive a final basket right after Christmas, a nice gesture to thank them and to give notice — Gigi's was going out of business.

"*Santa Claus is coming to town, oh yeah, Santa Claus is coming to town...*"

Preadolescent Michael Jackson poured from the storewide speakers, eliciting a half-smile. She preferred smooth jazz, but Renata insisted on holiday music from Thanksgiving to New Year's. Her optimistic, longtime friend assured her Christmas tunes made things more festive, which in turn led to higher sales.

Not likely, she thought.

It didn't surprise her that her dream would die at Christmas. She had never liked Christmas. Well, maybe when she was too young to know Santa was a fairytale and Christmas wishes rarely came true. She rubbed her jaw to ease the mild discomfort in her gums.

"Chestnuts roasting on an open fire. . ."

Nat King Cole's dulcet tones blanketed the room. She didn't want roasting chestnuts, open fires, Yuletide carols, Eskimo, or even mistletoe.

Well. . . She chuckled. A little mistletoe with the right guy underneath would certainly make her heart gay.

Renata flung open the office door. Fists on her hips, she said, "Why are you sitting there holding your face? Come on, chica, these baskets won't make themselves." Pointing to the extra-large, white wicker basket on the table between the desk and the door, she said, "What's that?"

"That's for Sylvia Jasper at WLUV. You like?"

Renata leaned in for a whiff. "Hmmm, nice. It's beautiful." She fingered the white, sparkly crinkled grass.

Gigi smiled. With a bevy of bath soaps, lotions, scrubs, sponges, and even a robe, the oversized basket was a spa lover's dream. Because everything in it was white and sparkly, she'd dubbed it "The Winter Wonderland." Radio host Sylvia would love it. The deejay had taken time to speak with Gigi at a recent symposium for entrepreneurs, introducing her to the station's manager and its social media coordinator. Gigi wanted to say thanks, even if she had little use for the connection now.

"Are we shipping this one?"

"No, I'll deliver it." She snatched a hard candy from the crystal bowl on her desk, more of Renata's holiday influence. Red, white, and green decorations festooned the whole place. Not even her office had been overlooked. Crinkling the cellophane between her fingers, she popped the sugarplum into her mouth and bit down. "Ouch!" Her hand cupped her right cheek and she frowned.

"What's wrong?" Renata floated over, her brow wrinkled with concern.

"I think I cracked my tooth," Gigi said, tracing small circles on her jaw.

"You'd better call your dentist. You don't want to celebrate Christmas with a toothache."

From where she stood, a toothache would make this year only mildly disappointing, which would be a tad better than usual. "How hard will it be to get an appointment this time of year? I'll be all right."

"About as hard as finding that video game I've been hunting for the past two weeks?"

Gigi shrugged. Frantic attempts to buy the hottest toy of the year weren't something she had experience with. After her ex's shenanigans—he'd dumped her the day after Christmas two years back—marriage and motherhood were at the bottom of her wish list. She just hoped her dentist hadn't shut down early for the holidays.

She opened her mouth to speak. "Ow."

Renata challenged her with her eyes.

With one hand plastered to her face, she said, "Okay, I'll call."

Chapter Two

The next morning, Gigi awoke to a stab of pain. "Ohhhh." Why did the worst things always happen at Christmas?

Granny would disagree. She had loved Christmas. Every year, Granny baked for two weeks, wrapped a host of gifts, cooked a big dinner, and corralled the whole family to attend the Christmas Eve service at the country church where she'd been a member for decades.

Gigi had loved that church almost as much as she loved Granny. She recalled the long, hard pews, the Sunday School attendance board, the pastor's billowy black robe, its sleeves trimmed with red velvet, and the stained glass windows through which she gazed until service ended. When Granny died right before Christmas, one year after Momma's stroke, so had Gigi's relationship with God and church. She believed in God, she just didn't trust Him. How could she trust someone who allowed so many bad things to happen in her life during what was supposed to be a season of joy?

She texted Renata that she would arrive a little later than usual, then popped two Tylenol with a mouthful of orange juice. Dressing took longer than normal, her toothache making her feel off kilter. She hoped the painkillers would kick in by the time she got to the store.

When she arrived, every space near the store, including hers, was taken. *One of the other stores must be holding a special sale.* She parked two rows over and trudged toward the door.

A few shoppers exiting the store nearly ran her over. Each had a bag emblazoned with the G3 logo. She could appreciate tiny blessings.

"Christmas time is here, Happiness and cheer. . ."

Four sets of shoppers inside the store curved the corners of her mouth. The phone rang and even as Renata excused herself from one couple to answer, the second line shrilled. Kaley looked at her and Gigi gestured for the sales associate to get it. She'd have taken the call, but she was in too much pain. Add toothache to her list of 101 Ways to Screw Up Christmas.

The phone rang again as fast as Renata hung up followed by several more calls. When there was finally a break, Gigi asked, "What gives?"

"Did you deliver that basket yesterday?"

Gigi nodded. "Sylvia wasn't there, but they assured me she would get it when she came in." Every word made her head throb.

"Oh, she got it all right. Sylvia's been talking about it on-air all morning."

She had? Gigi usually listened to the high-energy morning show, but she'd been so preoccupied by her aching tooth, she hadn't even turned on the car radio. "That's really nice of her."

"You bet your reindeer it is. The phone has been ringing off the hook. Everyone wants one."

Kaley chimed in, "Our social media hits and email are skyrocketing. That basket is hot."

Her brow puckered. "How many orders are we talking, 25 or 30?"

"Try closer to 75."

Her attention had been diverted to a customer fingering a pine cone basket, but she whipped her head back to Renata who was grinning like a Christmas elf. She shook her head in disbelief. Was this some kind of holiday joke? "We don't have enough supplies. I never intended to take orders for it."

"But boss lady, this is an answer to prayer. It's Christmas and people are willing to pay."

"How much?"

"Five hundred. You weren't here yet and I had to tell them something."

"*Five hundred?*"

"*Sí.* A little celebrity doesn't hurt. I checked inventory and placed rush orders. If everything comes in as expected, we can start shipping Friday, that is, if you find the baskets. That's the only item not in our system." A sliver of excitement snaked through her. It was probably too late to make a difference, but the extra revenue would help with the parting bonuses she wanted to give the staff. That is, if she could find the baskets to fulfill the orders.

"I got a sample from a vendor at that conference a few months back. If I can find his card, maybe he can ship some priority."

December 15. Ten days before Christmas, one week left to ship for Christmas delivery. Her mouth throbbed and a woodpecker was tapping on her head, but there was no time to waste. Looking at the increasingly crowded store, she felt a whisper of hope. *Don't get excited.* As soon as there was a break, she would call the dentist again.

Chapter Three

Four hundred twenty-nine orders and counting. Most of the supplies were now on hand with the rest expected that afternoon, but still no baskets.

Her jawline twinged. Friday and day three of the pain that had devolved into a dull throb. Why hadn't the dentist returned her call? She might have to take her chances on more Extra Strength Tylenol and one of Granny's old-fashioned hot toddies.

She couldn't believe G3 was in this pickle. She'd been planning a going-out-of-business sale. But now. . .

Maybe G3 wasn't doomed. Maybe she just needed a better marketing plan, one that ran through Sylvia and WLUV. She could also use a little more of Renata's faith.

Renata, her friend and partner. Not officially, but the Latina spitfire might as well be. She ran the shop as well as, if not better than, Gigi herself, and she was ecstatic about the sudden influx of business. If G3 survived, she would talk to her about a partnership. She wouldn't mind having a business partner. She'd been going it alone since the beginning.

Going solo – in business and in life -- was a lonely road.

The shrill ring of her cell startled her. She lifted the phone to her ear. "Gigi's Gifts Galore. May I help you?"

"This is the office of Dr. Kenneth Russell for Giselle Nelson."

Finally.

***

Fifty-four minutes later and perspiring only slightly, Gigi blew into the dentist's office. She waited no time before she was ushered into an examination room.

"All I want for Christmas is my two front teeth, my two front teeth. . ."

More holiday music. As she lay back in the semi-stiff chair, the sickly sweet tune wasn't lost on her. If she got out in under ninety minutes, the pain gone, her wallet only slightly lighter, and all thirty-two whites intact, she'd be satisfied.

She liked her pearly whites.

In walked Dr. Russell, his woodsy cologne leading the way. The outdoorsy scent reminded her of the candles in her Wonderland basket, only better.

"Happy holidays! What brings you here today?"

She gestured to her cheek.

"Ah, well." He snapped on a pair of latex gloves. "Let's see what's going on."

When she dared open her eyes, a surprising ripple of delight snaked through her. She stared into the most delicious face ever, even from behind the mask. Long and lean yet muscular, the good doctor wore close cropped, freshly edged hair with trimmed sideburns and goatee. Then there were those Hershey Kiss eyes. His chair-side manner did wonders for easing her pain.

He coughed and she jumped. Was she drooling?

"Ms. Nelson, it's good you came in. You cracked a tooth. If it breaks, it will mar that pretty smile, and we can't have that, can we?"

That kiddie song took on new meaning.

Wait. Was he flirting with her? All the Christmas season had ever brought her was heartbreak. Certainly she was hearing things, although the silkiness of his voice comforted her like peppermint chocolate cheesecake.

If wishes were fishes, Granny would say. If Christmas wishes came true, Daddy would be alive, Momma would be well, her business would be thriving, and she'd be deeply in love. She surely wouldn't be at the dentist, although the wink he tossed her made up for a lot.

"Anna will set everything up. I'll be back in a few minutes."

As he left, her phone buzzed. When he returned, she held up one finger. She finished her call and dropped her head. The good news? The new vendor had what she needed. The bad news? He couldn't guarantee delivery. He would hold the needed quantity, but she had to pick her order up -- eight hours away, in Atlanta. "Shall we proceed?"

An hour and seventeen minutes later, she arose pain-free and numb. "I can than you enuff, Docta Russ-thell."

"My pleasure. Be kind to that tooth and it should be fine. Any special plans for the holiday?"

She shook her head. "I haf to go to Alanna. Bith-ness."

"Enjoy your trip and be safe. I hear a storm is blowing in from up north."

Chapter Four

Thank God her younger brother was always up for adventure. Darius had agreed to accompany her to Atlanta. It would be a dog of a road trip—eight hours up from southwest Florida, picking up the baskets, then turning right back around—but what other choice did she have?

At the shop, her jaw still a little sore from her dental vist the day before, she checked in with Renata. "How many?"

"You don't want to know."

Gigi's eyes widened. "Tell me."

"683."

This couldn't be.

"Kaley and I will stage the products and packaging, and I'm calling in Stacie and the guys," Renata continued. "It will be all hands on deck."

"Good idea, and Renata?"

"*Qué?*"

"Stop taking orders."

As she prepared to leave, the rustle of the door caught her attention. Dr. Russell. What was he doing here? Unable to stop herself, she put down her bags, smoothed her hair, moistened her lips, and hastened to the front of the store.

"Hello, Doctor. How can I help you?"

"It's Ken, Ms. Nelson."

"If it's Ken, then call me Gigi. Are you shopping for a particular gift?" She tried to focus on his mission rather than his flirtatious chocolate gaze.

"I need a gift for my mother. What do you buy the woman who has everything she needs and much of what she wants?"

"You've come to the right place."

A short while later, Ken lingered, gift bag in hand, near a jewelry display.

"Is there something else I can do for you?"

A curious look came over him. "Yes, but more importantly, there is something I can do for you."

Chapter Five

No way. Allow Dr. Russell to travel with her to Atlanta? She didn't know him like that. He'd smelled her breath—although she always chewed mints before an appointment—scraped plaque off her teeth, and examined her gums, but she didn't know him. For all she knew, he was Dr. Delicious by day and Dr. Deranged by night. What did he use all those sharp, pointy tools for after hours? She'd seen a lot of "Criminal Minds." The cute ones were the worst.

"Why would you do this?" A surge of something hopeful exploded inside her as she imagined a road trip with this scrumptious hunk of manhood. Darius's commitment was half-hearted and came only after she promised things she'd be paying off for six months. Ken was here, ready, and she didn't have to bribe him even a little. She wanted to scream, "Yes!" but her good sense said, "I don't understand. What's in it for you?"

The depth of his stare drew goosebumps. A whisper, so ethereal she almost missed it, said, "Miracles come when you need them most and believe even more."

She wanted to believe. It had been so long.

He said, "Why? I get to spend time with a favorite patient, one I'm interested in getting to know better. I get to help someone in need, and I get to visit a frat brother who owes me a favor

"Your frat? What kind of favor?"

"He owns a charter plane service."

Chapter Six

Delicious, intelligent, adventurous, considerate. . . Dr. Russell's list of positive attributes grew every tenth of a mile.

He'd overheard her phone conversation in his office Friday. Instead of road tripping with her brother, she was tucked in the luxurious passenger seat of his car. They'd left Saturday afternoon after she was sure preparations were underway at the shop. He drove the whole way, and not because he didn't trust her behind the wheel of his sweet ride. He was that kind of guy. He also was the kind of guy who refused her offer to pay for gas, treated her to dinner, and chatted easily and confidently with her the entire way. "We're almost there but if you need a catnap, go ahead."

She stretched, embarrassed he'd spied her dozing. "I'm good."

"Yes, you are." His voice pitched lower and sexier than it had been all day.

Suddenly, she wasn't sleepy at all. The dazzle of his smile shone like the Christmas star, a beacon for her heart. She could power a ten-foot Christmas tree with the heat building within.

What was going on? She could only wonder. This was unlike any Christmas season she'd experienced in a long time. She just hoped what looked like glitter wasn't a lump of coal.

Chapter Seven

The next morning, she whipped out her cellphone and dialed Renata. In the background, she heard *"I'll be home for Christmas, you can plan on me. . ."*

"Hey, listen, we have the baskets. We'll be there before noon."

"Uh. . ."

Dread pooled in her stomach. If Renata wasn't feeling festive, something was wrong. Something big. "What is it?"

"Stacie quit."

"Why would Stacie quit a week before Christmas?"

"She got a better offer."

"Before Christmas? What aren't you telling me?"

"Jules surprised Stacie with an engagement ring and two tickets to Baja."

Jules, her stock guy and logistics whiz? "So they're both gone. What did Jules say?"

"He got a better offer."

"Because she said yes?"

"No, he really got a better offer. He hired on at the Retail That Shall Remain Unnamed."

The competition. She laid her device on her forehead. Fresh out of college, Jules worked for less than he was worth because she offered flexible hours, generous paid time off, and she sent his mother a free gift basket every month.

His mother was going to miss those baskets.

She rolled her eyes. Maybe she'd send one more, just to show she wasn't petty. "Who can we call?"

"I've called everyone I can think of. I got ahold of Quincy and he's going to round up a few of his friends."

Renata's brother's friends were the most talented college baseball team she knew. . .and possibly the most inept guys away from the diamond. She envisioned baskets everywhere, products spilled, trampled or ruined, and boxes shipped to the wrong addresses. "I'm not sure. . ."

"Don't worry. He's calling his *girl*friends."

Gigi hung up and burst out laughing.

"What's so funny?"

"We may have done all this for nothing. Half my staff quit when I have just under 700 baskets to build, box, and ship. Can you tie a bow?" She shook her head, the faint wisp of hope fading fast. "Never mind."

"Way to hurt a brother's ego," Ken said. "Taurean and I are at your service. We'll be your Guy Friday types until you kick us out."

"You really want to help?"

"He's got a layover until after Christmas anyway and my mother doesn't arrive until Christmas Eve, so if you need a couple extra pairs of hands, we're your guys."

"Well, if you're sure. . ."

"It will be my pleasure."

Chapter Eight

"I couldn't have done it without you. . .and Taurean." Too tired to smile, Gigi yawned.

"As I said, it was our pleasure."

She wasn't so sure, but she was thankful. With Quincy and his friends, Darius, Renata, Kaley, Ken and Taurean, it had taken two full days of non-stop basket making, but they'd just made it. The orders were boxed and gone, the final day to ship for guaranteed Christmas delivery. The shop was a wreck, so much so she'd put a Closed sign on the door. Short-staffed, she'd reopen in a day or so. The revenue from those baskets made up for the few lost in-store sales.

"Would you like to get out of here? I'll come back tomorrow to help clean up."

Was this guy for real? Could she keep him?

She retrieved her things, turned out the lights, and was about to shut down the stereo when Mariah Carey's sultry soprano floated through the air.

"I don't want a lot for Christmas, there is just one thing I need. . ."

In that moment, she knew exactly what she wanted. G3, a sexy dentist. . . Probably more than she was entitled to.

She returned to the front to set the alarm when a long arm encircled her waist. She tilted back and gazed upward. What was happening here? Something good, she hoped, although she was still too afraid to believe in the possibilities.

He pointed toward the ceiling. In the golden light from the street lamps, she saw it. Mistletoe. Renata's idea. She'd hated it, more of the season's sappiness that she'd never given in to. Before now.

He grasped her chin between two fingers and lowered his mouth to hers. He tasted of pepperoni, wing sauce and mint. An odd combination, but it worked. She sighed as he deepened the kiss.

Epilogue

In a few short days, he'd made her believe — in the spirit of the season, in the goodness of people, that maybe miracles weren't reserved for everyone else. God certainly had saved a few for her. G3 had a new lease on life, the death, illness, abandonment and disappointment of the past was past, and her faith was sparking anew.

Before the glowing Christmas tree in her living room, she tightened their hug.

"Taurean and I will be back after New Year's. I wish you would consider coming to Atlanta with me."

She was moving past her Christmas doldrums, but she wasn't quite ready to meeting family. There'd be time for that; she was sure of it. "I wouldn't want to alter your plans with your mother."

"She's going to love you when she meets you."

She loved that his vision for the future included her meeting his mother, that it included her. She rested her head against his chest and stared at the twinkling lights on the Christmas tree.

This Christmas, she got everything she wanted.

Patricia Woodside is an author and editor who loves all things romance, especially at Christmastime. Find her celebrating the holidays on Facebook, Twitter or Instagram and at her blog, readinnwritin.blogspot.com.

A Blue Christmas
By Jamantha Williams Watson

"Come here, Jesus!!! Looka here." Ollie breathed into the microphone. "Keep on playin' Jimmy." He nodded. "Keep right on playin', man. But I want y'all to know that the Christmas wind just blew in one of the finest, prettiest, sexiest, good God Almighty, devilish snowflakes up in heeeerrrre tonight." He took a handkerchief out of his jacket pocket and smeared it over his face. "She's back y'all. All the way back from Paris, ladies and gentlemen. It's Prince Edward County's very own Sweet, Sassy Roooooooooooose King."

Rose snaked her way through the crowd of admirers toward the stage.

"Bless your heart, sugar," she cooed to one man who extended his hand.

"Merry Christmas. I love you, too, darling," she said to a woman before lipsticking the word *Rose* on a paper napkin, inside the moist imprint of a glass. To Blue she nodded and gave a slow wink. He pulled the white hand towel out of the glass he was drying and set both down on top of the counter.

His eyes never left her.

Syncopated vibrations, staccato squeaks, funky, low bass tempos from all the blues, the jazz, the gospel music; tickling him from his toenails to the tips of the hairs on his head. All came alive as Blue stood there watching her. Way out there, somewhere, he heard sounds on his brass trumpet again. Man, whenever Rose came back to town he was Buttermilk Weeks, Mississippi Mae, and Dizzy Gillespie all in one. When Rose came home, Blue left and was back out again playing in those liquor- reeked houses in Newark, smoke-filled night clubs on Sugar Hill, and lilac-scented bedrooms in Flatbush. She was his very own musician.

Bee deep bee dop deeeeeee.

Daisy, the head waitress, jerked a menu out of Mr. Bernard's hands, fanned herself with it and flashed a mouthful of teeth.

"Hot damn! We 'bout to party tonight."

Rose swished and swayed her way to the stage. The lights in the room bounced tiny flecks of green and purple from the sequins in the singer's red dress and from the large diamonds in her earrings, necklace, and bracelet, while nearly every man in *Blue's Place* tried but failed to lick the anticipation from his lips.

Before Rose stepped on stage, she turned to the two boys who'd offered to carry her coat. She reached into her full bosom, pulling out two twenties. Then she patted the tops of the little boys' heads, and mouthed "bye-bye" as they ran out the door waving their money like flags.

When Ollie pulled the microphone off its stand and handed it to her, those in the room who were sitting hit the floor, grinning. Those standing braced themselves for the evening of a lifetime.

"Lord, I love coming home to my folks," Rose crooned, "especially at Christmas time."

"We love you, Sweet Sassy."

"Sing to me, baby."

"You know something," she said to her fans, then looked over to Ollie, "play me something slow, little quiet. Not too loud."

"Break it down, Rose."

She cooed. "You know something?" she asked, toying with her hair.

"What, baby?"

"Every colored citizen east of the Mississippi knows that when Sweet Sassy Rose wraps her fingers around a mike like this, baby, you are coming out of your shoes."

Bam!

Levi, the drummer, tapped the drum head one time. Rose gyrated her hip once to the right, then winked. "There just ain't no doubt about it." She flipped the hair out of her eye. "And when I yank my head back and slide my hand down my waist, like this here." She smiled, batting her lashes. "Y'all know you can expect me to howl *Hell of a Woman* stronger than Money Man Stokes ever dreamt. Ain't that right?"

Bam! Bam!

Levi drummed. The singer gyrated her hips twice to the left.

"And, when you...I say when you catch me gazing up in the ceiling like this, you know I'm going to slow it all the way down." She rocked her body from side to side until she was level to the floor. "Don't ya?"

The crowd hollered and cheered louder than they had all night.

"So, kick off your 'gators, grab you somebody; hell, do something 'cause Sweet Sassy Rose is back in here this Christmas, honey. And Lord only knows I'm going to make you feel it all the way down to the bone."

"Lord, Lord, Lord, girl."

"Good God, Almighty."

"Gonna put you on a plate and eat you up tonight, sugar."

"Lord, have mercy."

"River Hipped Sally, y'all." She nodded to the band. "Uh one, uh two, uh one two three." Rose belted out notes the walls hadn't felt in months. Irky propped a foot on his piano stool and banged while men and women danced as if tomorrow was not promised. By the time she had started singing about her lover sneaking out of the bedroom window before her husband had gotten back home, she heard a scream peel high over her low alto.   Satisfied that she could bring such pleasure to her audience, Rose smiled in the direction of the squeal. But it was the second scream that took her and the crowd by surprise as it dried "River Hipped Sally" down to a rat-a-tat-tat.

"Mother Fucka," City Slicker yelled before Chief punched a dent in his face. City Slicker stood, the front of his white suit now stained with vibrant splashes of red.

"Ah shit." He laughed, reaching in his hip pocket. "You done gone and fucked up now country boy."

"Watcha got?" Chief hopped into a Joe Lewis stance.

City Slicker answered by knifing a crooked smile from Chief's earlobe to the cleft in his chin, then two quick stabs to his chest. More women screamed. More men laughed. And Irky, who before the commotion even began, had placed one foot on the stool and raised the other foot in mid-air, lost his balance and lay in a 450-pound heap on the floor. He tried his best to roll out of the way of nosey onlookers and frightened teens who tried dashing their way through the only door that read EXIT.

"Tommy!" Rose cried to the city slicker who had by then taken two sharp blows to the gut, despite his opponent's wounds, and was curled on the floor like a newborn. Blue glared at Rose and thought of his pistol as he scraped his eyes over the crowd toward Tommy, the bloody city slicker, and he wondered how *this* faggot knew *his* woman. The throng who had only five minutes ago danced to a song about a woman whose hips were so ample, she had to share them with another man, now stood over the curled body of a man who was willing to cut his way into the heart of his lover.

While Chief lay underneath a small pond of his own blood, Tommy rolled over, facing the EXIT sign. But Paul Taylor reached down and grabbed a fistful of the man's white collar . He knuckled him between the eyes, until he, too, was knocked out like Chief. But it was after Blue slammed down the receiver on the telephone rocker that he noticed the city slicker beginning to stand. He reached under the counter and dug his hand into a small paper bag. The cold metal of the .22 against his sweaty palm simmered his temper a bit, but not enough to keep him from shooting two dime-sized holes through the carpet of his floor. At least that's where he thought he shot them. But he realized, after the, "Lord Jesus, I've been shot," rang from the ladies' room that he had made a very terrible mistake. Rose jumped off the stage, onto the floor, her dress splitting from ankle to thigh as Ola brushed past her through the ladies' room. Sure enough, Viola Witherspoon gripped the wall, too horrified to scream again as blood gushed from the side of her rear end.

"Everybody remain calm," Blue said, his hands raised high in the air, the gun on the counter spinning on its side like a bottle. Taking off his jacket, he leapt over the others to Chief, his best friend.

"You all right, man?" Blue balled his coat into a bundle and placed it under Chief's head, seeing for the first time the severity of his friend's cuts.

"Don't think he's going to make it, Blue," someone offered.

"Hell," Chief breathed, "I ain't going nowhere. Not tonight. I ain't dying," he coughed, "if that's what you're asking."

"Somebody get Mabel."

How did this foolishness, this mess get into his place? Blue closed his eyes and shook his head, answering himself with one word.

Rose.

He was so angry with her, he didn't know whether to hate her or love her. Sweet, slow, steady the way she liked it.

"Don't call Mabel." Chief coughed. "I'll be all right."

Looking up, Blue wanted to go to the restroom to see who it was who had actually been hurt, but he didn't want to leave his buddy. Not now. "Shhhh," Blue warned, looking down into a face he'd known all his life.

Chief coughed again then smiled at Blue. "May not make it this time, Doc. Don't know."

"You're going to be fine, Chief." Blue gripped Chief's hand harder. "Just fine," reassuring himself moreso than Chief.

"Your momma," Chief whispered and blinked.

"Yours," Blue said, gripping Chief's slippery hand. "Don't you leave me, boy. Don't you up and do nothing foolish like that. You hear me?"

Chief opened his eyes. "Don't tell Mab...," Before he could finish his sentence, his eyes closed.

Patting Chief's face, Blue tried to block out the screaming, the sirens, the blood as he knelt thinking of his next move. Once the police officer walked over asking a mouthful of questions, Blue felt helpless, watching guests flee from his establishment faster than they'd entered. When the guys came to help roll out his best friend in the ambulance, he stood to go with them but felt his legs give way.

"I'll come later," he mumbled. "Not now."

Glaring at Rose, Blue went to her and sat beside her at the table. He rested his head on it and moaned.

"He's not who you think," Rose whispered, sitting across from Blue, the club cleared of all but the two of them.

Blue tried replaying the entire night over and over in his mind, worrying about the safety of all his patrons.

"He's someone from New York. Wants to marry me, that's all. He had a thing for Sarah Vaughan...but..." She circled her ring finger around the rim of the glass of ginger ale, then pulled the marijuana joint from underneath her breast.

These things happen at other spots in town, Blue thought. People fought at *Farrar's* at *Chicken Shack*. But not here. He glared across at the woman who had caused all of the commotion in his club. Then he stood and leaned into her. "Just how the fuck did that city slicker get into my club in the first place?" He shook his head. "Don't answer that. Let me just be the first to tell you. I don't care who the hell he wants to marry, you, Sarah Vaughan, his own mammy…I don't give a fuck. I just know that when he gets out of that hospital I'm going to do either one or two things. Have his ass locked up, or kill him my damn self."

Flinching, Rose looked away. "I told him," she whispered. "I told him all about us." She inhaled the joint, then exhaled small wafts of smoke through her nostrils. "He knows all about me and you."

"And what will people think now? Dammit." He paced the floor. "Dammit, I should've gone up there to the hospital with that ambulance. But naw, Officer Morris had to keep asking me all those crazy ass questions. I should've gone right on up there to check on Chief. And Viola. Good Lord, Viola. God knows that was an accident."

Rose knew better than to keep bringing Tommy into the conversation, but she felt Blue needed to hear her apologies even if it would make him angrier…more jealous. Shaking her head, she sighed. Not another man on this planet, she thought, can do to me what Blue does. And yes, there are other men. Comes with the territory. But no man comes close to touching her in the places where Blue does. Not Tommy up in New York, not Tennessee Joe down in Memphis, not even Earl Wychette over in Lynchburg who's already inked my name on a three-year contract with Winbush Records.

No one.

She looked at the only man on the planet she found irresistible.

"Tommy is just so jealous, that's all," she reassured. "Doesn't want me looking at anybody, let alone going anywhere without him." She eyed Blue before continuing. "Sugar? I…I had to tell him about us. You understand that, don't you?" Tapping the ashes off the joint she swirled it along the inside of the ashtray. "Sugar?" Rose brushed her hand along the side of Blue's face.

"Don't touch me, woman," Blue spurned, slapping her hand away. "Don't you ever put your mother fuckin' hands on me again."

Deeply offended, Rose stood, pressing the cigarette into the ashtray, and blew up a cloud of smoke. "You know," she chuckled, "this has been a very long night. A very long night," she said before snatching the fur from the back of the chair. "I'll see myself out. Thank you very much." The thudding of her heels in the carpet echoed throughout the room.

"And," she walked back over and stood face to face with him, "don't try to find me."

"Wait," Blue turned, grabbed her arm, "don't go."

Tweee sweeeeeee tee bop.

"Why not?" She yanked her hand away. "What the hell do you need me for? Go on home to your wife," Rose fired back at him. "I'm sure she's already heard that her darling husband's nightclub has caught a lot of fire tonight."

"Dammit, woman. Don't you bring her into this."

Shoving her arms through the sleeves of her fur coat Rose shook her head. "You know? You men are all alike. Aren't you? What's that they say? You want your cake and you want to eat it, too? Yeah. That's it." She nodded. "Well, this is one piece of chocolate cake you can't have any more, Sugar Man. Go find yourself another sweet thing." And with that she walked toward the door.

Blue followed her, his eyes falling deeper in love with her back, its arch, the slenderness, the curve of it. And he knew right there, right then that he'd walk a thousand miles just to get a peep of her lovely back, just to hear her say no when she really meant yes.

Boo deep. Tweee sweeeeeee tee bop.

"There is no other woman but you."

She stopped walking and turned back to him.

"But," Blue tilted his head and walked toward her, "help me to understand. Dammit help me to understand how I can give you almost the entire world and you still need a circus clown to come up between us. Help me understand that." He was so close to her, he could bite her.

"Don't worry about Tommy, Blue. Let's talk about Loveline. What about her. Huh?"

Blue grabbed Rose's wrist and squeezed. "I should break your..." Clenching his teeth, he forced the words out of his mouth. "Is that what this is all about? My wife?" he said, blinking the anger out of his eyes. "What about Loveline? She's my wife. That's all," he said releasing his grip. "Baby you know that."

Her eyes holding his, Rose took a step closer to him. "Your wife, huh? And when are you going to leave your wife? She knows all about us. Hell, the whole world knows." She pushed past him. "You know what?" She threw up her hands. "I refuse to do this another moment. I'm leaving."

"Dammit, Rose." Without looking, Blue picked up a barstool and flung it into the Christmas tree, laying it on its side across the room. When she stopped in shock, he grabbed her by the shoulders and shook her.

"I give you everything. Everything I have. And this is how you do me?"

Ceramic Santas with rosy cheeks raced alongside red, gold and silver mirrored balls until they all halted, crashing into the legs of tables, chairs and one another.

"What else do you want me to give you? Huh?"

Her voice was husky with tears that streaked Maybelline's Velvet Black mascara down her cheeks.

"You!" She opened her arms to him. "Give me you. You're right. I have everything I'll ever want and need. But the one thing I don't have…," she lowered her lashes, "the one thing I want more than anything," she lifted her face to his, "is you, Blue. All I want is you baby."

With wide eyes and a tight mouth, Blue stared at the woman in front of him as if it was the first day he'd ever laid his eyes on her. This woman, this Rose could be placed in no other category of flower he'd ever seen. Sweet smelling, prickly, delicate to the touch but hard, Rose was unlike any woman he'd ever known.

Loveline was too delicate, too soft. She wasn't a puzzle for him the way Rose was. Rose he couldn't take apart and put back together so easily. She had a bite, a drive to her that even the average man craved. And he knew her. It had taken him nearly all his adult life, but he finally knew her.

Tweee sweeeeeee tee bop.

"You know I love you, baby. Not him, not anybody else." The tips of her long nails traced his lips, his neck, his chest where she drew eight's until he called her name.

"Rose?"

"Marry me."

Blue pulled her in to him and squeezed. The press of her wet mouth on his was really the only music he'd heard all night. This was where he wanted to be ever since he'd seen her glide onto that stage. This woman, he thought, was all the woman he ever needed. All the wife he ever cared for or dreamt of having.

"I need you," he whispered. "Only you. Every day. Every hour," he moaned, his fingers tousling her hair, his tongue tasting her face.

"Rose?"

"Leave her, Blue. Come back to me," she said kissing him with a ferociousness she'd never known. "Come back to me."

Blue yanked the mink from her shoulders, tossed it to the floor and picked her up in his arms. The seductive sounds she made as he carried her to the back room elongated his genitals and brought his mind to a very moist piece of chocolate cake.

"Merry Christmas, Rose."

"Merry Christmas, Baby."

Jamantha Williams Watson is an author of more than 100 books. When she is not writing, she enjoys performing, hosting her TV talk show and spending quality time with her family.

Mama's Key
By Jeida K. Storey

Janie shivered as she stood in front of the house, which should have belonged to her. The wind howled, stinging her ears and fingertips as she stood entranced by the two-story brick home. Covered in brilliant white Christmas lights and fresh fallen snow, the house sparkled beneath the moon's spotlight. The glittering ornaments of a Christmas tree shone through the bay window causing her to mourn the Christmas memories she never had the chance to make.

Janie trudged toward the front door. Each crunch of snow under her boots brought her closer to facing the life she'd left behind.

She stood frozen at the door. She looked down at the small gift box in her hand, feeling she didn't deserve to be on that porch, much less inside. She said a silent prayer, lifted her chin and knocked.

Janie heard the locks turn and her daughter's father swung the door open, effortlessly taking the wind from her lungs.

"Wow, you're here," Ryen said, pulling her into a hug.

Janie trembled from his touch.

"How long have you been out there? You must be freezing. Come on in and sit by the fire. Caryn, Janie's here."

Caryn sauntered around the corner, glowing like the angel atop the Christmas tree. Despite her stained apron, Ryen's wife looked like Michelle Obama stepping off the cover of Vogue magazine. "Oh, Janie. I'm so glad you could join us tonight. Welcome."

Janie marveled at the thirty-foot ceiling in the foyer, admiring the sparkling crystal chandelier. "You have some nice digs. Mighty gorgeous."

"Thank you. We're just sitting down to eat. Ryen, take her coat while I put the ham on the table. Good to see you, Janie." Caryn hurried into the kitchen.

Ryen stepped forward, but Janie raised her hand. She couldn't risk feeling his touch again. "Don't go fussing over me. I'm all right." She tossed the coat over her arm.

He smiled. "You look good, Janie. Been taking care of yourself?"

"Yeah, best I know how."

Janie heard laughter and an off-key duet as "Silent Night" by The Temptations began to play. "You sound like you have a house full."

"Just the kids and grandkids this year. Do you want to go in now?"

Janie looked toward the dining room and took a step back. She fiddled with the little gift box in her hand. "Would it be all right if I took a minute?"

Ryen nodded. "Sure. Let's go into the den."

Ryen didn't know what to expect when Janie walked through the door. He had protested the week before when Caryn said she'd invited Janie over for Christmas dinner after bumping into her in town. Having Janie around usually meant there would be family drama in her wake, but his kind-hearted wife convinced him to relent.

"I think she's changed, Ryen," Caryn had said. "She wants to make peace with you and Giselle. I think it'll be good for GiGi to see her mother."

Ryen watched as Janie took small steps toward the mantle. She stared at a baby picture of Giselle. She reached for the frame, but then pulled her hand back as if someone had swatted her with a switch.

"She's twenty-nine now," Ryen said. "Graduated with honors from Wayne State, received her law degree from Emory. Got married to a pastor last fall."

"You did a good job being her daddy," Janie muttered.

It's not like you gave me much choice, Janie. "We're so proud of her."

Ryen sighed. Janie looked beautiful as ever with her hair in a low ponytail and freckles dotting her nose, same as their daughter. There was a time when he'd loved Janie more than he wanted to admit. Before the drugs changed her.

Ryen met Janie on the hottest day of the summer in 1986. She was shooting pool with some friends, and one look at her long legs in those short shorts convinced him he had to have her. Ryen and Janie had only been together for seven months when she became pregnant. In the weeks leading up to delivery, Janie became depressed, but Ryen assured her they'd marry and raise Giselle, the name they'd chosen for their daughter, together.

Janie scoffed. "Now, Ryen, we didn't come from two-parent homes. What about that *is normal for people like us?"*

Once Giselle arrived, Janie seemed happier, but she refused to marry Ryen.

"Look, boy," she said. "You deserve a lady who loves you. That ain't me."

One night Janie showed up at Ryen's apartment with their daughter wailing in her arms. Tears streamed down Janie's cheeks, too, as she shoved Giselle at him. She put a gold necklace with a key attached to it around Giselle's neck and kissed her while Ryen soothed the child.

One look in Janie's eyes told him everything he needed to know, everything he feared. She ran out of the house and out of their lives three weeks before Giselle's first Christmas.

"We're ready to eat, you two." Caryn entered the room, distracting Ryen from his thoughts. "Everything okay in here?"

"Did you tell Giselle her mother is here?" Ryen whispered to Caryn.

Caryn shook her head. "No. I didn't actually think Janie would show, so I didn't bother telling her. Now, I don't know what to do."

"Maybe it'll be fine."

"Is all that whisperin' over there on my account?" Janie piped in. "You sure it's okay for me to be here? I can just leave my gift for Giselle and get out the way."

Caryn crossed the room and took both of Janie's hands. "You're family. You're not in the way."

Ryen cleared his throat. "Give us a few more minutes, darling. We'll be right in."

Caryn gave Janie's hand one more pat and left the room.

Ryen walked to the bar and took out two glasses. "Would you like something to drink?"

Janie looked at him like he was speaking Arabic. "I don't touch the stuff. I'm off everything now. Sober."

"That's one word I never thought I'd hear from your lips." Ryen smiled and filled the two glasses with fizzing liquid, handing one to Janie. "It's ginger ale."

Janie stared into her glass like she was looking for a wish in a well.

Ryen swirled his drink, clinking the ice cubes, thinking of the first time Janie had made an appearance at a family gathering.

Janie had not bothered to keep in contact with Ryen or visit Giselle, but Ryen knew all about her. The whole town knew Janie could be found slumming the streets. The pretty, light-skinned girl who used to make Ryen stop in his tracks, now walked the streets of Detroit strung out on crack and carrying weeds she'd snatched from people's yards. Sometimes she pulled them in a child's stolen wagon or pushed them in a wheelbarrow. Other times, she'd put them in her hair and pockets. Sometimes, if he saw her, he'd speak but she'd smile and try to sell him a dandelion for fifty cents. She didn't even recognize him. Pushing aside his feelings and shattered heart, Ryen focused on raising Giselle and by the time she was two, Caryn had come into their lives and became the only mother Giselle knew.

Ryen didn't see Janie again for seven years until she stumbled onto his mother's porch during Sunday dinner. Ryen had answered the door and recoiled when he saw her. The drugs had deteriorated her visage and her soul.

"Where's the girl?" Janie tried to force herself into the house.

Ryen blocked her. "Get on out of here, Janie."

"I want to see my baby. Move out my way."

Frieda, Ryen's mother, rushed to the door. "Don't let that woman in my house. There's nothing in this house that belongs to the likes of you. Go on and find a wagon to pull."

Janie didn't seem to hear her; she'd fixed her eyes on something inside the house. Ryen looked over his shoulder and saw Giselle staring back at her mother with wide eyes. Caryn held Giselle's hand and tried to coax her into another room.

"Giselle." Janie reached for her. "Come here. Come to mama."

Giselle's brows furrowed and she looked at Caryn. "Who is she?"

Caryn gathered Giselle into her arms. "Ryen, get her out!"

Ryen grabbed Janie's arm and tugged her away, slamming the front door.

He stuck his finger in her face. "You're not going to play this game. You don't get to crawl in here like this. That's my daughter in there."

Janie stood staring at the closed door. "She's my daughter, too."

Ryen nearly dropped his glass when he felt Janie's hand cover his bringing him back from that memory.

"You watching movies in that imagination of yours, huh?" She smiled.

He set his drink down on the table. "I was just thinking about what we've all been through. Some days were a nightmare, but even when those drugs made you someone I barely recognized, I know you still loved our girl. And I'm sorry that I kept her from you. It was selfish of me."

"You did a fine job protecting our baby from the monster in me. I ain't love myself. Sho' couldn't love on her. Not like you and Caryn did. All I want is the chance to try now."

He stood. "Well, then. How about we go out there and see your daughter?"

Janie's teeth began to chatter. Everything within her wanted to retreat. Ryen walked ahead of her and the room erupted with choruses of seasons greetings as he entered the dining room where everyone was seated. Janie hesitated, peering around the corner as a beautiful woman wrapped her arms around Ryen's neck. Her smile was wide as the ocean is deep, and her eyes were as shiny as a new penny.

Janie's fingers trembled as she brought them to her cheeks. *My baby.*

Janie hadn't seen Giselle in more than ten years, and had rehearsed what she'd say, but standing within a few feet of her, Janie was content just staring.

"Hey, Daddy." Giselle kissed Ryen's cheek. "Merry Christmas." She pulled away and a piece of jewelry snagged his sweater.

"Watch out now. My grandbabies bought me this." Ryen fiddled with the necklace clinging to the threads of his sweater.

"Sorry." She giggled. "You know I don't go anywhere without this necklace."

Janie gasped. She never expected Giselle to have kept the key she'd given her as a baby. She swelled with pride.

"That's right," Ben said. Janie recognized him from the photos as Giselle's husband. "GiGi told me it opens some music box. I've been looking all over to find one that fits."

Giselle tugged on the key, stood on her toes and kissed Ben's cheek.

Ryen looked toward where Janie stood behind the china cabinet. "Before we pray, we have a special guest with us tonight." Ryen reached out his hand.

Janie's heart thudded.

One of the children asked, "Is it Santa or baby Jesus?"

Janie shuffled into the dining room. With each step forward, Giselle's smile deflated.

Ben reached for her hand, but Giselle snatched away from him. She pressed her palms on the dining room table, dropped her head and took a deep breath.

"Dad." Her voice vibrated. "What is this?"

Ryen opened his mouth to speak, but Janie stopped him. "I came here to see you, Giselle."

Giselle rolled her head back until she was looking at the ceiling.

"Thought I might surprise you after all this time, you know."

Giselle shook her head and a guttural sound escaped from her lips. Janie watched everyone exchange confused looks.

Giselle's shoulders trembled, then heaved as she let out a laugh so loud it made Janie jump. She grabbed her sides and doubled-over until a single tear rolled down her cheek. Some of the children started to giggle, too, but Janie could hear the bitterness laced in Giselle's laugh.

Ryen rushed to Giselle's side. "Honey, I know you're in shock."

Giselle wiped the tear away as two more fell. "In shock? No. That doesn't begin to describe the *rage* I feel right now." Giselle approached Janie. "For those of you who don't know who this stranger is, this is Jane—Janie as they call her in the streets. My long lost mother who traded me for a crack pipe.

"Giselle," Caryn and Ryen shrieked in unison.

Giselle whirled around to face them. "You knew? You knew she would be here? Christmas is for family, and you let her walk up in here like the last twenty-nine years never happened?"

Janie shuddered.

Ben tried to comfort Giselle. "Babe, this isn't the time or place for—"

"Evidently it is. Other people in this room decided that for me." Giselle stepped closer to Janie. "You. Broke. Me."

Ryen found Giselle pacing in the den, holding onto her key. He and Giselle hadn't discussed her mother in years; he had no idea how large a grudge she held against Janie.

She didn't stop moving, so he took a seat and watched her for a moment. He remembered how he'd done everything he could to protect her, but he felt powerless against the rift Janie's addiction had caused.

"I'm sorry, baby," he said. "I didn't know you would react this way."

She stood still. "But you *had* to. How could you and Mom bring that woman into this house? I feel ambushed."

"We didn't think she'd come. But she did. And she's changed. I know you're angry with all of us, but don't lock yourself in a prison of bitterness. It's lonely in there."

Giselle sighed and plopped on the leather couch.

"You need to forgive Janie. I know she made some bad choices that affected us all, but she's ready to take responsibility for them. And she loves you."

Giselle huffed. "That's cute. If only she had loved me a little more than that crack."

Janie's voice filled the room. "Just because someone don't know how to love you properly don't mean that person don't love you with all they got." Janie walked inside the den and sat opposite Giselle. "I hope you know this ain't easy for me, either. I almost didn't come. I didn't know what you'd say when you saw me or what you might think. Hell, I'm scared now just sitting in the same room as you. But I'm not gon' run from you no more."

Giselle scoffed.

"I know you don't believe me. Can't say I blame you. You probably wondering what I'm here for in the first place, huh?"

"Damn, right," Giselle muttered.

"I ain't here to ask for nothing but a chance to explain." She took a deep breath. "I've been running all my life. From everything and everybody that ever gave me some sort of purpose. In my mind I was never gon' be somebody or go somewhere. I wasn't good at nothing but screwing and getting high. You weren't my first pregnancy, and damn sure wasn't my last, but you're the only one I kept. And I did that for your daddy."

"I don't want to hear anymore," Giselle said.

"Please hear me out before I lose the courage. I got excited about you when I started feelin' you kick all inside me any time I laughed. That made me feel real good. I even stopped smoking and snorting because I was real sure I could change for you. But my demons was just too fierce.

"Ryen wanted to marry me, but I wasn't no good for him. Being a mama was something I thought I could do, but when I saw all the things your daddy could give you that I couldn't… Well, I felt like the bottom of somebody's boot. So I did what I do best. I took off and left you where I knew you'd be raised right."

Janie let out a heavy sigh that turned into a wheezing cough. "I know I went about it wrong, but I didn't mean no harm, girl. I wanted to see you. To kiss you, hold you. I wanted my laugh to make you kick again.

"That coke had me good, girl. I kept doing stuff that wasn't no good for me. But I wanted better for you. I always thought about ya. I needed you to do something with your life and I knew you would because you had that man right over there helping you get there."

"I pity you," Giselle spat out. "You have a sad life and I want nothing to do with it. I've erased your mistakes from my story. None of this matters anymore." Giselle stood.

"It should matter. You're going to be a mama soon."

Giselle froze.

"You are?" Ryen looked at his daughter.

"I…just found out, Daddy. I haven't even told Ben yet." Giselle pressed her hand to her flat tummy. "How did you—?"

"You might not think I'm worthy, but I'm still your mama. And you'll have a baby soon and you won't be perfect. You'll make mistakes, but you'll never stop fighting for their hearts, even if you're the one who broke it."

Giselle's eyes narrowed. "So, that's it? You get to come back and just ask for forgiveness and everything gets tied into a neat little bow like the end of a sitcom episode? I don't think you understand what this feels like. I am one of the top attorneys at my firm. I make decisions. People respect me. My husband's church has five thousand members. I'm loved and respected wherever I go in the community. But for years I never had my biological mother in my life and I never understood how I could be so important to so many others, yet so insignificant to you." Giselle returned to her seat and dropped her face in her hands and wept. "Where were you? All those years. Gone!"

"I'm so sorry." Janie rushed to Giselle's side. She placed a hand on her back, and when Giselle didn't recoil, Janie wrapped her arms around her.

Ryen caught his tears with his thumb.

Janie cradled her weeping daughter's face in her hands. "I've been clean four years now. I ain't have much of a choice. It was gon' kill me. I used to beg for death, but I'll run like hell from it now. I've got something to live for. You, girl, it's you."

"I'm still hurt."

"I know, but I'm going to do everything I can to make that hurt go away. I love you. Even if you hate me forever, I will love you 'til I can't no more." Janie's voice caught in her throat. She brushed her tears away. "Well, then. I think I better be going."

"Don't go, Janie. At least stay for a meal," Ryen said.

"I've caused enough excitement. But I wanted to give you this, Giselle." Janie handed her the gift she'd left beside her coat.

"What is it?" Giselle asked.

"It's a promise that I'm not going anywhere this time."

Giselle unwrapped the gift and inside was a round, crystal blue music box.

"It was my grandmother's. Any ounce of fight in me came from her. I thought you might want it."

Giselle turned it over in her hands. "It's beautiful, but how do I open it?"

Janie handed her an odd-shaped key wrapped in tissue paper. "I told you. It's a promise."

With that, Janie walked out the door.

Giselle turned to Ryen with bloodshot eyes. "She's gone. Again." She sighed and tinkered with the music box. The lock clicked but didn't open. Giselle shook the box, but it remained closed.

She lifted her hand to her necklace and unfastened it. She held the golden key in her trembling fingers as she put it inside the keyhole on the music box. Nothing happened. "I don't know what I was thinking."

"Baby, I have to confess," Ryen said. "I didn't give you that key you love so much. It was Janie."

"What?" Giselle stared at both keys in her palm, then gasped. "Oh my God!"

Janie pulled her coat collar up as she walked down the driveway. She heard the front door slam behind her.

"The key!" Giselle exclaimed.

Janie spun around, tears streaming down her face.

Giselle rushed toward her, holding both keys together. They were puzzle piece matches, clasped together to form one key. She inserted them into the lock. It clicked and opened, allowing soft music to escape.

Giselle flew into Janie's arms, weeping on her shoulder. "All this time I've been searching and you've been holding what I've been looking for. And this is how I know you'll always come back. I hold the key."

"Oh, no, no." Janie sobbed. "You *are* the key, girl."

Jeida K. Storey is an Atlanta native where she received her Bachelor of Arts degree in English and Creative Writing from Georgia State University. She is a contributing author of the bestselling and award-winning anthology, The Ex Chronicles. Find out more about her by visiting www.jeidakstorey. com.

Red Heartstrings
By Cryssy Dee

Almost fearful of touching the tiny clothing on the rack, Jennisyn MacKay pulled herself away from the Christmas-themed toddler dress and prayed that she wouldn't have another breakdown in the baby section. She reminded herself that she was there for supplies and not to get distracted with self-pity.

She tried to remain focused as tears filled her eyes but refused to fall. Jennisyn took a trembling hand and placed it on her flat stomach, knowing that instead of life and promise, death resided inside her womb surrounded by adhesions and pain. As she took a deep breath to compose herself, she stepped back and slightly bumped into another person. When she looked up, she was face to face with a woman that was living the life she was supposed to have.

Jennisyn couldn't speak as the average-looking light skinned black woman protectively placed a hand over the rounding of her belly before quietly excusing herself. The woman didn't know her, but Jennisyn knew exactly who she was. As she tried to gather her bearings, she lost all sense of time or how long she had been standing there. Her heart shattered and she almost crumbled to the floor as reality reminded her that she was an aunt, a godmother, and a favorite babysitter, but not a mother.

Jennisyn would never be a mother.

Her once favorite holiday season was ruined and her visions of future traditions with her offspring would never come to be. She dreaded the Christmas joy or having to congratulate another mother-to-be at a holiday party on their blessing when her one wish of having a family would never be granted.

She touched her neatly placed high bun out of nervousness and knew that she wouldn't be able to accomplish the goals assigned to her as host of her best friend's baby shower. Looking for an escape, Jennisyn hurried out of the department store as quickly as she could without drawing attention to herself. She couldn't make it to her car quick enough. As soon as she entered the small space that shut her off from the world, she placed her face in her hands and sobbed.

She cried for her failure. She cried for her broken dreams. She cried for her ungratefulness.

Considered a brown-skinned beauty with natural hair pride, Jennisyn was less than a year away from being thirty yet, internally, she was ten years older, aged by endometriosis and polycystic ovarian syndrome, commonly known as PCOS. Two separate female disorders that robbed her of her dream of being a mother while crippling her health and affecting her entire body.

Ignoring the Texas winter's chill that had filled her car and through teary eyes, Jennisyn looked at her naked left hand where a romantic engagement ring used to be and sensed another loss.

Her passion for being a wife.

One year and an engagement party later, her fiancé quickly realized that she would never give him any sons or daughters, but instead, bear him with the burden of being her caregiver. All the love he'd given that had made her feel special and important, he took back and walked away to find another woman who could fulfill the job that she could not. No matter how much she tried, she would never be able to complete the circle of life.

The time of the year when families celebrated peace, love, and joy, Jennisyn was consumed with soul-wrenching pain and an emptiness inside her that would never be filled. From within her car, she wanted to scream out loud as depression graced her heart. With that came the questions that would never leave her mind. What made her unworthy to be called mommy? She was a good person with a good heart, right? How could less deserving women be afforded the gift of a lifetime when they didn't appreciate how special it was?

Some days were so rough that she had no choice but to share the cause of her tears with family, friends, or co-workers, only for her pain to be discredited by ignorant and irrelevant advice. Or worse, the suggestion of adoption. As if her desperation to feel the creation of life from within her own body would lessen with an unrelated baby in her arms. She didn't just want the aftermath; she wanted the personal journey to motherhood.

She wanted the choice that had been stolen away from her.

Jennisyn looked out the window to nothing in particular and knew that there would be no December magic to adhere to the desires of her heart and just like last year, the gifts under the tree wouldn't satisfy the happiness she longed for. Her hand trembled as she wiped her cheeks and tried to find the faith to restore her strength. She had prayed and coached herself all morning and thought she could handle the simple task of baby shopping, but it proved harder than expected, especially when she ran into the last person that she ever wanted to see.

It was Tuesday night and even though she had been avoiding the meetings for months, she knew where she needed to be. Jennisyn carefully drove out of the parking lot and let memory transport her to the one place where she didn't feel as alone. Her thoughts remained on the quick encounter from earlier as she drove.

Once she arrived at the church, she pulled around to the back of the building where non-members could meet up to use the space as needed. As she sat in her car, she saw familiar faces and as much as she wanted to just drive home and cry herself to sleep, she got out and entered through the side door.

"Jennisyn! Welcome back!" the head lady in charge called out. She was beyond her child-bearing years, but had never been blessed with any kids of her own.

"Hey, Sonica." Feeling less than friendly, Jennisyn tried to be polite.

"Today seems to be a down day for you. Am I right?"

"Yeah."

"Well, c'mon. We have new members and you can reintroduce yourself during share time."

Jennisyn felt like a stranger in a room where she used to cry out her frustrations and demand a cure when she knew there wasn't one. Instead, she gave a half-smile to the other women of different ages and backgrounds, all sharing the same agonizing grief. Seeing her once friend of convenience and circumstance, Jennisyn sat down next to Nessa, but felt the presence of sadness that loomed around her.

"I didn't think you would ever be back here after the last time we spoke," Jennisyn whispered to the woman that she hadn't spoken to in months.

"Another miscarriage," was all Nessa said before turning her attention back to Sonica.

Jennisyn knew that no amount of words of encouragement or condolences could mend the broken heart of the woman who had just lost her sixth baby. In their world, silence wasunderstanding.

Silence was respected.

"Let's get started, ladies. I'm Sonica and I'm the founder of The Dallas/ Fort Worth Chocolate Circle Support Group. We are sometimes called CC's and everything, within dignity, is allowed here. This space is for you to express your journey or your struggles without any judgement."

"Is the group named the Chocolate Circle because we're all black?" the unfamiliar face of a new member asked after raising her hand.

"No." Reva, the co-founder and Sonica's best friend, laughed. "The support for awareness ribbon color for endometriosis is yellow, but teal for PCOS. If you mix those two colors together you get brown, but chocolate seemed like a better description of that color."

Reva was middle-aged and the only mother by adoption in the group.

Sonica nodded, then added, "And it should go without saying, we don't speak about what was discussed here with anyone, especially online. Some of the things we will share are very personal. Moving forward, who wants to go first?"

"I will." A woman with a youthful glow raised her hand. "My name is Yalenna and this is my first time here."

"Hi Yalenna. Welcome and thanks for volunteering," Sonica stated.

"I'm twenty four years old and was just diagnosed with both endometriosis and PCOS a few months ago. I always knew something was wrong, but doctors made me feel as if I was crazy for suggesting that they actually do their job and find the root cause of my pain."

"Amen!" rang out from the twelve women who filled the small room.

"I've been married for two years and we've been trying to have a baby since day one. I come from a huge family and that's our tradition. I always knew that I would have multiple kids, but my body wouldn't conceive. We've tried every natural and old wives' tale that you can think of since our beliefs won't allow us to use modern day fertility treatments. I want to just go see a specialist, but my husband and our family won't allow it. I'm not praying hard enough, they say. My faith isn't strong enough, they say. At this point, I'm completely defeated and tired of feeling like a failure as a wife," Yalenna softly said as she wiped a single tear from her eye before sitting down.

Being gifted in the ability to speak in a soothing tone, Sonica responded, "Thank you for sharing with us, Yalenna. Speaking for the first time is always the hardest because all of your deepest thoughts are now being heard out loud. A couple of the ladies here have conceived naturally so I recommend that you speak with them after the meeting."

Yalenna just nodded her head as Sonica looked directly at Jennisyn.

Knowing that Sonica would stare her down, she loudly cleared her throat and started, "Most of you know but I'm Jennisyn. I used to regularly attend but after confirmation of my infertility and the ending of my engagement, I couldn't come anymore. Anyways, today was a bad day. I'm hosting another baby shower and it seems as if everyone is either using the season to announce their pregnancy or to celebrate their baby's first year. I can't escape the sadness that this month brings. Last year, I was to be married on Christmas day to the love of my life and I knew by this time, we would be having our first child. My life was set. My future was guaranteed to be everything that I prayed for. But, everything changed after my laparoscopic surgery. Lesions were discovered along my pelvic cavity and cysts were found on my ovaries. I was officially diagnosed with stage two endometriosis and PCOS."

Jennisyn took a moment to gather herself before sharing the rest of her story. "I literally went to bed one night, healthy and ready for the next chapter of my life, then the next day, I had both a progressive disorder and a hormonal disorder. Both were painful and chronic with no cure. Both caused infertility and stole the essence to make me feel like a woman. My hair thinned and my bladder became weaker. Acne covered my face, chest, and back. I gained weight uncontrollably while my stomach remained twisted with nausea and unable to digest food I once enjoyed. I was no longer able to sleep peacefully and when I did get any rest, I sweated so much that I soaked myself and the mattress. Moments of depression and attacks of anxiety fell upon me. But, the worst had to be the episodes of fatigue that plagued my body. I felt like I had run a marathon, then got hit by a bus. I would be bedridden with shortness of breath due to the exhaustion. I had zero energy that could last anywhere from days to weeks at a time and no one could understand why. I didn't look sick, but internally, I felt like death."

Jennisyn didn't know what else to say or how to end her emotional rant. She felt better and worse all at the same time.

"I'm just sick of being tired and tired of being sick." With that, Jennisyn sat down and wished to disappear from her surroundings.

"Thank you, Jennisyn, and it's nice to have you back again. We've all been there before, so know that we feel you," Sonica said, her voice full of encouragement.

As other women stood up to share their personal journey, Jennisyn tried to prevent from crying for them. Darlas, a successful professional turning 40, just found out that her husband got tired of waiting and cheated with his mistress to have a baby. Kenda, the biracial graduate student struggling to conceive her second child, could no longer afford fertility treatments as her health insurance barely covered any of the costs. And Stelle, the stay-at-home wife, had her church family forcing her to quit the group as they believed her infertility was due to her surrounding herself with other barren women.

Jennisyn had forgotten that some people believed being barren was a curse. As if she should be shamed into staying away from women who had the opportunity to give life. What made people think that she deserved the illness that overtook her body? What made them think that she could just pray it away?

People's ignorance frustrated Jennisyn to the core. They were uneducated when it came to a simple online search of the topic. They always blamed the woman, when there was documented proof that the cause of both disorders were unknown but commonly hereditary. Realizing that she had been lost within her own thoughts, she focused back on the group when she saw that they were all standing up to end the meeting. Jennisyn hadn't even heard any of the other topics discussed after share time.

"Remember, one of us is only a phone call or message away from support. I know you feel alone and we each suffer differently, but there's help if you want it, so find a buddy," Sonica said.

Nessa used to be Jennisyn's buddy, but her inability to get pregnant caused tension in their attempt at a friendship. Even though Nessa couldn't carry a child for longer than a few months, she had been closer in her goal of motherhood and Jennisyn secretly despised her for that. Jennisyn had no clue how it felt to have life growing inside of her and she desperately craved to know that experience.

As much as she wanted to walk over and briefly speak to Nessa, she knew that they were both in a state of hurt where a simple conversation would be a waste of both of their time. They weren't friends and they weren't suffering in the same manner. They couldn't console each other when Jennisyn didn't know what a miscarriage felt like and Nessa didn't know how it felt to never see a positive pregnancy test.

Together, they all recited the motto of the support group before leaving for the night. "To each its own, the journey begins. The cause unknown, the struggle will end."

"So, what happened that made you come back tonight?" Sonica asked, approaching Jennisyn from behind after the meeting had ended.

"I saw Atia today while shopping."

"Your ex-fiance's pregnant girlfriend? Did she speak to you?"

Jennisyn shook her head. "She doesn't know me, but I recognized her from the pictures he posts online. It's only a matter of time before he makes her his wife."

"I'm sorry. Are you doing okay?" Sonica reached out and gently squeezed her hand.

"I don't have a choice but to be all right. I can't change anything," Jennisyn replied with glum. She had been managing her sadness very well, but today was overwhelming.

"Especially with Christmas being right around the corner, this is a tough time for all of us."

Jennisyn remained quiet as she pondered over how the upcoming holiday would affect her for the rest of her life. Would she always be depressed when she should feel jolly? Would there ever be a moment where she didn't want to crawl into a ball and die when she saw a pregnant wife or the giggling smile from a baby? Could she ever think about her ex and his new family without feeling even worse about herself?

"Regardless, you have to forgive yourself. It's important," Sonica added.

To Jennisyn, forgiveness, at times, seemed impossible.

"Since this is a public group open to any woman with any preference, I can't ask this in front of them, but do you want me to pray with you?"

"Umm…no, but thanks. I think I need to do this by myself."

Jennisyn had spent the beginning of the year being mad at God for cursing her body. She was angered that as a loyal follower of His word, He would prevent her from the happiness that she sought. She may not have been the perfect Christian, but she always strived to be more like Christ. Then one day, during the summer, she remembered that God's Will wasn't for her to understand. Even though she still had her moments of doubt and the temptation to succumb to the weakness of mental and physical exhaustion, she had a mustard seed of faith. She didn't know how or when, but she still had a small glimmer of hope that God would heal her in His own way.

As she left the meeting and walked toward her car in the dark parking lot, Jennisyn tried to ignore how the cold weather made her feel even more alone but silently gave thanks that Dallas wasn't experiencing a white Christmas. She entered her car, locked the doors, and closed her eyes as she placed her head on the steering wheel.

She needed to renew her mind and cleanse her spirit of the damage that the day had inflicted. Jennisyn resumed her unwavering prayers for peace and purpose. Her newfound Christmas wish would be for acceptance and self-love in spite of the path that had been chosen for her.

With constant reaffirmation and daily prayers, she knew that in time, there would be another journey to happiness for the family that she desired. Maybe next Christmas, Jennisyn's want wouldn't be just a dream.

She placed her car into drive and proceeded towards her apartment complex. It was late and she was tired, but she could feel it. In her heart.

Hope.

Her lips curled into a smile as warmth filled her internally. At that moment, that was all Jennisyn had and all she needed to stay positive about the future.

Cryssy Dee is new to the writing world but can't wait to share her stories as they reflect self truth and her very own perspective of reality. She can be followed at Author Cryssy Dee on Facebook, Twitter, and Instagram.

Christmas Time is Here
By Candy Jackson

"I'm so durn excited I could just pee my pants."

My mother thought I was quite the character; it had been that way since I was a kid.

Oh she wanted a dainty little lady, but she got herself a ninja. She claimed that all through my childhood I climbed every tree, walked every creek and she couldn't keep me off the court b-balling with my crew, the neighborhood boys.

"Mommy, it's been so long since I've seen him."

My mother was preparing a feast for Christmas. She had the ham baking and the potato salad finished and chilling in the fridge.

We didn't have a big family, but we had enough neighbors to fill the house with joy.

"Well, what time is his flight arriving?"

I didn't even answer her question. I just buzzed around the kitchen barely containing my composure. It had been four years since I'd laid my eyes on my very best friend in the world.

When we were kids, we got into all kinds of mischief, so much so, our parents wouldn't even let us sit together in church.

We played together and went to school together and any time someone tried to come for me, well, because I was such a runt, he was the one who would fight for my honor.

We were so close there was never any doubt who would be sitting with whom at school or a football game or anywhere else.

"So, when did this super duper friendship turn into romance?"

I'd been avoiding her questions, but this one caused me to whip around nearly dropping the bowl of cake batter I was holding in the process. "Who said anything about romance?"

My mother walked over to me, and with her small hand, she patted my cheek. "Come on now, Jodi, you're my baby, my only girl. I know everything about you." She took the dishtowel she was holding and swatted my butt, then made a beeline to the other side of the kitchen.

We both burst into laughter.

But then, when my mom went back to basting the turkey, my thoughts went back to Idris and that night four years ago when he left for basic training.

I'd been so devastated when he first told me the news. This would be the first time we'd be apart. I mean, we went to grade school and middle school together. When our mothers thought we were a little too close, they decided to split us up for high school. It didn't matter though because our schools were right next to each other and because his was an all-boys and mine an all-girls school, so in the end, our schools did almost every function together.

They decided to throw in the towel when we both won scholarships to Georgetown University.

But, nothing had prepared me for Idris leaving.

My mother broke though what I was thinking. "Well, he's a fine fellow and you know, your father and I consider him family. And even if we didn't, he's eaten enough of our food to be ours."

Again we both laughed.

"You know how much we care for him, well, his whole family. I tell you, when Herbert passed and Emily had to make a way for Idris and his brothers, I knew we had to step in and help. I love that boy like he was my own."

"I know, Mama."

"So, when did this relationship turn into, well, a relationship?"

I wanted to tell her I had loved him my entire life. I wanted to tell my mama that if I could choose the perfect man , I'd choose Idris, over and over again.

But, I didn't tell her any of that. "I don't know really; it just sort of happened." I sat on a stool at the island and started cracking the hard-boiled eggs so she could make her legendary shrimp deviled eggs, leaving the cake batter as though it was going to make it's own way into the pan.

My mama wiped her hands on her Christmas apron and took the seat beside me. "You know, sweetie, you've always been such a sensible girl. I never had to worry about you and that was mostly because wherever you went, Idris was close behind. Sort of like where there's smoke, there's fire."

I was thinking, and I'm sure she was too, about the time when we decided to camp out in the back yard with his two older brothers and my two older brothers and they made us believe we had started a campfire.

Jude, the oldest of the bunch, had given us both two sticks and we rubbed and rubbed, but nothing happened. Just looking back, picturing those four getting a kick out of their youngest siblings actually believing we had started that fire, made me smile hard.

Well, we kept complaining that the sticks weren't working, and then Ivan, Idris' older brother, told us to go find bigger sticks in the yard by the big oak tree. We got over there and one of them used lighter fluid on the pile of sticks and nearly burned down the yard.

Our parents were at a community social and one of the neighbors called the fire station. By the time our parents got home, the entire neighborhood had surrounded the house.

It was only when Idris' father threatened to whip him did our brothers admit to pulling a stunt on us.

"You remember when he left for the military?"

My mother shook her head.

"Well, the night before, he told me that he couldn't picture himself with any other woman. Mama, it was the sweetest thing I'd ever heard. Anyway, he asked me to be his lady. He said when he got back we would announce it to the world."

"Announce what? That you go together. For Heaven's sake, you two are old enough to marry."

My mother said what my heart already knew, but I would wait for as long as it took. "Well, he said that he had something important to tell me. I've been sneaking around his mama, asking her what did she think it was. I'm thinking he's going to pop the question."

Mama got up, walked toward the refrigerator, and started pulling out more ingredients.

"Mama?"

"Well, I'm not sure, but what I do know is that marriage is a big step. Are you sure you're ready for marriage?"

I didn't even waste a moment. "Yes, yes, I'm ready."

It was almost as if my mother didn't hear me. She said, "You're a good nurse, Jodi. You've worked hard and now you're the head nurse of the prenatal ward. You're the youngest person in the history of that hospital to ever do that."

It felt like my mother was trying to talk me out of my desire to marry Idris, but why? I knew she loved him.

"Mama, what's going on? Why are you saying all of this?"

She turned to add something, but before she could muster a word, my nieces burst through the kitchen like two thunder cats with my oldest brother, Jude, and both of my sisters-in-law carrying trays of food and shopping bags filled with red and green packages.

We were still in the middle of hugging and kissing when the doorbell rang. I dashed out the kitchen, hoping it was Idris. I couldn't wait to lay my eyes on his handsome face. The last time we spoke, he sounded so down and out and I prayed that he was all right. He was such a caring, loving man and I wanted him home so I could show him some of the love he gave so freely to everyone else.

I opened the door and wouldn't you know it? Mrs. Saunders, Ivan, his wife, their three children, and Irvin's wife, in all her pregnant glory, were standing there giving me grins filled with Christmas cheer.

I felt a stab of disappointment not seeing Idris with them, but I hugged and kissed everyone just the same, hoping they couldn't tell.

Finally, as everyone settled in, placing gifts under the huge tree that my daddy chose himself, I was able to ask, "Hey, where's Idris? Has his flight arrived?"

When no one answered, I asked, "Was it late?"

Still, no response.

"Have you talked to him?"

Everyone's eyes were on me. It felt like there was some horrible secret that everyone knew except me.

My mind twisted and I came to my own conclusion: Had he fallen in love with someone else?

Finally Ivan spoke up, "Irvin and his boys went to get him. Don't worry, Jodi, he'll be here soon enough."

I literally exhaled; I knew in my heart he would never do me wrong.

Mrs. Saunders's busied herself in the kitchen with Mama while the kids stayed by the tree, shaking gifts and giggling as they tried to guess what was in the packages.

I figured I had to keep myself busy for the next thirty or forty minutes, besides there was still lots to do.

***

My nieces and I along with the Saunders' grandchildren set the table.

Our house felt like Christmas, the most wonderful time of the year, at least it would be this year.

Once we finished the table, I snuck off to my room because there was one thing I hadn't done - I had to wrap Idris's gift.

I knew it was a perfect gift. I knew because throughout our childhood, all he ever talked about was traveling the world. That's why it was no surprise to me when he decided he would go into the military. He knew with an education tucked safely under his belt, he would go in as an officer.

Joining the military was a way to honor his father, who had spent twenty years in the Army but never ranked past Corporal because he'd only had a high school diploma. Idris always spoke so highly of his dad, and how he had the courage to work his way up when doing so was twice as hard for a black man. I was so proud of him, I couldn't even get mad when he finally told me he was enlisting.

I took the envelope from my desk to have one last look at the two tickets that would take us to Paris.

I thought about how we would find our spot on campus, the tree where we both etched our initials and the Greek letters symbolizing Omega Psi Phi and Delta Sigma Theta.

I smiled and nearly cried, remembering how it was in that moment when he said the sweetest words I've ever heard, "Jodi I love you. I've always loved you."

Tears began to trickle down my cheek and my heart swelled as I thought about the man I planned to give my virginity to in Paris.

I dashed to the bathroom to freshen my face and heard the kids running on the hardwood floors in the hallway close to my room. When I opened the door my nieces, Lacy and Kallie were standing there, giggling.

"Come on, Auntie Jodi, it's time to eat."

I let each one take a hand and we headed down the stairs.

"Are you gonna sit at the kids table with us?"

I knew why Lacy had asked me that. I told her last year I would sit at their table because the grown-ups were all stuffy, but that was last year when Idris hadn't come home for the holidays. He was sent to Syria and spent his fourth Christmas away from me. I wasn't going to the kid's table this year and I knew Lacy would be disappointed with my answer, so I kept quiet and let them lead the way.

We headed down the stairs and before I got to the bottom, I noticed everyone was standing around the door. Mrs. Saunders let out a squeal and covered her face with her hands.

My daddy parted the family that had gathered around and then he said, "Welcome home, son, welcome home."

At last, my man was home, and if everyone didn't hurry and move out of my way, there was going to be a serious problem. Of course I said that to myself.

My mother turned, saw me standing there and stretched out her hand for me. Then one by one, everyone began to step away.

There in the center of our families was the most handsome man I knew. The love of my life was home, but he wasn't standing. Idris was sitting in a wheelchair.

***

Before anyone could stop me, I went to him and fell to my knees. I looked up to his face and my heart stopped.

His smile said it all.

I threw my hands around his waist and wept like a child as everyone started talking at once.

"How was your flight?" my mother asked.

"Did you eat?" his mother wanted to know.

"Man, you're a sight for sore eyes," my father said. But I didn't mumble a word.

I just held on as he rubbed my back telling me he was okay, he was just fine.

It took a while, but my dad was able to pry me from Idris. His mother was next to hug him and then his family and my family all welcomed him home.

My father made a space for his chair at the table and we all gathered around for our Christmas prayer.

My father led our families in prayer while I held on to Idris' hand on one side and my mother's hand on the other.

"Dear Heavenly Father…"

My father became choked up and suddenly Mrs. Saunders was leading the prayer.

"It is you, God, who is great enough to bring my youngest boy home. We thank you, God, for this mighty blessing. We praise you, God, for his safe travels."

Then like a chain reaction, everyone - including the children - said their own special prayer until finally it was my turn.

For a few seconds I couldn't speak, but then I opened my eyes to see Idris, with his handsome, golden brown skin and deep-set eyes, smiling bigger than any one of us. He squeezed my hand.

"Heavenly Father, mighty and powerful, I thank You. I thank You for bringing Idris home to me. I thank you, God for our families gathered here to witness this miracle. He could be anywhere in the world, God, but he chose to be here with me, God, and I thank You. Yes, You have given me the best Christmas gift of all: my man." With a roar of laughter my father proclaimed, "Amen!"

Everyone sat down and we began to pass the dishes. There were so many questions being asked, so many bowls of food, so many smiles and tears of joy.

We ate and we talked and we cleaned and we sang and opened gifts, and then when the kids decided to head to the family room to play with their presents, our mothers served coffee, hot chocolate and rum cake.

We all got comfortable and Idris began to tell us how he had lost the use of his legs. Of course his family knew - his brother had been working closely with his doctors - but because he was determined to walk again, he swore his family to secrecy so that I wouldn't worry.

"We were headed into secluded territory that we thought hadn't been occupied. One of my men heard a sound, but I wasn't about to allow him to leave the truck. They were my men and that was my job. Most of them were fresh out of basic training, and were not really understanding the importance of why I needed to go ahead of them. I had extensive training in explosive devices, and knew what to look for but one of my men pushed a huge tumbleweed over with his rifle and disturbed a seed bomb. I was able to knock him out the way, but it went off sending me several feet into the air and landed me hard on my back."

I sat on the floor next to him and gasped; Idris took my hand. I didn't want to cry because he was so strong and so fearless. I wanted to be brave too, but the tears began to fall.

"Don't you cry for me, Jodi. I knew I was going to get out of there alive because I promised you I was coming home. I'm home, sweetheart."

I rose up on my knees and laid my head on his lap as he once again rubbed my back.

"Are your injuries permanent, son?"

Before Idris could answer, his brother Irvin spoke up. "I've been keeping up with his progress weekly."

Idris interrupted, "Listen, man, I can talk."

Everyone laughed as Irvin stood and announced he needed more coffee, but Mrs. Saunders, my mother, and I were glued to Idris' every word.

"They say my injuries are reversible with a lot of therapy and hard work. Take a look." Idris stretched out one foot and moved it from side to side, and although it was slow, we all shouted, thanking God for His restoration powers.

***

After a few hours of talking and singing carols, the ladies went into the kitchen to watch a Christmas movie and the guys gathered around the television to watch the 'Skins whip the Dallas Cowboys. Idris and I went into the study and talked.

"Why didn't you tell me?"

Idris took my hand and pulled me to his lap. I giggled and snuggled up to him. "I didn't want you to worry. I know you girl. You would have been on the first thing smoking and I didn't want you to see me like that. It wasn't a pretty sight, but it was even harder reading your emails and not telling you what was really going on. You remember that night I called you?"

I remembered all right, because I hadn't heard his voice in over a month.

"Well, I came really close to sharing the bad news then, but I held back. The sound of your voice gave me the determination to press through. That's when I decided I had to get up out of that bed and try with all of my might to walk again."

I couldn't hold on any longer, so I closed my eyes and pressed my lips to his. "I've waited a long time to taste those lips, Mr. Saunders."

Idris wiggled around and dug in his pocket. "I've waited a long time for this." He pulled a light blue box from his pocket. "I know I'm not the man I was, I may never be again, but if you'll have me, I promise to be all the man you need."

"Yes, yes, yes!" I screamed so loud everyone came running, probably thinking something was wrong.

"What in the world..." Mrs. Saunders nearly jumped from her skin when she saw us lip-locked and kissing.

With everyone standing around us, Idris announced our engagement. "This beautiful woman promised to be my wife."

With hugs and kisses all around, it turned out to be the best Christmas of my life.

***

"Come on, Jodi, hurry or we'll miss our flight."

I tried to hurry down the steps, but there was no way I could move that fast, so I decided just to take my time. I didn't want to chance falling or doing anything that would prevent me from getting on that flight to Paris.

"Girl, if you walk any slower the Uber driver is going to leave."

The driver got out and put our bags in the trunk, then opened the door for us.

It was a beautiful and bright winter morning and all I could think about was the two of us finally going to see Paris.

Once at the airport, the Uber driver was kind enough to walk inside the entrance doors and find an attendant with a wheelchair. With only forty minutes to spare, we made it through security in record time (which was an added bonus because the wheelchair was on its last leg, no pun intended) and got to the gate on time.

Once at the gate, Idris passed our tickets to the attendant and helped me from the wheelchair. "Girl, you gain one more pound and I'll have to go back into therapy." Idris had been walking for the last five months and it was truly a blessing because after gaining almost fifteen pounds in my first trimester, I needed all the help I could get.

I looked up at my husband, who after nearly a year of therapy, was walking again. And then, I looked down at our second greatest gift as Idris placed his hands on my baby bump and gently kissed me. After being seated in first class, locking our safety belts and getting comfortable, Idris took me by the hand and pecked my lips. This would be our first holiday as husband and wife and by tomorrow, Christmas day, it would be spent in Paris.

With his lips close to my ear, Idris whispered, "Guess what, baby?"

"What is it."

"It's midnight. Christmas time is here."

"Merry Christmas, Idris, Merry Christmas."

Candy Jackson is an author hailing from our nation's capital, Washington, DC. Her debut novel, Pink and Patent Leather, can be found everywhere books are sold.

The Beat of My Drum
By Yvette Danielle

I thank God for my child. He has taught me so much in the short time he has lived on this earth. Even now, as I slip inside our simple apartment I can't help beaming with pride at Isaiah. He is on his knees in his Batman pajamas in the center of our scuffed kitchen floor.

Pots and pans are upturned and spread around him in a semi-circle. His little hands thump on them with two wooden spoons; his mouth is partially opened; nose crinkled up, and eyes are so tightly closed, I swear he's pushed them back into their sockets. His concentration amuses me, and when I see the tip of his tongue peeking out the corner of his mouth, I know it's gotten good to him.

My mother emerges from Isaiah's bedroom by the kitchen. "Hey, baby, when'd you get in?"

The Gospel Music Channel streams from my son's television.

"Hey, Ma, just now."

She watches me for a moment. "How was work?"

"Long and tiring, and so not worth the little money it pays me."

"Good thing it keeps a roof over your head and food on the table. Amen."

"Mmm hmmn," I reply. I want to avoid the sermon that is bubbling on her lips and threatens to burst forth any minute. Besides, my son's day will be more interesting. I put on my happiest face and wave to get his attention. "Hey man, what are you playing?"

"Hi, Mommy. I'm playing a beat to *My God Is an Awesome God.*"

I ignore the smirk my mother wears as she appears beside me. "You're getting pretty good at banging on those pots and pans."

"These are my drums. Can't you see," he remarks, as only a child can. "One day I'm gonna get an even better set and then I will play for God all the time… and you, too, Mommy." A huge grin stretches across his handsome face and melts my heart. "Well that's going to be really special and I cannot wait to see it."

Isaiah nods in agreement. "Did you call up the drum school?"

"No, sweetie, not until I get the money together first. Right now I just can't swing it for you to go. I need to find a better job, remember I told you that?" I'm looking straight at him so I have his full attention.

"Yes, but Mommy, don't worry. God will get you a new job with more money so I can go to drum school. I can just play these drums until He gets my new ones."

"Who?" I ask.

"God." His jaw is firmly set as he rests his chestnut brown eyes upon my face. He looks so much like his father I can barely maintain focus. "Right… Okay, it's time for bed. You have school tomorrow. No more talk about drums tonight. You hear me?"

"Yes, ma'am." Isaiah raises himself off the floor and wraps his arms around my waist. "I love you, Mommy. Goodnight."

I plant a kiss on his cheeks. "I love you too, man, now go say your prayers and lights out." I hold out my hand to receive his makeshift drumsticks. Isaiah runs out of the kitchen into his room and I follow behind a minute later.

"Now I lay me down to sleep, I pray the Lord my soul to keep. If I should die before I wake, I pray the Lord my soul to take. God, bless Mommy, Nana and my daddy, too, even though he's not around."

My chest tightens. I feel a supportive squeeze from my mother's hand on my shoulder.

"…and Lord, could you please give Mommy that new job you promised tomorrow? She needs it because she works so hard cleaning up other people's stuff. Thank you, God, for all the love You give and blessings we have, and for my drums and money for drum school. I promise to be good and play for You whenever You want, and Mommy, too, when she's not so tired. Oh yeah, and if I've done anything bad, please forgive me, but don't tell Mommy 'cause she'll punish me. In Jesus' name. Amen."

Edgewood Community Music School offers wonderful programs for children ages seven to ten years old. Its primary funding derives from wealthy benefactors and the contributions of parents whose kids attend. I hesitate before opening those magnificent doors that face out toward State Street, feeling wedged in between my son's desires and my mother bellowing how '*God will make a way*.' Now seated in the school director's opulent office, my instincts were right not to come.

Her greeting is standoffish. My modest appearance doesn't mesh with her stylish couture and I feel completely out of place. But it's too late to run out because she's reviewing Isaiah's application, so I force myself to stay put.

"So, Mrs.-"

"It's *Miss* James," I politely correct her.

"How old is your child?"

"Seven."

"And how do you pronounce his name?"

"EYE-ZAY-UH…"

"That's very… unique." Her plastic smile is radiant. "What classes are you interested in?"

"The beginner's drum course."

"Yes, well, we have a class for his age group starting in three weeks. The ninety-minute session runs for twelve consecutive weeks and meets twice weekly. Our tuition cost is five hundred forty dollars total or forty-five dollars a lesson. We require a two hundred seventy dollar deposit upfront at the time of enrollment and the deadline to sign up is in two weeks. Would you like to make your deposit now?"

My head is swirling in numbers. "Oh, uhm… Well do you offer any scholarship support or financial aid?" I ask as I clear my throat.

"No, our school does not offer such… assistance. The best we can do is work out a financial arrangement, but that's only upon receiving the initial deposit."

I pull my navy pea coat tighter around myself. "I see. My son has this incredible passion to play drums for God." A laugh escapes my mouth without warning. It is a mixture of embarrassment, irony, and pain. "I just want to give him that opportunity."

"I do understand your position, Miss James. Unfortunately, there is nothing more I can do until that initial deposit is paid. Our school's policy prevents negotiating any alternatives beforehand. That payment covers half of the student's lessons and shows the parent's commitment to their child's musical education." She pauses. "Can you obtain the money from other family members? The child's father, perhaps?"

This meeting is officially a wrap. "Thank you for your time." I rise and start toward the exit, then circle back. She watches with interest. "May I take that application, please?"

"Of course. I wish you luck." She hands me the paperwork. The gesture is dismissive and conversation ends when she diverts back to her oversized iMac computer monitor. I take my cue and hurry the hell up out of there. Luck certainly had nothing to do with this. I was going to need more than that. *Just where am I supposed to get that kind of money in two weeks?* If Jesus really is able to come through, now would be a good time as any to prove it.

***

Isaiah is on the front porch of my daughter's house wailing away on that old cookware set of mine. My grandbaby told me he wanted to learn the drums, and I saw an opportunity to get even with his mama for times she liked to grate on my nerves. Remembering Stephanie's face the day I brought them over still put me in stitches. But I would do anything for Isaiah, and the highlight of my day is watching him until she comes in from work. I poke my head through the open window to check on him. He's talking with a boy, who's about ten, leaning on the outer gate.

"You're pretty good. What's your name?"

"Isaiah."

"I'm Dwayne. You have a drum set?"

"No, just these. But I'm gettin' one from Jesus."

"What?" Dwayne says. I pull the curtain back some more and get comfortable on the living room couch. "I'm getting a new set from Jesus," Isaiah explains. "I'm just practicing with these for now."

Dwayne and I smile in unison. "So you want to play drums for Jesus - just like the little drummer boy."

"Who's that?"

"You've never heard the story?"

Isaiah shakes his head. Dwayne comes inside the gate and sits on the two front steps. Isaiah puts his wooden spoons down to listen.

"Well, some people say it's a Bible story, 'cause it talks about when baby Jesus was born, but my Dad told me it's an old African legend not found in the Bible. See, on the day Jesus was born, three wise men came to give gifts to him of gold, frankincense-"

110

"Franken-what?"

"Frank-in-cents. It's some type of oil. He got that and another kind called myrhh. Anyway, people traveled from everywhere to see baby Jesus and one of them was a little African drummer boy. He wanted to leave something too once he saw the special gifts the wise men had, but he was poor with no money or anything. So, later that night, the little boy went to the manger where baby Jesus lived and he played his drum for him."

Isaiah's eyes grow big. He clenches the wooden spoons at his side.

"The drummer boy played his heart out, as best he could, and baby Jesus looked up smiling and touched him with his hand, then went to sleep. The legend says that anyone who stops, prays, and remembers Jesus Christmas day will hear the drummer boy playing that night, until all of God's children are asleep in peace."

"Wow, that's a cool story." Isaiah jumps to his feet. "That's gonna be me! My mommy will start her new job and have the money to send me to drum school soon."

I raise my eyebrows at Isaiah's remark. *Stephanie got a new job and didn't tell me?*

"How do you know?" Dwayne asked.

"I prayed for it."

"Did your Mom teach you to pray?"

"No, my nana did. She says, 'Don't go to bed 'til you pray and thank God first.'"

I'm trying to hold back from choking on my own tears. *Yes Lord*, I internally shout. *Bless these babies!*

***

Three days pass and I am no closer to having the school's deposit in time. Isaiah is overly amped about going, especially since befriending Dwayne, an older boy from the neighborhood. When he asked if I started the new job he prayed for, it tore me up to say no. He looked so disheartened. Seeing him that way made me silently wish a man was around to help provide for him. A knock at the front door jolts me from my private thoughts. When I open it, I see Dwayne standing next to an attractive, much older version of himself. *God, you're funny.*

"Yes?" I ask. Thank goodness I changed my clothes.

"Miss James? Hi, my son tells me you have a very talented drummer living in your house," the man says with a dimpled smile.

Now I am blushing. "Well, if you call beating on cookware a talent, I guess he's right."

Hearing laughter, Isaiah materializes from his room. "What's so funny, Mommy," becomes, "Hi Dwayne! Who's that with you?"

"Isaiah, don't be rude."

"Sorry."

The man raises his hand. "It's okay, Miss James, no offense taken." He turns to Isaiah. "I'm Dwayne's father, Mr. Murray." He extends his hand for Isaiah to shake. "I was just asking your mom about you playing the drums-"

Isaiah butts in. "I practice every day with these." He proudly pulls out his wooden spoons and demonstrates his skills by air drumming. I'm embarrassed, but Dwayne's father is too preoccupied with Isaiah's moves to notice.

"You play well."

"Thanks. I wanna play for Jesus like the little drummer boy Dwayne told me about."

Dwayne flashes a smile, and he and his dad share a look between them. It saddens me knowing Isaiah won't have such father-son bonding moments.

"My nana calls it natural talent 'cause I've never had lessons," Isaiah continues. "But I'm waiting for God's blessing to my mommy for me to go to drum school."

I put my arm around Isaiah's shoulder and squeeze. "Okay, man, I think you've bent Mr. Murray's ear enough." The smile on my face is tight. "If you let him, he'll talk you into unconsciousness." I kiss the top of my son's head. "So, what brings you by Mr. Murray?"

"Please, call me Trenton – Trent, for short," he says. "I am the youth pastor of our church and run the children's music ministry. When Dwayne said he met a seven-year-old who wanted to play for the Lord, I just had to meet him myself. Do you have a church home, Miss James?"

"Stephanie, please, and uhm… no." I look away. "I go with my mom sometimes when I have the energy, but I work a lot and Sunday is my only day off. But Isaiah usually goes with her every week."

Trent mercifully interrupts my rambling. "Well, Dwayne has something he'd like to give your son if that's okay with you."

Excited, Isaiah blurts, "What is it?"

My interest is piqued too. Dwayne chuckles. "I have an old drum set just sitting in our basement. It used to be my dad's, and even has drumsticks that are painted gold." He winks at Isaiah.

"*Yesssssssssss*," Isaiah squeals. He jumps around, drops his wooden spoons and bear hugs Dwayne. I am moved by their generosity and the immense happiness my son displays.

"I really don't know what to say or how to thank you-" I begin.

"I do," Isaiah proclaims. "Hallelujah, hallelujah, *hallelujah!*"

***

Trent and Dwayne invite us to youth service that Sunday. I decide to go to show my gratitude for Isaiah's awesome gift. Trent proposed bringing the drum set to my place afterward. I planned to make lunch while they set it up. I must admit service is pretty great. The congregation is filled with young kids, teens, and a nice mix of adults close to my age who are there supporting the youth. Trent is delivering today's message, and Isaiah is captivated by him. He is rather charismatic and, as the service winds to a close ninety minutes later, I really didn't want it to end.

Lord, we thank You for the many blessings You have given each of us, big and small. Father God, we honor and praise You for the awesome sacrifice You made for us through your son, Jesus. Thank You for showing us just how strong the family tie can be - we know a family who worships together in the house of the Lord and the presence of God is a powerful thing… and today, God, I feel Your Spirit telling me there is someone here with a need only You can fill… but this person doesn't believe You are God Almighty, who can do all things…God says He cannot make a way when you are in the way. Your faith unlocks the blessings for your family. A child cannot do it for you. But today, it is because of your seed -this child- that God releases to you what is yours. To show you that He is and has always been your provider... your first love... and a Father to the fatherless. So right now, if you can believe that...Step away from your pride and move out by faith... Come, receive your gift from the Lord...

I cannot hide the tremors or tears erupting from my eyelids like water behind a broken dam. My feet stagger and I am not ready for this complete meltdown happening as I press forward. My mom is shouting from the sidelines with the rest of the church, Isaiah at her side. But Trent is the one with a bird's eye view from the pulpit. By the time I make it to where he stands, I am an absolute sniveling mess.

He compassionately leads me into a prayer of salvation and repentance before doing the strangest thing: he reaches into his pants pocket and removes a wad of cash from his wallet. "Stephanie, God has given me something for you." My heartbeat is a talking drum as he counts out two hundred seventy dollars and places the money into both of my hands. My knees give out. I am utterly broken. The last words I remember hearing are, "I am doing this out of obedience to our Father, who always keeps His promises."

***

We had a high time in that youth service today, yes indeed. I watched my child give her life to the Lord -*hallelujah*- and my grandbaby witnessed the miracle of God's blessing firsthand. *Glory to God.* Stephanie admitted once we were back in the house that the blessing she received from Pastor Trent would pay for Isaiah to start music school. She hadn't said a word to anyone. Not even me, *her own Mama.* I told her He'd make a way, because if there's one thing I know to be true about God, it is this: He is good all the time.

***

My stride is confident when I stroll into the school director's office the following week in a black Tahari suit my mother bought to celebrate my new job. I am now the office supervisor of the cleaning company I work for.

"I'm here to enroll my son into your music school. We spoke last week," I added, handing her Isaiah's application. "I'm Stephanie James."

"Yes, I remember you… so you wish to *enroll* him?"

I dig in my oversized purse and dramatically pull out a handful of cash. The director tries not to gawk at me.

"I believe you said the cost needed up front is two hundred seventy. Right?" I hand her the bills. "And that only covers half of the tuition?"

She busies herself counting to avoid eye contact. "Yes, that's correct."

I go into my purse again and withdraw more money. "Then I would like to pay for my son's tuition in full."

Her face has fought a losing battle and her mouth drops. "Well, this is certainly a surpri-… I mean good news."

"Yes, my Father came through for me."

The director rises from her desk chair and walks around to my side. She seems dazed and leans against the edge for support. "Are you all right?"

"Well, to be honest, Miss James, since your last visit our Board received a substantial donation from a former student of ours to use for an annual scholarship. It's to be named 'Abraham's Seed' and will provide children of low-income families the opportunity to take classes here."

My hand covers my chest as she continues. "This donor wants public anonymity and expressed strict prerequisites. Awards shall only be given to a child whose parents take initiative to inquire about Edgewood's programs. They must show the same heart and desire to enroll the child as the child has to learn here.

"It's been approved, and the first full-year scholarship can go to the parent who's met these criteria. You, Miss James, are that parent."

I have to sit down. *This cannot be happening for real.*

"It's the most eccentric request I've ever heard," she maintains, "and the Board agrees, but considering the value of the gift…" She waves her hand dismissively.

"I taught here when this donor attended. He was from a poor household and wanted desperately to take lessons. He'd hang around and just watch because his mother couldn't afford to pay our tuition or buy an instrument. One of the teachers nevertheless took sympathy on him and privately instructed him, free of charge, even shared his equipment.

Afterwhile, a stranger heard him play during a concert and bought his first instrument, delivered here to Edgewood, upon making some inquiries. This student practiced faithfully every day after school. He was truly gifted and one of the finest musicians I ever heard play." She closes her eyes momentarily, her thumb and index finger cupping her lips and chin. A reminiscent grin unfolds beneath her hand.

She regains her composure. "So you see, Miss James, your money is no good here for at least one year. Your son's tuition is covered, and he can start taking his lessons in two weeks." She retrieves the cash from her desk and hands it to me.

I want to jump on this woman, hug her tightly and shout, scream, cry and dance out this joy bubbling over inside me. But instead I calmly and politely thank her as I stand to leave. This time is even more humbling than the last. Stopping at the door's threshold, I turn toward her one last time. "May I ask what instrument this student-donor played?"

"Drums. With golden drumsticks."

I smile as I walk away, knowing my own little drummer boy would sleep that night in perfect peace.

Yvette Danielle lives in Raleigh, North Carolina. Her first published story, Pursue.Conquer.Destroy is featured in the award-winning anthology The Ex-Chronicles, also with Brown Girls Books, and is a national bestseller. Her love of writing started early in her adolescent years, and she attributes an active imagination to her colorful style of storytelling. She is currently working on her debut novel. Visit her website, www.yvettedanielle.com and connect with her on social media via Goodreads/Facebook Page: Yvette Danielle, Twitter @ydanielle and Instagram @yvettedanl.

Merry Christmas Mama
By A. Rozelle

December 23

"Coming, Mama," I mumble. Auto-pilot kicks in and I rise from my sleeping position far more slowly at the age of forty-three than I would have at twenty-three and will my eyes open. My feet find my slippers under the bed; my hands find the robe hanging on the bedpost without my having to look for it. I'm standing, with one houseshoe on, half in my robe before it hits me: Mama's gone. I buried her three days ago.

I kick the houseshoe off, shrug off my robe, pull back the crumpled sheets and comforter, and more or less roll myself back into the still-warm spot where I'd *finally* managed to hunt down sleep around 4 a.m. I already know I won't be lucky enough to find it again so instead, I lie awake and look around the room my son, Marlin, grew up in. The room in *my* house that became mine when I moved Mama — who was recovering from a stroke - into the house two years ago.

My spacious, gorgeously decorated and light-filled master bedroom became Mama's because, unlike my current digs, it has a bathroom that was necessarily close when time was of the essence, which it usually was when Mama wanted to be independent and make her own way to the "potty." She'd reverted to calling it that after the stroke, when speaking was difficult for her. It was painful to witness her struggle to make words match up with thoughts, her fight to make one side of her body do the things it had always done so easily - the normal life functions we all take for granted until they're nearly impossible to perform.

My room, the room I used to share with a long gone ex-husband, Kenneth (who is now sharing a master bedroom with a twenty-three year-old, one-hundred-pound massage therapist somewhere on the other side of town), the room where I nursed my now twenty-one-year-college-student-with-no-declared-major son, became a hospital room away from the hospital when I moved Mama in.

The walls are still lined with shelves full of bottles, medications with names I can't pronounce. Every organic, all-natural, new-age pill, potion, cream, and tincture my forty-seven-year-old, too-busy-building-a-Black-owned-law-firm, older-sister, Sheryl, insisted on FedEx-ing to my doorstep, when a visit from her would have been so much more healing to our mother.

From the hospital bed to the wheelchair in the corner, from durable medical equipment of every shape, size and weight, to the specially made and installed hand rails, the tub chair, and still more bottles, tins, and jars filled with things to promote healing and prevent another stroke (Mama's second stroke was the one that moved her out of her own home, and put her in my care), my room, much like my life, became my mother's. Who else was going to make the sacrifice?

Certainly not Sheryl, who is so "busy" being the pillar of the upwardly-mobile, "new black", mega-church-attending segment of the community that she has no idea where her husband is most nights, or where (and certainly not *how*) my teenaged niece and nephew are spending their winter break days. Not my younger brother, Dennis, who, at thirty-five, *still* has not embraced the reality that rap is no longer a viable career alternative for him.

That left me. As usual. And why wouldn't I take in my own mother? It's what you do. It's the right thing to do. I have had to remind myself of that fact many, many times over the past few years.

I manage to wiggle into a comfortable position. The sun is just rising and I can see the outlines of my re-housed things in the closet: stilettos I haven't worn in I don't know how long; blouses, skirts, slacks I haven't pulled out of the dry-cleaner plastic since I brought them home; bags, scarves — everything I managed to fit in Marlin's single closet. The rest of my things are divided between the back of what used to be my walk-in and the hall closet.

Since Sheryl is so busy, she's written a check or two to help cover costs, but Dennis? The occasional visit is the depth and breadth of his contribution. So why wouldn't I take a leave of absence from my job? Use my savings to make sure Mama had the things she needed? Say goodbye to Malcolm, the love of my life, in order to care for her? Who else was going to do it?

I close my eyes and try to shoo away the idea that at some point, I'll need to clean out both rooms. Put Mama's stuff in bags, boxes, and trash bins. I'll have to make arrangements to do something with that monstrosity of a hospital bed.

Thinking about *my* bed, my extremely expensive Serta mattress, which now belongs to my rap-tastic younger brother and his umpteenth live-in girlfriend, always takes me to the same place. The same memory. The memory where, three years ago, on a morning very much like this one, I lay in the arms of Malcolm, the only man in the world I've loved since I'd realized my ex-husband was Satan himself. While Malcolm and I were catching our breath, basking in post-coital afterglow, I had promised him that my taking care of Mama wouldn't become my entire life.

Yes, of course I'll make sure my siblings help out, I told him. *Naturally, there'll be therapists and in-home care.* I tried to convince both of us. *Obviously, Mama will recover, get back to being herself, and then we'll pick up right where we left off. Maybe move in together.*

Little did I know at the time, not only was I lying to him, I was lying to myself. My siblings seemed to disappear whenever there was a doctor's appointment, therapy session, caseworker visit. Right about the time Mama's condition worsened and I took a leave of absence, Malcolm took a job. In Seattle. And I was stuck.

As I lay in bed, trying to repress memories that always make me cry, trying to swallow the lump that forms in my throat when I think about what used to be (or could have been) my life, sunlight filters into the room, and I realize that the day is moving forward. If I'm not careful, this day, like so many other things in my life will get away from me.

Of course, this *is* Texas, so when I finally *do* crawl out of bed and open the blinds, there'll be nothing resembling a white-washed, television-worthy holiday scene. Just plenty of dormant St. Augustine grass, the occasional cloud overhead, but mostly, sunshine. Sunshine I am not in the damned mood for.

Out of the corner of my eye, I catch sight of the huge vase of vividly colored flowers on top of the dresser, oddly out of place among the Lebron James and Michael Jordan posters Marlin left behind. For my own sanity, I had to remove the near-naked versions of Ashanti, Beyoncé and some

Hispanic-looking chick with wet and wavy hair. And even though there are more flowers in Mama's room than I know what to do with, and even more greenery in the living room and den, these flowers, the orange, bright pink, purple and red roses with baby's breath and crisp, bright green leaves were delivered to me. For me. With *my* name on the card. A card that reads:

Niecy,
I was so, very sorry to hear about your mother's passing.
Please, don't hesitate to call me if you need me.

Malcolm

The flowers had arrived just as I was getting in from meeting with the funeral planner. Although I didn't think I had any tears left, I must've soaked my pillow through that night. An overwhelming emotional mixture of grief, regret, sadness, and anger, so much anger, has left me drained. But every time I look at those flowers, I feel a little of the old me return, a hint of my life coming back.

I finally decide get out of bed. It hits me that I'm in the house — my house — all alone. For the first time in more than two years.

December 24

"I'll be right there, Mama."

This time I remember, as soon as I open my eyes, that Mama is gone, and there's no need to leave my bed. Except that there is a reason to get up, since I have about a million and one things to do today to salvage Christmas. Funerals have a way of dampening holiday cheer. I roll over and admire the flowers again.

Malcolm was the promise of a new beginning for me. Our long-time friendship had grown from the early stages of two co-workers encouraging each other through hard times to two consenting adults, sharing thoughts, dreams, struggles and a bed. Back when I still had time for moments of relaxation, my time with Malcolm was my opportunity to reset. To regain my sense of balance. To recharge. But the ever-growing list of Mama's needs devoured all of my attention. And there was less and less time for us.

It's now been five days since the flowers from Malcolm arrived, shoved into my hands by a harried-looking white man with a scraggly beard and dirty fingernails. I'd had to drop whatever I was doing at the time to answer the door, so it wasn't the most pleasant of interactions.

I was sure it was yet another bouquet from Sheryl's Inter-Faith church family - a huge conglomeration of ministries, networks, and pomp-and-circumstance that Mama refused to attend when she was living. But that was Mama. She loved the tiny building, set far back from the street on the south side of town that housed her home church. You almost had to pack your own gun to navigate the neighborhood, but Mama found solace in those hard, varnished wood pews.

Sheryl'd had an actual hissy fit — I mean a real, live *hissy fit*, when I insisted we have Mama's service there. She even offered to cover all the expenses if we would move the funeral to *her* church.

I had laughed and said *absolutely not*, but informed her that we *would* be discussing Mama's expenses at some date in the very near future. The insurance barely covered the casket and grave site. I paid for the marker myself. Who else was going to?

****

I don't know *what* I was thinking. I'm not a fan of crowds. Or grocery shopping. Or Christmas music. Yet, here I am, *un*joyously surrounded by all three. Between the screaming kids, long-as-hell checkout lines, and the bumper car activities in the parking lot, I am *beyond* ready to get home. Joy to the World. *Not.* More like *Jesus Be an Amazon Gift Card.* Because this year - I just cannot. I used to love Christmas. And Mama always made sure that no matter how broke we were, I received two separate gifts: one for Christmas and one for my birthday, which is also on December 25th. My siblings and I had more than a few serious fallings out over that fact. But my birthday wasn't the only reason I loved the holiday season. Because of the holidays, the house was decorated the entire time between the day after Thanksgiving, when we would all help Mama unwrap the ornaments she'd inherited from Nana, until the day after New Year's. Popcorn strings, twinkling lights, and gift wrapped packages, the scent of *real* pine mixed with the aroma of pound cakes and sweet potato pies baking, greens stewing on the stove, honey-glazed ham roasting. Christmas meant *family*. The holidays meant *home*. But the last few years have really changed things.

****

I feel like I've missed a huge step. When Kenneth and I divorced, I was heartbroken, but also full of optimism and glad to be free. I was *Neo-soul Niecy with the natural hair*. Then I met Malcolm, and there were slow, sensuous nights when we made love to Jill Scott and Musiq Soulchild CDs while patchouli candles burned and Marlin was off visiting his father. Malcolm gave me hope. He made me want to be better. Do better. But he also wanted a commitment I wasn't ready to make.

Somewhere between the fabulous, mahogany brown sista who was contemplating locking her hair and starting a new career, and the burnt-out, overweight, utterly confused soul I've become is the woman I was meant to develop into. Somehow, that development was arrested, and I became responsible not only for my bad choices, but also for the mistakes of everyone around me.

And that included Mama, who refused to take her high blood pressure meds and would not even entertain the idea of altering her diet. My own eating habits aren't much better these days. And while my hair is still natural, most of the time it sits on top of my head in a tangled puff that's lucky to see hot water and shampoo once a week. What happened to me? Where did *I* go? I make my way to the grocery store, my last stop of the day. I have a roast to braise and bake, yams to candy, greens to clean, and rolls to brown. Our first Christmas without Mama is going to be hard on all of us, but at least we'll eat well. One thing I *do* know is that I have to hurry up and get out of this hot ass store before I scream.

December 25

My alarm goes off, and I realize three things. One, this is the first time since Mama died that I've slept through the night. Two, I have one hell of a hangover. I guess drinking Jim Beam while cooking Christmas dinner was not one of my most brilliant ideas. And three, I apparently fell asleep with the vase of Malcolm's flowers sitting on the floor next to the couch. I discover *that* fact when I get up to go to the bathroom and kick it over. Cold water on your toes at 6 a.m. will wake you right on up. I stumble my way into the shower. I'm mid-lather when I remember - *Oh shit! Tell me I did not...*

I rinse, hop out of the shower and run, soaking wet and naked as the day I was born, to confirm what I already know — my cell phone is on the coffee table. I push buttons until my worst nightmare is confirmed. *I called him.* I try to swallow the rising panic, ignore the fact that my stomach is lurching, and check the length of the call: 0:54 seconds. *Cool.* I take a deep breath. *After all, what could I have said in less than a minute?*

I can't, for the life of me, remember, although I obviously left a message of some kind. My stomach lurches again. Last night's bourbon is making its way out, and I'm trying to make it back to the bathroom at top speed. By the time I get myself together and take a couple of Tylenols, the call is coming back to me in flashes.

I recall the excitement I'd felt searching for his number. I remember initiating the call and the phone ringing. I remember calling up the liquid courage I'd acquired, willing Malcolm to pick up, then feeling disappointed yet relieved when I got his voice mail. Worst of all, I remember my little speech.

"I miss you. I'm sorry. I...I." I also remember that I cried. Hard enough that I could barely enunciate the words "I need you." All I can do is hope the message will be lost in what will surely be plenty of holiday calls and voicemails. I try to convince myself that he will never hear it.

****

Neither of them have bothered to say either "Merry Christmas" or "Happy Birthday" since they walked in the door. But the conversation begins as soon as Sheryl's lengthy blessing concludes, and she has served her two sulking teenagers (they wanted to go to Aspen with their dad), and Dennis, has filled both his plate and that of his unexpectedly expecting girlfriend.

"I still can't believe you funeralized Mama in that clapboard...shanty of a church." Sheryl's lips are pressed tightly together as she spoons up a hearty serving of mashed potatoes and douses it with gravy. "It was an embarrassment. Mama deserved better than that."

My head continues to throb.

And that's when Dennis, mouth full of ham, chimes in. "I'm sayin'!"

That's the last straw. I lose it. "In case neither one of you remember, Mama didn't like Inter-Faith. And since neither one of you selfish bastards was actually here enough to know *what* her last wishes were, *I* made the arrangements. Just like *I* carried her from doctor to doctor. *I* moved her into MY house and left MY job to make sure MY mother was comfortable in her last days on this Earth."

Stunned silence. I swear I see grins sliding across the downcast faces of my niece and nephew. Dennis's girlfriend mumbles something about having to pee and creeps out of the room. I was sad about it before, but at this moment, I'm mighty glad Marlin, who is spending the holidays with his dad, stepmother, and new baby sister in Hawaii, wasn't able to be here.

But these two...sitting at *my* table, eating food *I* shopped and paid for, prepared and served by myself, in the home where our mother took her last breath (neither of them made it until she was already gone), *have the audacity to complain*? I don't know if it's the hangover, the grief, sheer fatigue, or a combination of all three, but the devil is about to have his way at this dining room table.

"And since we're talking about what Mama would've wanted-" I'm stopped mid-rant by the ringing doorbell, followed by rather insistent knocking. I stomp through the living room thinking it'd better be the Baby Jesus, his mother, Mary, Joseph and all three of the Wise Men on the other side of this door. I fling it open with extra attitude, and forget to take my next breath.

"Happy Birthday, Niecy."

It's him!

That smooth, soul-stirring baritone. My name always did drip like honey from his beautiful lips. I was screaming like a wild banshee a second ago, and now I can't find my voice at all.

"I must look crazy as hell," he says, trying to smooth his shirt. *Not even.* "Just got off the plane..." His voice trails off. "How? Why are you here?" He smiles. And my knees go weak. "You called."

"I called," I repeat.

"You said you needed me." I nod. *It's true. I do need you.*

"Here I am." He opens his arms and I fall into them, tears trailing down my cheeks. When I finally have the willpower to untangle myself from his embrace, I look behind him and see a shiny, bright red Corvette parked in my driveway. "Believe it or not," he says, a little embarrassed, "it was the only thing the rental company had left."

"Wait one second," I tell him. I don't even invite him in, just leave the door open and walk straight past my siblings, who are still sitting at the table, apparently waiting for me to continue my tirade. I head to my room, grab my purse, jacket and key ring. I remove the house key and hand it to Sheryl on my way past in the opposite direction.

"Lock up when you leave," I tell her, eyes on the tall, close-cropped caesar-cut, non-shaven, dark chocolate, jeans-and-wrinkled-shirt-wearing Christmas miracle standing in my living room, permeating it with the heavenly scent of his cologne. A scent that still sends my mind to places no decent woman should be thinking about.

I turn back to address the crowd once more. "And make sure y'all turn off the stove. I won't be back for a while."

For the first time in years, I feel weight fall off my shoulders. My mind clears with every step I take toward the two-seater freedom wagon in my driveway. I notice there's a small green, red, and white wreath attached to the grill, and I'm sure, with every fiber of my being, that Mama has kept up with her tradition from beyond the grave. Two gifts.

For Christmas, a gorgeous, cherry-red Corvette, as good a chariot as any, to take me away from the place where I've lost both my mother and myself, and for my birthday, the love of my life, who flew all night from half the continent away just because I drunk-dialed and admitted something I never would said in a sober state: I needed him.

I look toward the sky, where I know she's watching from behind some cloud, when she should be getting herself checked into her heavenly mansion, and whisper "Thank you, Mama. Merry Christmas."

A. Rozelle is a freelance writer and author whose work has appeared in The Dallas Morning News, The Dallas Weekly and Rollin' Out Magazine. She is currently hard at work on her second novel. You can find her at www. arozelle.com.

My Heart's First Wish
By KP Holley

"Dang, y'all, hush. I'm trying to win fast money." I yelled and threw my hands in the air in disgust. Behind me I heard groans and could imagine the side eyes. I jumped up and spun around glaring at the person I just knew was the culprit. Jo Ann glared right back at me and even had the audacity to shoot her middle finger up. I couldn't stand her. She was well over 6 feet tall and her whole body was covered in tattoos. Well at least the visible parts. I shuddered thinking about what she was covering up.

Once Steve went to commercial, I turned my attention back to the break room. Laila and a very pale, red headed girl (I think her name was Angie, but she'd be New Girl until someone else came along) were on the love seat, of all places, grinning and sitting too close for my taste. I shook my head and chuckled.

"Happy birthday to youuuuu." Ms. Carolyn came marching through the doors singing as if she were leading a parade. In her hands was a little plastic saucer with a blueberry muffin on it, topped with one unlit candle.

All the girls rushed over, joining Ms. Carolyn in singing, *"Happy Birthday, Dear Stephanie."*

Do not cry, do not cry, I willed myself.

"Happy Birthday to youuuuuu." They sang all off key, but it was sweet.

"Go 'head, baby girl, make a wish." Ms. Carolyn placed her soft, wrinkled hand on my shoulder in a loving gesture.

Inhaling the scent of the Palmer's cocoa butter she used to moisturize, I closed my eyes and remembered the last time I was given that request. I was actually thankful to Jamie for interrupting that thought by hollering out in her Jamaican accent, "What 'dey too cheap to spring for ice cream, mon?" We all laughed.

I thought I was off the hook until a petite woman carrying a Bible came walking over to my table.

"So, how does it feel to celebrate your birthday with Jesus?" Rhonda asked.

I sucked my teeth and looked out of the window, letting nostalgia take over me.

***

My birthday was never a big deal to me until the year I turned six years old in the first grade. My teacher, Mrs. Swanson, sent home a note giving my mother permission to bring cake and ice cream to my class during the last day of school before holiday break. She thought this was a reasonable request that would be honored with delight. I knew differently but hoped my mother, San, would surprise me and participate. I was jittery all through class, jumping up running to the window and watching the door like a hawk. The 10:00 bell rang and I knew she wasn't coming. I'd be lucky if she remembered early dismissal at noon.

Mrs. Swanson glided over to my desk and crouched down low so only I could hear her. "Stephanie, I'm sure your mother got busy at work and couldn't leave the store with this being the holiday season and all." I nodded and smiled slightly but kept my head on the desk. I knew that wasn't the case considering San hadn't worked for as long as I could remember unless working on my six-year-old nerves counted. Embarrassed by my family's financial situation, I made up the story of San being a manager at JCPenney's.

"Okay class, unfortunately, Stephanie's mother will not be able to make it," Mrs. Swanson explained. One group of girls laughed and pointed at me. I dropped my head to hide the tears.

"There's still a treat waiting for you in the cafeteria," she sang. Everyone's eyes lit up, including mine. We were excited because Santa was coming to town and making a stop to visit us after lunch.

When Santa arrived, it seemed like the line went on forever. Finally, it was my turn. I ran into Santa's arms, laughing.

"What would you like for Christmas, Stephanie?" he asked, pinching my cheek.

My eyes shot up and my mouth flew open. "You know my name?" I said in surprise. I thought back to San saying, "There ain't no Santa, just like there ain't no Jesus." I still believed in Jesus, though, because Miss Faye, our neighbor, made sure I went to church on Sundays.

He laughed a hearty laugh. I leaned in close and whispered in his ear. His facial expression was a little weird but he nodded. That was good enough for me.

December 25th, Santa did not deliver, thus beginning my hatred of fat, bearded white men, joy to the world, the free world, the Third World, and even Disney World for that matter. I blacked out the dates of the calendar from October 31st to January 1st. All that changed when I met EJ Richardson.

***

I had been chosen to attend one of the most prestigious high schools in the city for my senior year. It was something I'd been looking forward to, but the first day could've gone down in the record books as the worst day of my life. I decided on a crisp, white button-down Polo shirt and a khaki skirt. After combing my chin-length bob and applying a glossy Wet'n Wild to my lips, I grabbed the only designer bag I owned, a black Dooney & Burke that I had "claimed" in the unclaimed lost and found box. It doubled as a backpack. I yelled out, "I'm gone," to San, but didn't get a response.

After waiting for almost ten minutes, I finally saw the bus coming, but it was not slowing down. The driver of the jam-packed bus made some gesture pointing behind him and kept right on going. When the next bus came, I thought I was lucky, as it was relatively empty and the A/C was blowing snowballs. Good. I was scared I would sweat out my perm if I stood outside any longer.

My relief in the situation turned into immediate regret when somebody's broke down uncle decided he just had to sit next to me.

"How ya doin' this mawnin?" He smiled showing rotten teeth. He reeked of beer and cigarettes. I politely nodded and pretended to read the street signs.

"I got two doughnuts. You want one?" he asked nudging me in the side. Shaking my head like a wild woman, I nearly knocked him over to get off at my stop. I had been holding my breath the whole ride. Reaching down for my bag, I realized I left it on the bus. "Wait, hold up, my stuff," I yelled, banging on the side of the bus as it pulled off.

I looked around the campus in awe taking in the huge oak trees and lush green grass. I walked by a window and almost fainted in horror at my appearance. There were sweat stains forming under my arms. My hair had gone from bob to bimbo and thanks to Stinky Donut Dude, I had a blob of grape jelly on my skirt.

I spent the whole day explaining to administration why I didn't have my schedule, my student ID or my books. I was beat and ready to go home.

"Excuse me," I mumbled to the group of guys sitting on the stairs. No one moved so I said it again louder and started to walk in between them to get down the steps.

One of them had the nerve to say, "Whoa, hold up, girl. You don't have to act like that. You almost knocked me over."

I didn't look back, just sucked my teeth and gave a sarcastic, "My bad."

This fool decided to stand up and get in my face. Just great. My pepper spray was in my bag, too.

"Calm down, Miss Lady. I don't mean any harm. I'm a gentleman." He took my hand in his. I couldn't pull away if I wanted to. "I'm EJ, and you are?" His face beamed a 60-watt smile. I looked his 6'5" frame up and down, opened my mouth, but forgot my name.

My new friend walked me to the bus stop and jumped on, too. I told him about my morning fiasco.

"So this dude harassed you on the bus and might have taken your purse?" His eyebrows creased and his voice showed anger.

"No silly, he didn't harass me. He was really polite actually. I left my purse, carelessly trying to get away from his stinky smell." I waved my hand in front of my nose and laughed; EJ didn't.

"I think I'll start picking you up for school to make sure nobody bothers you. Okay?" He smiled and put his arm around me tighter. I just nodded and leaned in closer to bask in the scent of his cologne.

After the first couple of weeks, EJ insisted I change a few of my classes so that we could have more time together. I even joined the cheerleading squad so I could go to all the games.

Once football season was over, I quit the squad and got a job at the library.

My best friend, Carla, thought that was crazy, but I told her how much we loved each other.

"Girl please, we can't all be Beyonce and Jay-Z. Somebody gotta be Lil Kim and Biggie," she said one day while we were hanging out in the band room. "I guess if it works for y'all, more power to you but I'm too young to be tied down." Carla slung her long hair and puckered her lips. We laughed hysterically.

"What's going on here?" EJ walked up and startled me.

I leaned in to give him a kiss. He didn't kiss me back. He and Carla stared each other down. They were always at odds.

"Girl, let me go. I have to get ready for my date." She skipped off singing." *I love it when you call me Big Poppa.*"

"What did I tell you about hanging with her?" He glared at me. I looked away.

Carla and I had been friends since elementary. He only wanted me hanging out with his friends' stuck up girlfriends.

"I'm not going to tell you again. She's bad news and I don't want her around."

I wanted to protest, but instead, I just smiled, took his hand and let him lead me out of the band room.

***

San and I were invited to Thanksgiving dinner at EJ's house. Since he and I had been dating, I'd spent time with his family, but always made a point to change the conversation when anyone asked about my family. We hadn't seen my father in years. My mother put him right up there with Jesus and Santa in the unreal department.

That Thursday, San walked into the house unrecognizable. She was dressed in a leather skirt suit and matching boots. Her hair, makeup and nails looked like she had spent the day at a top-notch salon. I blinked twice, star struck. Then the real San made her presence known.

"I know you're not wearing that," she said, pointing with disgust at my orange sweater dress and brown flats.

"Wh-what's wrong with it?" I stammered, all of a sudden feeing like the inadequate, lonely little girl I used to be.

"You the one always 'round here bragging on these high class folks and their big ole house, I figured you might want to at least look presentable." She rolled her eyes.

I refused to let her know she was getting to me.

"This is Michael Kors and it was a gift from Mrs. Richardson," I smirked. *Ha, that'll show her,* I thought.

"Humph whatever, probably a hand-me-down that Goodwill wouldn't take." She lit a cigarette, laughed and then walked off.

"Why do you hate me?" I screamed down the hallway behind her. I didn't recognize the voice that came out as my own.

She turned around slowly. San had a reputation as a fighter in the streets. I'd seen her take down women and some men much bigger than her.

"Nothing I've ever done has been good enough for you, except for dating EJ." I lowered my voice a little but the words came out in sobs.

"First of all, I don't hate you. And as for your precious EJ, let me tell you something. You better hope you don't mess it up." She started toward me. "I had an EJ, too." She took a drag from her cigarette. "His name was Stephen, your father. "

I leaped to get closer to her. "My father?"

"Stephen and I were in love." Her face softened as she remembered another time. "Spent every free minute together, then I got pregnant with you." She said "you" like it was a four-letter word. "I planned our June wedding and named all six of our children."

My face visibly dropped. I didn't know what was more shocking I had a father or the fact that San actually wanted six children, me included.

"As it got closer to my due date, he stopped coming over as much. Christmas morning, my water broke. I took a taxi to his house on the way to the hospital. His roommate told me he had moved out two weeks before."

My mother did something I'd never seen her do; she got teary-eyed.

"Oh, San, I mean, Mom, I'm…" As the words caught in my throat, I reached out to her. She brushed by me and walked out of the door.

A little while later, EJ picked me up. I spent the evening with the Richardsons in a daze. San never brought my father up again and neither did I.

***

"Heyyyy Ms. Faye, how are you? Happy Holidays," I said hugging the elderly woman's neck.

"Well, if it ain't Miss Stephanie Sunshine." She smiled a gap-toothed smile using the nickname she had given me years before. She scolded me about not coming to church anymore.

"I've missed my Zion family, but I've been going to St. Paul with my boyfriend."

"St. Paul?" she asked wide eyed. "Ain't that a Catholic church?"

"Yes maam, my boyfriend is Catholic and when we get married, I'll convert my religion," I told her proudly. She mumbled something about priests and young boys and closed her screen door. I shrugged and went inside.

Since EJ was out of town with his family enjoying the slopes of Colorado, I decided to go visit my home church, Zion Travelers. Service was great. Afterward, one of my childhood friends, Thomas, walked me the few blocks home. As we rounded the corner I saw EJ's car parked. I ran to the house. He opened the door and scooped me up, laughing and tickling me. I had totally forgotten about Thomas standing right there.

When I found my manners, I wiggled out his arms and said, "Silly me. Baby, this is Thomas, he goes to Zion-" Before I could finish, EJ was barreling down the steps like a mad man, charging at him. I looked on in horror. He rammed into him as if they were on the field and playing for opposing teams.

"Oh my gosh, EJ, what are you doing?" I screamed. Thomas regained his balance and prepared for a fight. The two men were like gladiators. San came to the door with a gun and fired a shot in the air, which got everyone's attention.

"Now EJ, I know your folks got money to get you out of jail but I'm sure you'd rather be skiing."

"And Thomas get home before your mama come around here talking smack." She pointed the gun in Thomas' direction and smirked.

He scowled at EJ and slowly walked away. EJ jumped in his car and sped off. Chasing him did no good. I sat outside until well after midnight hoping he'd come back. I brought in my birthday on the steps, crying and cold. When I did go in the house, I walked into a living room decorated with lights and a huge Christmas tree. I had never seen one in my home.

"You gon eat this cake, Anna Mae?" San laughed at that tired joke. My heart sank even more as I traced heart-shaped birthday cake that sat on the table. The scent of red roses filled the room, and the sight of boxes of all shapes and sizes wrapped in shimmer paper, brought tears to my eyes.

"I counted. The boy got eighteen gifts. I guess for your eighteenth birthday," San said.

I shook my head and went to my room.

A few days later EJ came over. As we sat in his car, arguing, I imagined I was anywhere but there doing anything but that.

"We're just friends," I pleaded. I had been saying that for at least the last fifteen minutes.

"You and your friends," he scoffed.

"I hardly ever see Thom…" I stopped. He shot me a look that said, don't even say his name. "I don't see him and I won't ever see him again. Can we please drop it and focus on us? Are you excited about going to New Orleans to watch the Sugar Bowl with your dad?" I steered the conversation to something he loved, football. It worked. We were back on track, for now.

***

Our high school love was solidified when EJ got a football scholarship to Lousiana State University and all but demanded that I give up my scholarship to Jackson State University and follow him, which I did. And then, I followed him to Atlanta after college, where he was going to play football for the Falcons.

I was extremely lonely since he was always on the road. That's why when my old friend, Carla, called to let me know she was in town, I immediately invited her over. We hadn't hung out in forever.

"Girl, you have given up everything for this man," Carla said after I brought her up to date on everything going on with me. "His mama chose your house, for goodness sake and what kind of color is mauve for a kitchen?" She made a face. I threw a towel at her and laughed.

"Whatever, heffa. EJ has given me a good life. I live in a mansion. Yes, he's a little temperamental, but it's all I ever dreamed of. I can't mess this up."

I thought back to San telling me at the wedding and every chance she got, "Girl, do not mess this up." Of course she had a lot at stake. EJ had set her up with a nice condo.

I uncrossed my legs and scooted closer to her, "Can you keep a secret?"

Before she could answer we both gave one another the side eye.

"Okay, nevermind. I know you got loose lips but I'll tell you anyway. You're going to be an auntie."

Carla was estatic, rambling on about ordering Greek paraphanelia for her niece-to-be since she pledged in college. I secretly hoped this was the news EJ needed to get back on track. I didn't tell her about the thot that left her panties in an envelope at the guard's station with a note for my husband that said, "For the memories."

***

Things started going downhill in 2013. EJ had torn his ACL and was out for the season. He stayed in a funk for weeks. The only thing that brought him out was news that I was carrying his child.

Prince Elijah Jackson Richardson was born in the spring. His chocolate brown skin, curly hair and beautiful sweet eyes caused everyone that met him to marvel in delight. The grandparents doted on him, even San who insisted she was too young to be called Grandma.

My birthday was coming up and I couldn't wait to get my post baby-snapped-back-body out of the house and hang with friends. Like always, EJ did the most in planning. There was a huge party at the downtown Atlanta club he owned, featuring performances by my favorite R&B and rap artists, cuisine catered by world renowned chefs and entertainment by choreographed dancers. The all-white affair was a paparazzi sensation.

I was on cloud nine from the night's events but my husband fumed the whole ride home.

I raised the partition separating us from the driver and straddled my husband's lap. "Thank you so much for the best party ever. I love you." I kissed his face and ears, working my way down his neck. He sat there, emotionless. Feeling defeated, I moved back to my seat to endure the rest of the drive home.

I motioned with my finger to follow me to the bedroom as I undressed in the foyer. Instead he stopped at our well-stocked bar and poured himself a drink. I walked by hoping he would slap my butt like he used to. I was not prepared when he grabbed my hair and kissed me very aggressively, biting my lip hard, but there was no passion.

I pried away from his tentacle-like hands.

"Damn it EJ, that hurt," I yelled, wiping the blood from my lip. "Look, I had a wonderful time tonight, as I always do when I'm with you but you're drunk and you're treating me like crap. What is the problem?" I softened my voice as looked him in the eyes, pleading for answers.

"Who invited Rufus?" He pushed my forehead lightly with his forefinger.

I was confused and my face showed it. "Of course, I invited Mr. Rufus. He's our gardener. He's been with us forever. I figured he would enjoy the party as a member of the family."

"What was that dance you and Rufus were doing?" he asked.

He couldn't be serious. Mr. Rufus was over sixty years old. His Chicago two-step had turned into a Stone Mountain half-step ages ago.

I threw my head back and laughed uncontrollably. "Boy, bye."

Things took a turn for the worse as my husband threw his drink in my face and slapped me so hard I almost hit the floor. I couldn't believe what was happening. Although I'd seen his temper more times than I'd ever hoped to count, over the years, EJ had never laid a harmful hand on me.

"Oh, my God!" I cried, scrambling away from him.

I was terrified. I ran into the kitchen where he knocked me down, kicking me and calling me awful names. I saw the same rage in his eyes as I did the night he attacked Thomas. Thinking this could be the end of my life if I didn't get away, I found the strength to push from under him and run to the other side of the kitchen. He had me cornered. The next thing I remember is hearing our nanny, Sofia, screaming.

The man I'd loved since the day we met lay on the tile floor lifeless, a bloody kitchen knife stuck in his chest. The police hauled me away from our home, scantily dressed, dazed, and confused as I fought to see EJ.

Surprisingly, San was in the courtroom during the trial. She pulled me in close, kissed my face, and said she knew all along I would blow it. I should've expected that from her. The love I had for EJ did not die with him. My in-laws have custody of our son, PJ. They don't answer my calls or letters, an effort to have a relationship with him. The only constant has been my girl, Carla. Along with her legal team, she's working on an appeal. She vowed to help me get home to PJ. For now, I can see my sweet boy's face on pictures she sends every month.

***

"So, you're really not going to celebrate your birthday?" Ms. Carolyn asked, snapping me back from the memory I traveled to on a daily basis.

I released a heavy sigh. "Celebrate? I'm spending my thirtieth birthday in prison," I said. "I have fourteen years left on my sentence. You tell me what I have to celebrate."

"Them," she said, motioning toward the door as she smiled that loving mama smile that left her lips and reached her eyes. I looked in the direction she was pointing and smiled, too, waving at the two girls and two boys and the middle-aged woman with them, all dressed in matching Santa hats and tee shirts that read, 'We love you, Stephanie.'

Through therapy, I learned that EJ's abuse started long before he ever laid a hand on me. His need to control the classes I took, the friends I hung around with and the way I wore my hair were a part of his abusive nature.

A few months into my sentence, I received a letter from my old high school counselor offering support and encouraging me to use my story to help students through a healthy relationship class.

"What did you wish for, Ms. Stephanie?" New Girl asked, breaking me out of my trance.

Before I pushed my chair back to go hug the kids, I took a deep breath and replied, "The same thing I've been wanting and wishing for since I was six years old. To be free."

My Heart's First Wish is KP Holley's debut published work. She earned a Bachelors of Science degree from Jackson State University in mass communications. During her newspaper career, she contributed to many departments of the Clarion Ledger, Jackson Advocate, Hattiesburg American, Jackson Free Press and American Gazette, respectively. KP, a native of New Orleans, resides in Arlington, Texas with her husband, Ramon, and three daughters.

A Silent Night?
By Terri Ann Johnson

Chapter 1

As I watched the snow fall, painting a beautiful white blanket on the ground, I thought, *I couldn't have picked a more beautiful day to die.*

My hospital suite had a view of M Street in Georgetown and even as I was five floors above street level, I could still see the festive decorations of the holiday. Beautiful silver and gold-trimmed garland adorned the stores on the block outside of my window. I could hear the Salvation Army Santa Claus sounding the call for donations and his hearty, 'Ho, Ho, Ho.'

Turning my head away from the joy that felt like it was seeping through the window, I faced the hospital door and remembered the conversation that led me to this place.

***

I sat in Dr. Price's office waiting for her to enter. The pictures on her desk told me that she had a beautiful family with a sense of humor. The Christmas pictures of them wearing silly, ugly Christmas sweaters almost brought a smile to my face. Almost. I heard a gentle tap on the door. Dr. Price walked in holding medical folders. As she put them down on her desk, she reached to hug me. I appreciated the warmth of her initial greeting. As she sat in the chair behind her desk, she gathered her medical folders in front her and smiled at me, but only for a second. The immediate change caused a slight chill, even though it was one week before the Fourth of July.

"Mrs. Jackson," Dr. Price began with her hands folded on top of her desk. "I know that the last few months have been rough. But, I have some serious news."

I took a deep breath, bracing myself for what she had to say.

She continued, "Your stomach aches and missed cycles are not due to depression and grief. You are pregnant, my dear."

That news didn't elicit any kind of response from me. At least not the kind of response that usually came from a woman who heard that she was about to bring a new life into the world. I couldn't be happy. Not when I'd suffered the loss of one life, the loss of my heart, just a month ago. Not when Brian wasn't here to celebrate this with me. Even if he were alive, though, my husband and I had always known babies were not in our future because of my medical history. A pregnancy could kill me.

My silence made Dr. Price stand, walk around to the other side of her desk, and sit down in the chair next to mine.

"Don't think the worse," she said.

I shook my head. "I don't know how this happened. Brian and I were careful. We took precautions against pregnancy," I told her.

"Precautions are not one hundred percent reliable, but we can now take precautions to keep you safe. I already have a plan. We can medically induce a coma to minimize your chances of having an acute seizure during childbirth."

"That will help?" I asked, hearing the hope that was inside my heart now inside my voice. "Will that save my life...and our baby's life?"

When the doctor paused, I knew that she wasn't going to tell me what I wanted to hear. She was going to tell me the truth. She said, "This option will give you a fifty-fifty chance." Then, she stood and returned to her side of the desk. Looking down at a calendar, she said, "If you decide to keep the baby, I already know exactly how we'll do this. I'll keep you on bed rest to monitor you and then," she paused and looked straight at me, "we'll bring you in the week before Christmas.

That'll be your thirty-seventh week, so you'll be with us the last three weeks and during that time, we'll figure out when to induce labor."

I took a deep breath. "This is a lot to consider. I'm on an emotional roller coaster. I've had to deal with Brian's death and now, I have to think about a new life." Without thinking, I placed my hand on my belly. "I'm not sure that I can get through this," I said, wanting to cry, but my eyes were tired of crying and no tears dropped.

There was so much compassion in her eyes and in her voice when she said, "I had another patient whose medical history resembled yours. She is alive and well and so is her three-year-old son." She paused, giving me time to think about that.

A son. That woman had a son. Would I have a son in Brian's image? Or would we have a baby girl who would have been the apple of Brian's eye?

Dr. Price said, "Spend a little time thinking about it. About what you want to do." Another pause. "If you want to have the baby, we have a plan." She let another beat go by. "And if you don't...." She looked directly at me. "We'll talk again next week. How does that sound?"

I knew what she was saying, asking if I was considering an abortion. But I already knew what I was going to do. "Dr. Price, I don't need any time." I took a breath and once again pressed my hand against my center. "I'm going to keep my baby."

The brightness of her smile was her approval.

I continued, "And I'll follow your instructions. My baby will be coming around Christmas and what I know is that Christmas is a time of miracles. I'll step out on faith."

This time, she nodded her approval and agreement.

"I just have one question," I said.

"Whatever you want to know."

"Can you induce me on Christmas Eve? Hopefully, I'll wake up on Christmas Day looking at a little baby," I said.

Now her eyes sparkled with her smile. "Mrs. Jackson, my team and I will do everything in our power to make that dream a reality."

***

I turned my head, once again taking in the view of M Street and the shops below where I knew folks had dropped some serious coins to make sure their loved ones would be happy in the morning.

My eyelids felt like cement blocks were weighing them down, but I fought to stay awake. I wanted to take in everything, on what could very well be my last day alive.

There was a fifty-fifty chance.

At least my HMO had chosen Georgetown Hospital and hooked me up with a private suite, no extra charge.

The creaking of the door startled me from my thoughts, though I didn't have to turn to see who was entering. I didn't know why, but the door only creaked when Nurse ReAnn entered.

"Ms. Lachelle, I have your ice chips," said Nurse ReAnn as she gingerly laid the cup on the tray.

Every time I looked at her, I had the same thought: she looked just like Willona from Good Times.

I thanked God for Nurse ReAnn every day. Even when I didn't speak to her for days at a time, she didn't pay that mess any mind. If I didn't talk to her, she'd just start humming, sounding like the folks at my grandmother's church, maybe *Angels Watching Over Me*, by that Hawkins lady.

I let her hum, even though that was it. I was so mad at God that I didn't want anybody to come into my room. She knew it, but, she still came in, opening the blinds, watering the plants, humming her tune.

I'd been in the hospital for three weeks now, and when I first came in, Nurse ReAnn called me Mrs. Jackson. But she'd transitioned from calling me Mrs. Jackson to Ms. Lachelle. She never mentioned it, but I think someone told her about Brian. Even though it had only been seven months since Brian died, I liked *Ms.* better anyway and when she started addressing me that way, I began to soften up and let Nurse ReAnn take care of things. Even Tracy and Vanessa got their information about me from her. I mean, they're my best friends, but I didn't want their stress right now. So, I told them, "Get the 4-1-1, from Nurse ReAnn or don't get anything at all." They chose the former. "Ms. Lachelle, I know you feel that keeping you in here for the past few weeks has been a stretch, but with your medical history, we want to get you through this, okay?" asked Nurse ReAnn, bringing my thoughts back to the present.

I gave Nurse ReAnn the side-eye because I could've stayed on bed rest at home and not come in until today for the birth of my baby. But then, I tried to smile because she had kept me so comfortable.

It was hard to smile because I felt almost paralyzed. It was also hard to keep my eyes open or even to move my lips. From the TV that hung in the corner of the room, I heard Steve Harvey say, "And the number one answer is," but I couldn't open my eyes enough to see what rolled over on the board.

Finally, I allowed my eyes to completely close, then, a second later, frantic shouts came from Nurse ReAnn. "Code Blue! Code Blue!"

Over her voice, there were beeps and alarms, and then other voices before there were more beeps and alarms.

Something was wrong. That was my second to last thought. My final thought: *Jesus, Jesus, Jesus!*

Chapter 2

A cool, light breeze woke me up. The smell of salt raced up my nose. My fingertips buried themselves in what felt like soft sand. I was in heaven; I was sure of it.

If I could have mustered the courage to move, I would have covered my eyes and peeped through my fingers to glimpse at my eternal home. But, I wasn't that brave.

The sounds were heavenly though. Crickets chirped; I heard waves. Then, I couldn't help it -- I blinked and saw stars twinkling like dancing diamonds in the sky. I blinked again, but this time, I shifted my eyes from left to right to get more of heaven's view. I saw the glow of the moon, and the glitter of the light bouncing from the water.

With the speed of a sloth, I opened my eyes wider.

Nurse ReAnn glided toward me, her feet barely touching the water beneath her. She looked beautiful in her yellow heavenly gown. The light of the moon emanated from her as she came toward me, smiling as her wings spread wide behind her. When she got close enough, she touched my hand.

"Hi, Ms. Lachelle," she said.

At first, I didn't say anything. *Can dead people talk?*

"Ms. Lachelle, you're not dead," she said as if she read my mind. "You are in a suspended state, between life and death. God knew that now was the time because you trusted me on earth. He knew you'd trust me here with our task."

"I'm not dead?" I asked.

"No, but this state cannot last long or you will die. I am your angel and I will facilitate our task. God has watched your faithfulness over the last few months. He wanted to reward you."

"Reward me? Why? I haven't been faithful. I wanted to give up. There were days when I didn't even know if I was in my right mind."

"But you didn't give up. You prayed, you kept the faith; now God wants to reward you." Nurse ReAnn raised her arm and for the first time, I moved. I turned my head in the direction she pointed and saw a bright light leading to the moon. Then I saw his face. It was painted on the moon. My man, my love, my dead husband, Brian.

"My Chelle." I heard Brian's velvety tenor voice call me in that way that I thought I'd never hear again.

"I know you have been hurting, missing me. I've seen your tears and cries. But, through it all, you kept the faith, all for our baby."

"Brian." I was finally able to breathe his name. But I didn't want to do too much else. I didn't want to miss a moment with my love.

"Chelle, I need you to want to live. I didn't have a chance to fight for my life. I want you to fight. Fight to kiss our baby girl. I want you to tell her how much her daddy will always love her." He paused."I will love her to the moon and back."

"Brian, I am sad and scared, and you aren't here. I know I should be happy, but there are some days when..."

"Shhh. God is faithful. Remember, He began this good work in you and He will continue His work until it is finished." He paused as if he wanted that scripture to settle inside of me. "Will you fight for your life so that our daughter has one parent in the flesh?"

It's hard to fight. That takes energy. Brian was my energizer. His smile gave me life. Without him, life doesn't seem worth living. "I'm torn between wanting to be with you and wanting to be there with our baby."

"That shouldn't be a conflict or a contest at all. You have to choose life -- your life and our baby's life."

I knew Brian's words were the truth, but I had to tell him my truth as well. "I want to be happy, darling, I really do. And there were days when I almost was, but I didn't want to betray you."

"That wouldn't be betrayal. I want you to be happy. I've felt your pain; I've seen your tears. But, for the sake of our daughter, you have to let go of the hurt and pain, knowing that a part of me is still there with you and will always be with you. You just have to remember that God always has a plan."

As soon as Brian said those words, our eyes locked and together, we recited, "For I know the plans that I have for you, plans for good and not for disaster." It was a scripture, our favorite scripture that we'd recited together so many times before as we made plans for our future, what we thought would be a long life together.

There were tears in my eyes when he said, "My Chelle, our baby girl has a future. Please give her the future that God has promised."

I was getting ready to ask him how I could do that when Brian's face began to fade. "No, Brian!" I called to him. I wasn't ready to let him go again.

"Ms. Lachelle." I heard Nurse ReAnn calling my name, but I didn't want to hear anything she had to say. I wanted to stay with Brian.

But the nurse said, "I must get you back. You cannot stay in this state much longer."

I blinked back tears as I thought about what my husband had said. If I fought, if I fought to stay alive for me and our baby, a piece of Brian would always be with me.

"Come on, Ms. Lachelle," Nurse ReAnn said, taking my hand.

I nodded, and inside I made a vow to Brian. *I will fight for my life and the life of our daughter, I promise you. I won't waste these gifts that God has given me. The gift of seeing you one more time and the gift of our daughter. I will do everything I can to show God that I appreciate this time that He gave us.*

As Nurse ReAnn pulled me away, my eyes stayed focused on the moon, even as Brian's face had completely faded away. As my nurse took me back, I closed my eyes and now talked to my daughter. "Baby Girl, we've got some work to do!"

Chapter 3

I was asleep, but I was awake. I could hear everything that was going on, but I couldn't say a thing. I could see, too, even though my eyes weren't open; they couldn't open.

It was scary, but then, it was not. I felt calm, I felt peace. I felt as if I should just lay there and listen to the doctors so that they could do their work -- the work for me and my baby.

"Mrs. Jackson's vitals have stabilized."

That was Dr. Price's voice.

"Let's begin inducing the coma, medically."

Oh, my God, it was happening. I tried to smile, but nothing on me would move.

Dr. Price said, "If she remains in stable condition, throughout the day, we should be able to give Mrs. Jackson a very sweet Christmas gift, the gift that she wanted."

The doctors went on to discuss when they would reconvene and then, I was left alone with just the machines that beeped with each of my heartbeats, and the nurses, who kept up a regular schedule checking on me. I waited to see Nurse ReAnn, but she wasn't among the staff. I hoped that she would be there when it was time for my baby to be born.

Hours later, Dr. Price came back into the room and I wanted to shout when I heard her tell the team, "She's strong enough. We can do this." Then, she leaned over me and said, "Hang in there, Mrs. Jackson; you're strong."

I wanted to tell her that I was strong, even stronger than she knew since I saw Brian. There were no doubts now -- I would do this.

I heard one of the nurses say the time. I felt the gentle movement of the bed. The wheels squeaked as they rolled me down the bright hallway. I started to feel anxious. I reminded myself to stay calm. Breathe. Just breathe. Finally, we arrived in the operating room. Although they placed my bed under a light, it was cold.

"Mrs. Jackson, I know you can't hear me, but we will begin your cesarean section now. If you were awake, you would feel me tugging, but you wouldn't feel any pain." I didn't feel anything, but I smelled something burning. Half of the staff was focused on Dr. Price's hands while the other half was focused on the machines' monitors, blinking and beeping. No one seemed concerned about the smell. Again, I told myself to breathe, just breathe.

Suddenly, everyone in the room heard the loud cries of the baby. My baby was breathing. The doctors and the nurses screamed a collective "Yes." Dr. Price delivered my little Christmas package to a nurse. As she cleaned her up, a tear streamed down her cheek, as I heard her say, "The miracle of Christmas."

"Let's get her to the NICU for examination," said Dr. Price. I was glad that Dr. Price detailed what would happen in the operating room because her instruction to the nurse would've alarmed me if I didn't know that all premature babies were taken to the neonatal intensive care unit immediately after birth.

For the first time in a long time, I was happy. This is why Brian wanted me to fight. He wanted me to live to see the plan that God had for me.

Chapter 4

"Mrs. Jackson, Mrs. Jackson," I heard a voice yelling. My eyes widened enough for me to see a nurse opening the blinds. I squinted as the light filtered through.

"Merry Christmas, Mrs. Jackson." My eyes shot open. Then, I remembered and I lifted my hand to my belly. "Faith," I whispered through a raspy voice, calling the name that had come to me in my sleep.

"Shhhh," the nurse directed. "Your baby girl is here, weighing in at five pounds and three ounces and very healthy. Her lungs are strong, trust me. She gave us a very determined cry," she said, laughing. I smiled, but then suddenly, I was overcome with exhaustion. Right before I closed my eyes, I wondered, *Where is Nurse ReAnn?*

In my sleep, more dreams came to me -- Nurse ReAnn and Brian. Had I seen my husband? Had I dreamed him? My questions were many, but my sleep was filled with peace.

When I awakened, the sun's rays brightened my room and my eyes fell to the white bassinet beside my bed.

"Oh," I whispered as I pushed myself up. Leaning over, I looked at my baby. I had a baby. Life had new meaning. I had someone to love again.

As I lifted her into my arms, I spoke my first words to her. "Hi, baby." I cradled her protectively. Her little eyes opened and she gazed at me as though she knew me. As I stroked her smooth skin, I said, "I wish that I had been the first person to hold you. But, rest assured, I'll never let you go. I took in the soft, pale pink, preemie onesie that she was wearing. "Where did you get this cute little 'Baby's First Christmas' bonnet?" As I stroked the bonnet, I noticed the yellow wings on the side. That made me blink, and I remembered -- Nurse ReAnn...in my dream...and her wings.

"It wasn't a dream," I whispered.

As I secured Faith in my arms, I hit the call buzzer. Just a few seconds later, a nurse came into the room and I paused. "Where is Nurse Reann?" I asked the nurse who had entered my room, a woman I'd never seen before, wearing red bifocal glasses.

She glanced over her bifocals. "I don't know a nurse here by that name, Mrs. Jackson." She frowned. "Are you okay? Can I get you anything?"

I shook my head. I didn't need anything else. God gave me a beautiful Christmas gift.

Turning my attention to the joy in my arms, I spoke to my daughter. "Baby, I hope you like the name Faith because without faith, nothing is possible. We've been through a lot and with God, we'll get through anything. We have a heavenly angel, your dad." Then, I paused. "No, we have two heavenly angels, your daddy and our nurse. They will always watch over us."

As I rocked Faith in my arms, I heard Eddie Kendrick's smooth tenor, falsetto voice singing *Silent Night*.

I sang along: *"Round yon Virgin Mother and Child Holy Infant, so tender and mild..."*

For the first time, I smiled. I really smiled. "Faith, we had anything but a silent night."

A Silent Night?

'A Silent Night?' is Terri Ann Johnson's debut as a writer. She has loved books since she was a young girl. Her love for reading blossomed into a desire to write. Terri is a mom to her son, Joshua, and loves to travel with him, family and friends. She is a Finance professional in Washington, DC and is working on her first novel. Terri is a member of Delta Sigma Theta Sorority, Inc.

Unwrap the Gift
By Sonya Visor

It didn't take schooling, even though I had two college degrees, to understand the foolishness of a size eighteen woman trying to use a size ten coat from the Macy's rack as a shield. I just grabbed what I could in a moment of desperation because I wanted to wait and reintroduce myself to the one who "got away" seven years ago — Brian Jacobs.

Well, he didn't really get away from me. Technically, we were never together, but in my world of "what-ifs" we were inseparable. We shared a special moment back in our college days, but I never capitalized on it. Back then, I didn't think I was good enough for Brian. But now I could see it coming to pass *if* I lost the weight by our class reunion. Everybody was coming to town for Christmas and I needed a miracle.

"Hmph, Drea. You've only lost *two* pounds. You need more than a coat hanger to cover up," said Sasha. She's my blunt cousin who shortened my name from Andrea years ago. She waved two fingers in front of my face and said, "Tsk, tsk."

Sasha would never win the Miss Congeniality award, but I loved her anyway. Even though Sasha spoke the truth, she didn't have to say it out loud. Especially when she knew why I was ducking and dodging *him*. Sometimes I had to remind myself that she remained in my inner circle because she understood the meaning of the word loyal.

"He's coming. He's heading this way," Sasha said through clenched teeth.

Sasha maintained her flawless composure while pulling my arm. She said from the corner of her mouth, "*Don't* embarrass me."

I yanked my arm back and said, "Hush." I crept over to a pillar and peeked out to see where he was. The second Brian turned in my direction I ducked back, hoping the pillar did more for hiding me than the coat hanger. *Great.*

"You look silly lurking between the clothes racks," Sasha hissed. "You can't hide all of that trunk of yours *anyway*."

That was easy for her potato chip-thin self to rattle off. People like her never understood my struggle. So yes, I was playing peek-a-boo to stay off of the radar until I found my twenty-three pound thinner self.

Sure, some said my body had sex-a-licious appeal because I had hills and valleys in the right places. But I also had some built-in borders from the hard labor of lifting and eating Oreos, pizza, and itty-bitty wings on lonely-nights, family-nights, and girl-nights. My palate didn't need an excuse to be put on duty.

"Speak to the man or walk away," Sasha said with clipped words. "You're better than this."

Ouch. She was right. The extra pounds I'd been carrying made me sensitive and contributed to my low self-esteem.

I could inspire others, but didn't have anything to give myself. Being dumped this last time because I'd gained weight brought me to a gutter in my heart that only God himself could clean.

Now I couldn't even receive compliments from people without wondering about their sincerity. People would go on and on about my shine, and they weren't talking about oily skin either. Most of the time, I had to convince myself to believe them.

Why was he still there? I studied Brian as he sifted through the clothes racks. He was probably out Christmas shopping for his sisters since he was in the women's section. I needed to escape before he made his way across the aisle.

Sasha jerked her head toward the store entrance and I waved my hand at her as I moved to the left. I hoped Sasha had enough sense to divert the man's attention while I strutted out of this department. I had to get to the escalator in record time.

A mere three inches from stepping out of the store's entrance and into the mall, I froze when I heard, "Drea, is that you?"

I paused, then prayed. Not really sure what I rambled off to the Lord, but I knew my utterances were a plea for help.

"Drea…it's me…"

I couldn't escape since she'd called my name. So I did an about face and pretended to be surprised even though I knew the voice belonged to Brian's sister. I adjusted my coat to hide my hills and borders. I didn't need my food binges being exposed.

Before I could get a word out, she wrapped her arms around me and said, "I'm so happy to see you."

"Oh. *Hey,* Tammy," I said cheerfully while trying to match the thrill in her tone. I broke her embrace to adjust my belt that had fallen off *again.*

"You look great." Tammy's eyes swept over me. She had always been kind. Despite her compliment, I noticed how her eyes locked on my hips. "Brian's around here somewhere."

I ran my fingers through my hair and said, "You look gorgeous as usual." There was nothing more to add, so before I walked away, I said, "Good seeing you."

"Wait. You *are* coming to the get-together, right?" Tammy raised her eyebrows. She had reasons to be skeptical. The woman I once called my friend I'd just brushed off and all I'd said was bye and see you later? I released a heavy sigh. I'd better get my head straight.

"Sure. I'll be there." I hugged her once more for assurance.

"Oh, look who's here." Tammy peered past me causing my heart to race like I'd just finished the one hundred meter before she said, "*Sasha!*"
Whew.

"I saw you earlier, too." Tammy's smile held that twinkle that made her so loveable and easy to hug.

"Girl, trying to get this shopping done," Sasha smiled and nudged me, "but I'll call you later."

We kept moving until I smelled cinnamon pretzel nuggets and stopped. Auntie Anne's goodies were whispering my name.

Sasha mumbled as she shoved me past those extra calories, "See…it wasn't so hard to see an oldie-goldie?"

I jerked my head around and glared at her. "Don't you get it?"

Even though disapproving words weren't spoken, I often felt judged by the stares of others. Mostly from people I hadn't seen in a while.

"You need to get your ex out of your head. You're not that big." Sasha placed her hand on her hip. "That man done gave you a complex."

I didn't want to go there, so I snatched her arm and dragged her toward the exit. We made it to the other end without incident.

"Stop pulling on me." Sasha yanked her arm free.

"But—"

"But nothing. You've changed," Sasha scoffed. "Now that I see how you're behaving, I regret getting that invite. *And* we have three weeks to go."

"If I reach my goal, I'll be there." I averted my eyes.

Sasha snorted. "Urgh."

It was time for me to ditch Sasha so I could take the next step in my plan. I'd come back later to go to GNC nutrition store to purchase their brand of diet pills. I couldn't do it now. She'd play the social accountant by collecting all of the data, and if it didn't add up, she would challenge me and frazzle my nerves.

"Have you considered the man might not mind the extra weight? He's dated curvy and even heavier ladies before."

"So now you're finally admitting I'm big?" I huffed and practically sprinted in my effort to get away from her. She was too stubborn to leave me be, so I braced myself for an argument.

As expected, Sasha caught up and blocked my next step. I tried to go around her. Exasperated, I said, "What?"

Sasha wagged her finger in my face. "You better not do anything drastic. Nothing is worth risking your health. No pills. Promise?"

Dang, she knew me all too well. I tightened my lips and proceeded to open the car door. "Hurry now. I have a delivery." I planned to deliver *her* right to her doorstep.

I decided to hop on the diet wagon tomorrow. Tonight I was having a farewell party to my high carb friends. I'd start with sugar butter Christmas cookies and top it all off with my homemade hot chocolate.

Sasha didn't need to know my business. This challenge was between me and my future physique. I would become smaller any way I saw fit.

****

It had been eight days, five hours, and twenty-six minutes since my last real meal — the kind you chew, munch, and savor. Today I allowed myself three soda crackers, spaced evenly throughout the day. Because last week I couldn't shake loose the right amount of pounds, now I had to delve into drastic mode.

Sasha's daunting words lingered in my mind. "No, pills." So I tried the liquid diet route.

Every organ in my body screamed for nourishment and to break away from the no-food-jail I had locked them in. Maybe if I could gather up some umph to actually get out of bed, then I could get some low-sodium soup to take the edge off. But not until after my weigh-in.

The first two weeks I knew I'd done well with inches, but these last few days had been tough to budge the scale. With what I was putting my body through, I needed privacy this past week. Thankfully, I had a legit work-from-home job.

Yesterday Sasha called and begged me to ride with her to pick up her Christmas order. I agreed to go to make her shut her mouth because I was having a hunger attack and she could be relentless.

Lightheadedness hit me as I inched toward the edge of my bed. Eating would fix the problem, and I needed some fixing before Sasha picked me up. Sasha was always prompt when she had something *she* wanted to do.

Glancing in the mirror, I frowned at my reflection. Disheveled was not an adequate description, because an unmade bed looked better than I did at the moment. I looked dusty, and as my mom would say, ashy. Ash meant I looked close to dead.

I managed to stand up, but wobbled and sat back down before trying again. The second time around I was a bit steadier.

I walked over to the fridge and pulled out ingredients I'd bagged to make my green smoothies. The plan said I could have three smoothies a day, but instead I sipped one over the course of the day. I would try to drink a few more ounces to get rid of the faint feeling that the diet plan said should have disappeared two days ago.

I reached for the mixer and stopped mid-air as nausea hit me. I placed my hand over my chest, which thumped like a booming drumline. My phone rang and I could see Sasha's face flashing, but the pounding made it impossible to answer. She called again. This time, my parched mouth rebelled, so I swallowed to help moisten my throat. I mustered a faint, "Hey."

"What's *wrong*?" Sasha bellowed.

"I'll be all right," I said to calm her. I didn't need any Sasha hype.

"Which diet is it today? The first week was the popcorn diet or something ridiculous. The second week it was some powdered mess. What's it this week? All-you-can-eat broth?"

"Ha ha. You're not funny." Hearing her go on like that made my head pound even harder. I pressed my fist against my forehead.

"I need my Drea back. This is the last day of your crazy get-a-man-plan, right?"

"Two more days."

Sasha's comment made me pause. It challenged my motive and I didn't like that. Wasn't I doing this for myself? I guess in some way I thought this weight loss was for me.

"Oh, and about that, Brian probably won't be there."

Seriously? All this agony and he wouldn't even be there?

"Why? What happened?"

"His mother was rushed to the hospital."

Shock stunned me for a moment. Brian was a dedicated family man. I knew the relationship he had with Mrs. Jacobs was solid because they remained close to this day.

"You still there?" Sasha asked.

"I'm here."

"All this craziness was for what?" Sasha's tone mocked me. Even though I couldn't see her, I knew she wore a smirk.

"I'll go see him at the hospital." I made a mental note to pray for Brian's family. I remembered how hard it had been for me when I lost my mom.

"Keep the faith, girl," Sasha sang. "I'll be there in ten."

"What?" I panicked as I disconnected the call to go weigh myself. I hated when people had to wait on me.

I peered at the numbers between my feet. *Yes!* I didn't know if the adrenaline burst came after I saw the numbers or because of my quest to see Brian. Regardless, enough energy pumped through me to get a shower and get dressed.

The doorbell rang and I reached for my purse. In a flash, I saw the living room tilt vertigo-style, then spin three times as I stood clutching my handbag. Not sure if I would timber left or right, but everything went slo mo, like I was having an out-of-body experience.

I hit the floor, knocked out in a boxing match of my own making, only there was no one to count to ten or cheer for me to get up. Darkness came in like a swift wind and engulfed me as I surrendered to it.

****

"How you feeling?" Sasha placed her hand on my shoulder.

I glanced around the hospital room looking for nothing in particular, and then, I cast my eyes back to Sasha.

She waved her hand in front my face as I sat on the bed. "Why are you looking through me? You feel weak? Maybe you're being released too soon."

"I'm fine, Sasha." I pushed her hand away and finished putting my shoes on as I waited for my discharge papers. And the sooner the better than to deal with *her*.

"For someone who is being released today but only a few days ago could have gone into a *coma* and left for dead, you don't sound *too* thankful to be here." Sasha's eyes watered, but I remained stoic.

I did, however, feel the sting of a tiny arrow to my heart from that statement. She was right. Gratitude that she'd taken charge by calling 911 washed over me. But that still didn't give her the right to tell Brian my story.

If I spoke my thoughts out loud right now, I might cry. Worse, I might lose it and go postal on her. I didn't know if she cried because I almost died, or because she felt guilty about talking to Brian. She must've thought I was out cold because of the stuff hooked up to my arm when they first admitted me.

I decided to play along before I told her I knew she had shared my life story with Brian like a news anchor on the Fox 6 News. I heard every word Sasha said. Especially when she blurted to him, *"She did this for you… To. Get. You."* And Brian's reaction echoed in my mind as well. *"Maybe, I was wrong about her."*

"Look, I have to tell you-" Sasha said.

I huffed. "Tell me what? The same thing you told Brian when you thought I was asleep and couldn't hear you? About how many diets I tried hoping to win him over?"

The guilt on Sasha's face told me all I needed to know.

"I mean how sick are you?" I ranted, but slowed down when I felt my chest tighten. I didn't need to have to redress in a hospital gown and be hooked back up to tubes of any sort.

"Look, I told the man that you two needed to talk." Sasha stood with hands on hips and continued." I explained because I didn't want him thinking you were strung out on drugs the way your face was sunken in and all that."

I touched my face. It wasn't that bad, was it?

"Maybe I exaggerated a little." Sasha shrugged.

I retorted, "Sasha Brown, you would've had a fit if I had told Randy anything you'd told me in confidence. You have a lot of nerve thinking you didn't serve an injustice by telling Brian *why* I wanted to lose the weight!"

She folded her arms and averted her eyes. I rested my case.

"Okay, so you heard everything *I* said, but did you hear Brian's response?"

Oh, I heard him. I glanced at the bulletin on the wall, then scowled at her. Of course I was embarrassed that he found out I did this to myself. Yes, I created an unhealthy situation just to look good for him. But did Sasha have to shame me? She'd ratted me out like she was facing ten years in the prison yard if she didn't spill her guts.

"Okay." Sasha paused and added, "When he saw you laying there all tubed up, he whispered in your ear something like don't leave me."

"Wait…what?"

"He said, 'Don't leave me," Sasha repeated, but this time with a slight neck roll.

I blinked back a flood of hope because it could've meant anything, like don't die.

"Before you go down 'silly lane', he said he shouldn't have let you get away."

"Stop lying — you've done enough teasing," my voice squeaked.

"I'm not lying and you know it." Sasha rolled her eyes.

157

Really?

The thought of what I'd lost made my eyes pool. I'd been a fool. I wouldn't travel that road again. Food comforted, but never helped me before when I'd lost faith.

"She's not playing you. I said those things."

Was I hallucinating? That voice. *His* voice.

I turned my head to face the doorway. Brian stood next to his sister. He held flowers and offered them to me. "It's *good* to see you awake, Andrea."

I felt like a four-year-old caught writing on the wall with crayons. I put my head down.

"Your size is not who you are. If you think that's all that matters, then you're right...it's not *you* I want." Brian said.

Had I made him angry? Ruined my chances? I swallowed hard.

Brian glanced away, before returning his focus to me. "I'm more intrigued with the treasure on the inside, *not* the package a beautiful soul is wrapped in. I've played that record before and need a new song."

On that note, Brian walked out without a good-bye, a see-you-later, or glancing backward as the three of us watched him exit.

Did I really need a man who would leave me like that? "You can't just sit there on the bed like...like...you are the boss from the Devil Wears Prada. You have a heart." Sasha always demanded action.

"What am I supposed to do?" I said as my eyes flooded with tears.

Tammy smiled and said, "Go after him."

I struggled with what to do. Inwardly the answer was crystal clear, but I couldn't do it. "I'm not running after him." I pressed my lips together.

"Seriously?" Sasha clucked her tongue. "You're choosing to hold onto your pride after all this? Even *I* get what God wants for you and *you're* the Christian. You heard the man. Where's your faith?"

"What does my faith have to do with him walking out?" I pointed to my chest.

"Pride. It's a dose of death for a single woman and it'll have your butt at home thirty years from now thinking...on the night before Christmas when I stood in the hall." Sasha chuckled. "I'm not—"

"Mark my word; you'll be watching couples walk by when you know it could have been you," Sasha said.

"The Bible says, he who finds a wife, not *she* who finds a man." I frowned.

"You're going all scripture on me? Uh…uh…what about the one…be ye humbled or get humbled."

We all snickered at that one.

"Stop stalling," Tammy said. "He's still up in Mom's room."

"What if it doesn't work out?" I asked. In my heart I knew I could be honest with him. Then what?

"Girl, go claim your gift." Sasha beamed. "Or you'll never know."

I nodded. "But I have to sign my release papers?"

"I'll go get the nurse," Sasha replied and exited the room.

Tammy nodded. "It's room 221, just be *you*. We got you."

Before leaving, the nurse had rattled off instructions, something about a follow-up appointment, but it was all a blur. As I tried not to hyperventilate, past rejection feelings of self-doubt tried to crowd me. I resisted and took a deep breath and straightened myself up.

I glanced at Sasha and Tammy, who both agreed to stall the nurse with my wheelchair ride to the front door, then got onto the elevator. After it dinged, I stepped out and approached the door to his mother's room just as he stepped into the hallway. I had another whirlwind of emotions, but this time it wasn't darkness reaching for me, but the light.

Brian stood and opened his arms to me. He said with a cheeky grin, "Santa wants to know if you've been naughty or nice."

We hugged and shared a hearty laugh. I broke into a joyful cry because God had given me more than a man-gift to unwrap. No, it wasn't about Brian; he was just the bonus prize. It was me. I had more on the inside to give than I realized. Now I understood that if I focused on the real me, I could receive the gift of a second chance. I hadn't taken Brian seriously when he asked me for a date in college, but *baby* let him ask me out again; it would be on!

Known for pushing the envelope by writing about taboo topics, Sonya Visor is the author of Love Me for Who I Am, a novella about a woman battling an addiction to sex. Readers can contact Sonya at sonya@sonyavisor. com and find more books by visiting her website at www.sonyavisor.com • Facebook.com/sonya.visor • Twitter.com/sonyavisor •TruU • Goodreads •Pinterest.com/unmask1

The Letter... A Christmas Wish
By Tomeka Farley Daugherty

Wesley

Opening the door to their weekend getaway, Annie deeply inhaled before saying, "All of this for me, babe?"

Closing the door, Wesley walked up behind Annie wrapping his arms around her torso. Nudging her head to the left, Wesley started placing tender kisses from the nape of her neck down to her shoulder. Each kiss intensified Wesley's desire for Annie. Annie pushed her firm butt into the center of Wesley's genitals grinding slowly to whatever imaginary song was in her head. Giving him his own private dance.

Before long, they made their way to the bed with each of them tugging and pulling at each other clothes. The heat between them ignited a burning desire once their bare skin connected. This time no protection would stand in the way. The two became one, one hot ball of fire, hands, legs and body twirling around feeling, touching, biting, and doing everything imaginable to control the flames that were blazing out of control. Foreplay was out the window, it was time to get down to business.

Wesley looked into Annie's eyes, no words were needed. The non-verbal exchange was louder than a freight train. Today, at this moment, they were taking their commitment with one another to another level. No condoms needed, just skin-to-skin contact. Wesley entered the confines of Annie's walls with ease.

"Ooooohhhh." Wesley closed his eyes, pushing himself deeper. They always used protection, but with no barrier between them, Wesley felt like a virgin again. The feeling was unreal.

Annie refused to close her eyes. She seemed to want to remember every expression that came across Wesley's face as she allowed him to take full control of her secret garden. Opening her legs wider and wrapping each of them around Wesley, Annie looked to prepare herself for the best ride of her life.

Annie

Dear Wesley,

It's been eight months, two days, nine hours, and nineteen minutes and counting since I heard from you. A lot of time has passed and several unknown answers just hang in the air on your disappearance. I'm still hopeful that you're out there somewhere, trying to find your way home. I have to remain hopeful and believe you will return one day soon. But with each passing day, it's becoming harder and harder to believe that you just may be gone. You being gone, that's unacceptable. It seems like you're still here with me. When I close my eyes really tight, I can hear you whispering in my ear and feel you caressing my skin. I miss you so much. I tried to wait until your return, but this can no longer wait. I didn't want to tell you like this. My plan was to tell you in person once you came home.

I'm pregnant.

✷✷✷

The holidays were upon them, displaying a variety of lights and decoration lining the streets in Media, Pennsylvania, welcoming all to come and partake in the festivities. Annie loved being a part of a town where many visitors found themselves coming for different reasons. While others found the slogan of "Everybody's Hometown" inviting, Annie actually admired calling this place home.

Home. That one word used to lighten her heart, but that was before the recent events. Annie pushed her back into the hardness of the train seat. Looking out the window, the sky was crying. It was as if it were releasing the tears that Annie tried every day to hold inside. Annie placed her hands on her protruding stomach reminiscing on her last encounter with Wesley.

✷✷✷

"You put your foot and toes into that. Dinner was good, babe."

Annie placed the last dish into the dishwasher. "Glad you enjoyed it."

"Do you need any help before we hit the hot tub?"

"I got it. I'm about done anyway. Go ahead and get the hot tub ready for us."

Annie dried the last dish, placing it back in the cabinet. She couldn't wait to get to the hot tub for more than one reason. She was ready to relax and the hot water would do wonders right about now. Wesley and Annie were enjoying every moment of the cabin. Making love in all five bedrooms, the living room, on the kitchen counter, the back patio, even the pool table. This weekend had been purely divine and that's why Annie immediately decided to step outside of her comfort zone. Annie walked into the bedroom and dug into her luggage, pulling out the sweet surprise.

Making her way to the hot tub, Annie stopped in mid step when she saw the trail of candles in front of her. Placing her hand on her chest, Annie tried to slow down her speeding heart that was racing because of the revealing lingerie she decided to put on.

Gripping the sliding door, Annie inhaled, letting it out slowly and saying to herself, *"You got this girl. Now go work this nightie."* Annie just stood there and Wesley didn't mind because visually he appeared to be treasuring every curve of her body. Annie admired the flames dancing to their own tune while highlighting the black box sitting in the center. Looking up, she made eye contact with Wesley and her heart melted into a million of pieces.

Could this be it? Could this actually be happening? Was he proposing? Annie looked from the box to Wesley then back down to the box. They talked about getting married many times, but would this weekend be it?

Over the music that was playing in the background, Wesley confessed his love.

"Annie, we were meant to be together. Without you, my life would be incomplete. You bring out the best in me. Because of you, I walk differently, dream harder than before, and aspire to be a better person."

Wesley stepped inside the heart he made of candles, picking up the little black box just before he kneeled down onto one knee asking, "Annie, will you marry me?"

As the tears rolled down her face, she answered, "Yes."

Placing the two-carat sapphire engagement ring on her finger, Wesley kissed her hand before standing to his feet.

Annie leaned into Wesley for a passionate kiss. She rolled her tongue over his lips just before he opened his mouth welcoming her inside. Minutes later, gentle kisses turned into forceful ones, each of them trying to feast the internal burning. They broke away to catch their breaths. With each breath they took, the desire in their eyes grew. Wesley scooped Annie into his massive arms making their way to the hot tub to enjoy their final days in the cabin.

Seven days later
Wesley

Duty called and Wesley was expected to report back to his first love, the sea. As a child, being a US Navy Seal was a dream that Wesley turned into a reality shortly after his first year of college. Being out in the open sea, seeing miles and miles of nothing but water, listening to the waves crashing, assisting in disasters, Wesley enjoyed each mission. But being away from his parents and his woman, Annie, was always hard.

The sea was calm and quiet, almost too quiet. What a perfect time for Wesley to close his eyes and get some rest. The newbies were doing well and would be ready to take command of their new posts soon. Wesley closed his eyes before his head hit the pillow. He felt exhausted from the top of his head all the way down to his feet. Wesley slept for hours before his sleep was interrupted by a loud commotion. A commotion that immediately sent Wesley into ready mode, but it was too late.

"Command the entire area! Now, now!"

Understanding the harsh command, Wesley stood to his feet, just as the door swung open and the gun was pushed into his face. Wesley's thought was to reach for the gun and disassemble it, but that thought instantly changed as the gunman stepped closer, placing the gun to his temple. Another gunman appeared in the doorway ready to fire if he made any quick movement.

"Hands up! Move and you die," the second gunman replied.

His ship was overtaken by Somalian pirates. It looked like a war field as they made their way through the main common area. Wesley's blood was raging like a wildfire with anger. He needed to do something. He tried to hold his breath because no matter how much you tried, you could never get use to flesh burning. Looking to his right and then his left, he saw several veterans and newbies lying motionless. Dead on his watch. Wesley came to one conclusion. He had to get home, so if that meant complying with their demand - to make it home safely, that's what he would do.

Annie

Before the tear could fall, Annie swiped the moisture away. There was no way she would have an emotional breakdown in front of strangers, especially strangers on the train. Her stop was next. It would just have to wait until she got home. Annie gathered her things, stood and made her way to stand in front of the train doors, ready for them to open. As Annie stood there with others gathering around waiting as well, she thought to herself, *Annie, get it together, you have to remain strong. You're carrying a piece of him that you will always have and love. It's Christmas time, your favorite holiday. Anyway, it's been months now. If he was still alive, they would have found him by now. That's what the commanding officer constantly told her when she fired off with her list of questions. All of your letters have gone unanswered. All of your prayers have fallen on deaf ears. It's time to accept your new reality.*

The doors opened and the people who'd gathered around Annie, stepped by her as she remained standing there. She felt like a ton of bricks had settled around her feet, however, just as the doors were about to close, Annie mustered up enough strength to push herself through the other side.

The wind from the speeding train magnified as the train sped away. Blistering like a windstorm, blowing the loose papers in sight, the wind spoke, "Don't give up!"

Whipping around Annie was perplexed. Did she just imagine someone saying something to her? No one was there. It was obvious Annie was exhausted and delirious, too. She didn't even notice when the last letter she wrote to Wesley, the same letter she carried around with her, fell out of her belongs and was being taken away by the cyclone of wind.

Turning back around to head home, Annie came face to face with an elderly lady. Her facial features were strong, showing her years of struggle, but she stood upright, tall for her size. She looked familiar. Annie felt like she knew her but just couldn't recall from where. The elderly lady moved closer, reached out her fragile hand. In an attempt to touch Annie's face, the elderly lady hand landed on Annie's stomach.

Annie was livid. Elderly or not, this old lady was invading her personal space. Annie was taught to respect her elders, but this lady had clearly lost her mind. And not only that, but she was transferring her energy to Annie's baby because baby Wesley was kicking up a storm now.

Then the lady spoke, "I'm alive. I'm still alive. Don't give up on me."

His voice, her voice. Her voice was Wesley's voice. Her features were no longer of an elderly woman, but of Wesley, standing tall in front of Annie, touching her stomach and communicating to his son.

Wesley

Wesley squinted his eyes, trying to adjust to the light. Today made eight months, twenty days, ten hours and five minutes since being held captive. Each day was a struggle to carry on, to remain alive. Each day, Wesley agonized over a new way of escaping, but fatigue was his current first, middle, and last name. There were many days when he went without food or something to drink. The surrounding leaves provided him with little to no nourishment, but enough to get through the next day.

During his hostage taping, initially, Wesley would hold his head a certain way to allow the sun to reflect off his background to send signals, anything, any clues to pick up his whereabouts. Wesley would blink several times, trying to send codes through his eyes. Everything he thought was working to bring him back home was just keeping him further away.

In the aimless hours, Wesley thought of his childhood, of his parents, Annie, and his future, the future that was promised to him when he proposed to Annie. He dreamt they would live together growing old with one another. These thoughts were what kept him going. Especially during the moments where his manhood was tested. He wasn't just some average person who'd been captured. He'd spent years preparing for something like this to happen. But just like Wesley prepared, training for danger and every other potential situation, these Somalians did the same thing. He witnessed their training strategy and when a loophole presented itself, Wesley pounced on the opportunity to free himself, facing death with each attempt.

Early on, Wesley knew how valuable he was during the hostage negotiations, but as time continued to pass, his value lessened with each day. And today's conversation between the two leaders proved it.

"*Kaliya dilo isaga. Waxaan ma helin wax lacag madax furasho ah weli.*" (Let's just kill him. We haven't received any ransom money yet.)

"*Tani waxay noqon doontaa dhejinta ee la soo dhaafay, waxay yeelan doontaa toban saacadood in ay bixiyaan ama uu dhinto.*" (This will be the last taping. They will have ten hours to pay or he dies.)

Annie

Annie barely made it up the steps before collapsing on the front porch. She sat there, shaking uncontrollably, as fresh tears mixed with the dried up, stained tears that already took residence on her face and down her chest. She wrapped both arms around her stomach, holding baby Wesley and praying.

Annie didn't know how long it was that she sat there in the same spot. Praying and crying. Praying for a miracle, her Christmas wish of Wesley returning safely.

As a car drove up, the head lights reflected Annie's shadow on the house, but she didn't move. She still didn't move when the woman emerged from the car.

"Oh, my goodness. Hurry, Senior." Wesley's mother, Pearl closed the distance between herself and Annie.

As Wesley Sr. put the car in park, Pearl sat next to Annie, clutching her to her bosom, comforting her as she wept. Wesley Sr. stood there ready to provide whatever support was needed for his daughter-in-law and soon-to-be-born grandson. Even though Annie and Wesley weren't married, once Wesley proposed, she officially became a part of their family.

Pearl nodded her head, and then, she, Annie, Pearl and Senior went into the house to the dining room table. Pearl sat next to Annie, holding her hand, giving her all of the strength she had inside while Senior looked through the cabinets in search of the pot to boil water for some tea.

Minutes later, Annie took several sips of her tea before she outlined the events that had taken place. Pearl and Senior looked at one another, looked at Annie, and then looked at baby Wesley moving up a storm inside of his mom.

The road for Wesley's return wasn't easy, but Wesley Sr., Pearl, and Annie weren't giving up. The day after Annie told Pearl and Wesley Sr. what happened, Senior contacted his son's commanding officer for answers. During the conversation, he learned that the final ransom request was just recently received, requesting thousands of dollars or his son's life would no longer be spared.

Commanding Officer Washington wanted to respond and try to explain, but he knew better. Whenever a captain like Mr. Wesley Senior Spoke, no matter when they served, you shut your mouth and took whatever lashing you received.

Wesley Sr. wanted to honor his son's wish of never using his rank or contacts when it came to his son enlisting, conducting special assignments or more. It was important to Wesley Jr. to make a name for himself and Wesley Sr. honored his son wishes, until now. It was time for Wesley Sr. to take action, so he made the necessary call to get things in order.

Seconds turned into minutes and minutes turned into hours, everyone who was once in charge of his son's rescue was placed on administrative leave. Wesley Sr. took over the negotiations by watching all video recordings. Immediately, Wesley Sr. recognized the location where the Somalians were videoing, due to the special assignment he held when he was in the service many years prior. Wesley Sr. contemplated on his next move. Would he just focus on rescuing his son or would he make each person involved pay with their lives?

Rescuing his son was the most important thing to him right now. Therefore, that was where Wesley Sr. placed all of his resources, too.

One Year Later

Wesley thought about this moment many days during captivity. It was actually what kept him going. He stood at the alter waiting patiently for the doors to open to reveal his soon to be wife. As Wesley waited, he placed his oversized hand inside his left wedding suit pocket, feeling the ridge of the letter. There was no need for him to pull the letter out to reread it. The words recited themselves over and over in his head. It was the letter...a Christmas wish that Annie wrote to him one year, eight months, two days, nine hours, and nineteen minutes ago, the letter that he received in the mail one week after he arrived home.

Home. Wesley was home. He chuckled to himself when his son, Wesley Sutherland III came bouncing down the aisle just before the doors reopened announcing Annie's arrival. As Annie walked down the aisle in her wedding dress, Wesley held his son's hand and his heart filled with gratefulness.

Last Christmas, Annie's wish was for him to come home. But this Christmas, Wesley's wish was for them to live a life full of pure happiness.

Tomeka Farley Daugherty has always had a passion for writing. Her first published story, Deception At Its Finest is featured in the anthology Single Mama Dating Drama, also with Brown Girls Books. Tomeka is the CEO of her own travel business, It's Your Destiny; www.itsyourdestiny. paycation.com. Tomeka is married to Stanley Daugherty. They collectively have four amazing children and welcome the first granddaughter to their loving family. Tomeka is currently working on her debut novel. Visit her website, authortomekafarley.wixsite.com/website and connect with her on social media Facebook: @TomekaFarleyDaugherty & Twitter: @ DaughertyTomeka.

Please Come Home For Christmas
By Joyce A. Brown

CHAPTER ONE

Richard Jones ended the long-distance phone call by casually extending an invitation. "We'd like for you and your wife to spend Christmas with us. I have plenty of room, so you can stay with me. The rest of the family would like the chance to meet and get to know you."

There. The request was out in the open. All he wanted for Christmas was to share the overwhelming joy he felt at being reunited with the son he released without ever seeing him.

For the past four months, he'd been trying to explain to his family and friends that the baby he and Sandra Blake-Symonds had placed for adoption had "found" them. Back then, the two sixteen-year-olds weren't capable of parenting.

Introducing thirty-seven-year-old Donovan Wright to his mother, sister and brother was the answer to a prayer. Encouraging Donovan to become acquainted with Richard's daughter his half-sister, Amber, and the rest of his family was the next step in the process of Richard publicly claiming his son.

"Man, that's not going to work." Donovan's voice interrupted his musings. "This is the first Christmas since my mom lost her sister. My mom was her caregiver. We're meeting up at my aunt's house on Christmas Eve to decorate the place, cook Christmas dinner, and open the house for family and guests."

***

Richard thought back to the day his son reentered his life.

"Richard." Sandra's voice was clogged with tears last July. Her words were slurred, but exuberant. "This Jennifer Wright woman just called me, saying her husband, Donovan, is my son."

"If this is another scam..." The hair stood up on the back of his neck. A myriad of emotions washed over him — anger, confusion, fear, and irritation warred within him. This was not the first time Sandra had called with "news" about their child. Over the years, she'd hired one shyster after another who promised results about getting around Illinois' sealed adoption laws to find their son. At least they knew the boy had been adopted after Richard's mother demanded a meeting with DCFS. Questions bombarded Richard's mind — was this a set-up? How did he even know this was his son? What did the man want? Why now? He would only know what this was all about if he met Donovan Wright, talked to him face to face.

Over the hastily-arranged dinner meeting, Donovan looked at him out of eyes that matched his in color and shape. They even shared the same slight lisp. No DNA needed. This was his son.

"Thanks for meeting with us." Sandra openly wept, unable to do more than clasp Donovan's hand.

"This has been a long time coming," Richard said. "Is there anything at all that I may do for you?"

Donovan wrapped his arm around Jennifer and said, "I don't want anything other than information, man. I've had a good life with people who love me and have always had my back. I'm educated and I have a great career. I own a home and I have a beautiful wife. We'd like to have children, but I need to know more about my genetic history first."

"I see," was all Richard could muster, as tears stung his eyes.

That hot July night, they began a tentative relationship. Richard made regular phone calls. He bought expensive watches as gifts for Donovan and Jennifer's second wedding anniversary. He was determined to show his son how much he wanted him in his life now.

CHAPTER TWO

Rosalind's phone beeped as she pondered whether to journal or cry about the pain of the holidays without her beloved sister. Rosalind's sister died on July 3rd, after a three-year battle with ovarian and colon cancers.

The rest of the family was out, enthralled with Black Friday shopping. She finally picked the phone up.

"Hi Mom, did I wake you up?" Hearing her son's voice lifted Rosalind's spirits.

"No, I was writing. What's going on?"

"Richard wants me and Jennifer to spend Christmas Day with them, to meet the rest of the family." Donovan's deep voice was hesitant.

Rosalind closed her eyes and sighed. The past four months had been like repeated trips to Cedar Point, the Roller Coaster Capital of the World. Since meeting Richard Jones and Sandra Blake-Symonds, the people whose DNA he shared, their actions had imitated roller coasters as they fought for a place in his life. Both had travelled to Georgia to spend time with Donovan, getting to know him and sharing their individual life experiences, since they hadn't been a couple in years. More gifts arrived for his birthday and the contact between them continued.

The turbulence, the ups and downs had left Donovan wondering if he'd made the right decision to seek them out. All he'd wanted was medical information and for his biological parents to know he was okay. He had no idea he was opening Pandora's Box.

Finally, Rosalind said, "Absolutely not. Are they crazy?" Still reeling from her sister's passing, now, she was wrestling with two new people. She was trying to navigate the minefields of holding on tightly to her son versus sharing him with the people who gave him life. She'd always known this meeting would happen one day; Donovan always knew he was adopted. They had discussed finding his biological mother when he was a teenager. They'd planned to list him on the Adoption Registry.

But then, following the loss of his father, those plans had been stalled. Now, with her mourning Regina's death, this was the absolute worst time for his parents to be thinking about taking Donovan away for the holidays.

"I didn't think it would turn out like this," Donovan told her. "I just wanted to know so that I could move on."

Rosalind knew this was the real reason why he'd wanted to find his parents. The death of his father and his aunt, both from cancer, reminded them that his DCFS file didn't contain any medical information. They didn't know what diseases or health issues he might face in the future and he had told Rosalind that before he considered fatherhood, he needed some answers.

"Nothing is ever as simple as it seems or as complicated as we make it," Rosalind said. "Once they laid eyes on you, there was no going back."

Television and movies made "reunification" seem so simple. The adult adoptee finds a birth mother, hears her explanation, they embrace, and the screen fades to black. But what Rosalind and Donovan had discovered in this process was that life isn't that simple.

"I already told them no way."

Rosalind sighed with relief. Christmas was a mega experience in their lives with multiple Christmas trees, decorations throughout the house, and enough food to feed a small army. Family and friends stopped by constantly and there were presents for everyone. New pictures were taken. Old photos were put on display for the stroll down memory lane. And the whole time, they listened to Christmas music, and Rosalind's favorite -- James Brown's *Santa Claus, Go Straight to the Ghetto.*

For the past two Christmases, Donovan and his wife, Jennifer, flew into O'Hare Airport, spent a night or two at a luxury hotel on the Magnificent Mile, shopped, and then caught a bus to Rockford on Christmas Eve. They'd spend a couple of nights with Rosalind, and then catch a flight back to Georgia where they spent New Year's celebrating with their friends before returning to their jobs as fifth-grade teachers. It was a tradition they hadn't planned to break.

"What do you want to do? They are not going away," Rosalind asked. She knew this because she'd spoken with Sandra this past July, listened to her tearful explanation that she'd been forced by her parents to place Donovan up for adoption, yet had continued to search for him.

In exchange, Rosalind shared highlights of Donovan's life, scanning pictures dating back thirty-five years to the present and mailing them to Sandra so she had a timeline of his development and achievements. The pictures showed Donovan with the family who had loved him without reservation since the day he arrived. Rosalind and Donovan shared a unique bond from the moment the DCFS social worker placed him in her outstretched arms and she wanted Sandra to see and understand that.

Rosalind said, "You need to tell them something you can live with."

"I guess we can go the day after Christmas. They want us to spend the night with them. But, no way am I spending the night there. I intend to spend some time with Frank."

The thought of that made Rosalind smile. Frank had been his college roommate during his freshman and sophomore years. They retained that brotherly bond and got together during the holidays. Donovan was caught between two competing realities and three competing families—the family he'd grown up in, Richard's family, and Sandra's family.

"Would you feel better if I came along? I want to meet these people, too."

"Yeah." Rosalind heard the whoosh, Donovan exhaling the breath he'd been holding. "Richard mentioned inviting cousins and close family friends. That's too many new people at one time."

"I'll go in for a moment, meet them, and come back later for you and Jennifer."

"Thanks, Mom. See you for Christmas."

CHAPTER THREE

December 26th
Richard opened his door in Chicago's Pill Hill neighborhood, expecting two people and saw four. His smile, reminiscent of Donovan's, was friendly and welcoming.

"Sorry we crashed your party. I'm Dr. Rosalind Wright, Donovan's mother, and this is my sister, Kathryn. We're taking them to the hotel later and thought we'd come in and say hello to everyone first." Rosalind's words tumbled out one after another. The jazzy vocals of *It's Feeling Like Christmas* poured out of a surround system and filtered through to the front door.

"Come on in," Richard said. "You can meet the family before the rest of our guests arrive."

Donovan stood close to Jennifer. He hung back, as if unsure of his footing. Jennifer whispered something for his ears alone and he calmed down. Richard took the heavy coats, hung them in a closet, and led them toward the spacious kitchen. Richard revealed that he had been listening to his son during their many conversations, and he said to Rosalind, "Donovan says you have an extensive art collection," as Rosalind looked at three original African-themed art pieces on the wall.

Rosalind's laughter expelled some tension as they discovered a topic in common. "My purchases started out small and snowballed. Almost every wall in my house has multiple pieces of art in some pretty unusual groupings." The vibrant statement pieces were tastefully framed. "I like these."

"If you like, I can give you the artist's card," Richard offered.

Rosalind held up a hand to stop him. "No thanks. I really do need to stop purchasing art."

Jennifer told Richard, "She's already given us enough art to furnish our home. We need to find Art Buyers Anonymous for my mother-in-law."

Jennifer's remarks caused Donovan's first real smile since they'd left Rosalind's sister's house two hours earlier.

Christmas decorations and the aroma of roasted meat, greens, and sweet potatoes reminded them of why they were here.

"This is my mother, Mrs. Virginia Jones." Richard pointed to a spry, gray-haired woman who Richard told them had single-handedly cooked the feast. To his mother, Richard said, "This is Donovan's mother and aunt, Rosalind Wright and Kathryn…I didn't get your last name."

"Leonard," Kathryn announced, looking at the various pots. "I love soul food."

Richard addressed his mother. "Mother, this is Donovan and his wife, Jennifer."

Donovan moved slowly from behind Rosalind and walked around the kitchen island to the now smiling woman who reached for both of his hands. As Richard recited Donovan's degrees and awards, Ms. Virginia stood straighter, pride evident in her face.

Ms. Virginia clasped Donovan's hands forcefully as she told him, "You come from good stock. All my children and grandchildren are well-educated."

Donovan flinched and pulled away slightly. The flared nostrils and steely brows were pure Papa C. Calvin Wright, the father who insisted he get a college education. Two years ago when making his wedding toast, Donovan acknowledged to the majority of his friends that he was adopted, that Calvin and Rosalind Wright raised him as their son — that love trumps blood!

Ms. Virginia continued, oblivious to what Donovan was feeling. "Richard, show him the pictures of his grandfather and the rest of the family."

"We'll do that later. I want him and Jennifer to take a ride with me to pick up Amber." Richard's next words were addressed to Rosalind and Kathryn. "Amber is his sister and she's excited to have another big brother. We won't be gone long."

Richard pointed to high-back chairs at the granite kitchen island. "Sit down and make yourselves at home. You ladies should really stay. We've got a couple of hours to get acquainted." Richard issued the sincere invitation.

Rosalind looked at Kathryn who nodded her agreement.

"Would you like some coffee or a soft drink?" Richard inquired.

Rosalind spoke for both of them. "Something warm to counteract the wind and cold would be wonderful. Kathryn's car heater was no match for today's below-freezing temperature."

Richard poured two steaming mugs of coffee, setting them in front of the two women, "Would you like cream and sugar?" He opened the refrigerator and brought out brand name cream. He picked up the sugar bowl and placed it on the counter in front of the two sisters.

Kathryn reached for the sugar, and Rosalind, for the cream.

"Sandra's on her way over here. That will give the two of you some time to get better acquainted. Sandra's really appreciated the information you've shared with her. She shows those pictures to any and every one she can corral."

"Thanks for the invitation. We'll have a moment to get acquainted without you and Donovan around."

Donovan pecked her on the cheek and they went to grab their coats before heading out into the cold.

***

"We been praying for this reunion since we found out he was adopted," Ms. Virginia told Rosalind as soon as the door closed behind Richard, Donovan, and Jennifer.

"How did you find out about the adoption?" Kathryn probed.

"Once I got over my initial hurt that Richard signed those papers, I went down to DCFS and wouldn't leave till someone talked to me. The social worker told me he was already gone." Ms. Virginia glared at Rosalind, "Why didn't you ever try to look for me?"

"Why would I do that? I had what I wanted." Rosalind knew most black people practiced a form of adoption that was an open arrangement between the parties. But the state's legal system enforced a wall of separation between the adopting parents and the biological family. When Donovan came into their lives, he was her only focus. She didn't dwell on his past. Rosalind made a mental note to remind her social work students of the consequences of divulging confidential information.

"We were wild with grief and didn't know how to undo this terrible thing. I did something incredibly stupid. I sent my daughter, Charmaine, down there to Peoria to look for y'all." Ms. Virginia's unresolved hurts were making the situation uncomfortable, but no way was Rosalind going to be made the villain for Ms. Virginia's family's choices.

Kathryn sent Rosalind a look that clearly said, "Don't go off on this woman."

Rosalind sucked in a deep breath, remembered why she was here, and spoke as calmly as she could. "My husband and I were told the parents voluntarily terminated their rights. There was no reason for me to consider that anyone else in the family wanted him." Taken aback by Ms. Virginia's tone, Rosalind breathed in smells of mouth-watering goodness being prepared for the feast, exhaled, and centered herself with the instrumental version of *The Christmas Song*.

"Sandra could have brought him here if she didn't want him," Ms. Virginia continued her rant.

Within the next five minutes of hearing Ms. Virginia's recitation of events surrounding Donovan's birth, Rosalind surmised that Ms. Virginia blamed Sandra for everything, had whitewashed her son's behavior, and now wanted to claim her grandson.

177

Throughout her professional career, Rosalind had counseled teen mothers, conducted home studies for adoptive parents, and sat in courtrooms when rights were being severed. It was never cut and dried. Everyone had a piece of the story. Her unique position as adoptive parent and social worker often proved useful in dealing with complicated family situations. Rosalind hadn't planned on conducting an intervention involving her own son.

Rosalind put on her best professional manner and slid into the mediator role. "Ms. Virginia, did you tell Sandra that your family would like to raise Donovan? Richard shared with me her father called, asked him to come to the hospital, sign the birth certificate, and marry his daughter."

Sandra and Richard had gone their separate ways when the pregnancy was discovered. Sandra's family was angry that she'd become pregnant out-of-wedlock at sixteen.

"Them kids were too young. My husband said he didn't have to marry her," Ms. Virginia countered. She pulled out an envelope bearing the DCFS logo out of her pocket. It was crammed with papers that she spread out on the table in front of Rosalind and Kathryn.

"What about signing the birth certificate?" Rosalind needed to remain calm and deescalate this situation. She didn't want to ruin this day for Donovan. "Establishing paternity would have given Richard grounds to oppose both the foster care placement and the adoption process."

Ms. Virginia rolled her eyes at Rosalind, turned down the flames under her pots to simmer, and sat down heavily on the stool across from them. "If he wasn't gonna marry her, he didn't see the need to sign it."

How many times had Rosalind heard that line? Make the woman the villain. Ms. Virginia's son was not responsible for the decisions Sandra made until the moment they affected her personally. "How did that work out for y'all?" Rosalind's sarcastic nature was taking over. Time to sip her flavorful nutmeg-spiced coffee and lean back in her seat.

Unlike the prodigal son who left home, squandered his wealth, and returned looking for scraps from his father's table, Donovan was the son, grandson, brother, nephew, and cousin this family had never met. The family had longed to find him, to no avail, until a fateful night five months earlier when the prodigal's wife called his birth mother to ask if she "had given birth to a boy and placed him for adoption."

At that moment, Richard's brother and sister-in-law walked in the back door, accompanied by their two daughters. Ms. Virginia made the introductions, saying, "That's the woman who raised him."

"No," said Rosalind. Lord, help me to hold my tongue she silently prayed as she smiled. "I'm Donovan's mother. My name is Rosalind."

CHAPTER FOUR

"Did you ever think we'd be sitting here, together?" Richard asked, his jubilant voice and face turned to Rosalind and Sandra who were seated on either side of him, eavesdropping on conversations of guests tip-toeing around the family drama even as they savored the hors d'oeuvres and libations.

"Not at all," Rosalind responded, her voice full of acceptance. Earlier, the sight of Donovan standing between Richard and Sandra in the kitchen surrounded by his biological family erased all questions about where he'd come from. The puzzle pieces fit. Donovan looked like Richard but had Sandra's body type.

Rosalind's tears flowed as she shared with them, "Every Christmas I would 'talk' to Sandra, hoping telepathy and a gracious God would calm her spirit and assure her that 'her little boy' was surrounded by a family who loved him and provided for him. That she would know how much I cherished the gift she had given me." Rosalind patted Sandra's hand.

Then Sandra dabbed a tear and mouthed the words, "Thank you."

Rosalind Wright chuckled, and continued, "Unfortunately, I didn't consider sending that same prayer out to you, Richard."

"It's okay," he assured her. "When I was mentoring young men through the One Hundred Black Men program, I wondered if somebody was mentoring my son. I prayed he was all right." Richard gazed out of the window. Thirty-five years ago, he rode several trains and buses from his parents' home on the southside to the Cook County Courthouse to sign release-for-adoption papers. Immense sadness, guilt, and disappointment plagued his steps that day. A son he'd never seen. That little boy's mother calling, pleading, "Sign the papers so he can go to a good home. If you don't sign the papers, he'll grow up in foster care." She'd already signed them.

Richard thought he was doing the right thing. At sixteen years old, his dream was to be a musician, traveling the world playing drums as part of a successful band. Feeling like a failure, Richard signed the papers. Months later he realized there had been other options — his family would've welcomed the child into their family. By the time Ms. Virginia contacted DCFS, she learned that he'd already been adopted. It was too late. The deed was done.

Nearly thirty family members and close friends who responded to the invitation to "come and meet my son" were ready to enjoy their second Christmas feast in two days. Bluesy Christmas music filled the room, punctuating conversations.

Across the room, Richard's best friend, Anthony was gazing at the dessert table and chortling to his wife, Niecy, "Wouldn't miss this sweet potato pie for nothing." As frequent guests, Anthony and Niecy knew the quality and quantity of food that was being served. He stage-whispered to his wife, "Who knew we'd be sittin' in the best seat in the house, witnessing a reunion of sorts between Richard and Sandra and their son?"

Niecy tried to whisper, unsuccessfully, "I hope the two mommies don't claw each other's eyes out."

A late arrival, another female friend came into the room and hugged Ms. Virginia. "Where's my honey-baked ham and peach cobbler? I brought my diabetes medicine along for later if I pass out."

The crowd roared.

Donovan said the blessing and everyone demolished the succulent feast. Forks tapped plates and moans of enjoyment filled the dining room as Richard's wish was being granted.

"Look at Richard," Ms. Virginia stated. "He got exactly what he wanted for Christmas — to know his son."

Richard observed Rosalind smiling as she watched her son and his bride exchange kisses. She'd shared with him that Donovan had also hoped for this day and this clarity about his beginnings.

Donovan stood, taking Jennifer by the hand. "Thank you all for such a warm welcome. Jennifer and I really appreciate it. We've had a great time but we have to go."

"Why the rush?" Sandra asked. She'd been quiet most of the afternoon.

"I'd like to let today's events soak in and spend some alone time with my lovely wife. It's not too late for one more Christmas gift."

"What's that?" Rosalind looked at her son, pleasure in her eyes.

"Now we can get to work on expanding our little family."

Joyce A. Brown is an idependently published author of women's fiction. Like her FB author page, Joyce A. Brown.

Merry Little Christmas
By Dwon D. Moss

Melody

"*Santa Baby, just slip a sable under the tree, for me. I've been an awful good girl, so hurry down the chimney tonight.*"

I sang along with Eartha Kitt while grabbing the towel off the rack. I made sure I was careful not to fall since I was pregnant.

It had been a long journey to get where Cliff and I were. Cliff made sure that I was treated like a queen from the moment we said, "I do." He didn't give me the world on a silver platter, my baby gave me the world on a platinum platter. Now, he was just as thrilled as I was to have a baby. He wanted a boy to carry on his name and I just wanted a healthy baby.

Since the doctor assured Cliff that it was okay to have sex, I was going to give him the works tonight. I put on a lacy tank top and some maternity boy shorts. I swayed my hips side to side and hummed, "*Somebody rocking knocking the boots.*" I laid across the bed and wiggled. Wiggled because my butt was eating my boy shorts and turning those panties into thongs. I must have wiggled myself to sleep because when I woke up, the blinds were open and the sun was shining.

Just as I was about to get up to shower, Cliff opened the door with a tray full of turkey bacon, eggs, grits and toast.

"Don't forget that we have a doctor's appointment in two hours," he reminded me.

I scrunched up my nose. As if I could forget.

I scarfed down my food and took another shower. I wasn't going to the ob/gyn with unfresh lady parts.

Cliff

"I promise to see you soon. Are you available tomorrow?" I whispered into the phone while Melody was in the shower. I kept the conversation going, whispering the whole time, until I heard the water stop.

Melody yelled, "I'll be down in a minute."

I barely heard her because my mind was on the phone call I'd just made. In the seven years of marriage to Melody, I'd stayed true to our marriage vows. Temptation presented itself several times, but I somehow managed to fight it.

But not this time. Chrisette was different from the others. I couldn't stay away from her. I tried to, but it was hard. Both of us were working long hours and I was spending more time at work with her than I was at home with my wife. Chrisette had ambitions and goals. She challenged me and that intrigued me.

Don't get me wrong. Melody had her own achievements and goals, but after seven years, she didn't excite me. Truth be told, I was ready to leave my marriage. I just didn't know how. Melody was the most loyal and sweetest soul on earth and if I left her, especially while she was pregnant, I would look like an ass. The problem was, since Chrisette had come into my life, everything about Melody got on my nerves. The man in me was only staying for our baby.

Melody

I could hardly contain my excitement on our trip to the doctor. Maybe today, we'd get to find out if we were having a boy or a girl. The baby was breach during our last visit and he or she wouldn't get in position for us to get a good view.

As he drove, I looked over at Cliff. I expected him to be excited, too, but he had a strange look on his face. An unfamiliar look. I was sure he would be smiling after this doctor visit. I reached over and grabbed his hand, so excited that we were taking this journey together.

Cliff

Melody just grabbed my hand, intertwining our fingers and all I could do was think about my lust for Chrisette but love for Melody.

Melody

I was thrilled the moment I got on the examination table. I knew everything would be all right, because I thanked God in advance for positive results. The nurse, Mrs. Williams, shared my enthusiasm. We continued to chat as she squirted cold gel on my stomach. She moved the ultrasound probe over my belly and I heard the thumps of our baby's heartbeat. It was in sync with mine.

"All right now," Mrs. Williams said as she slid the probe over my belly. "Let's see what we have here."

I tried not to hold my breath as we waited to hear the news from the nurse. All I wanted was a healthy baby, but I was so excited to learn what we were having.

Cliff held my hands while we waited.

Keeping my eyes on the screen, I watched the image move back and forth. Then, the nurse announced, "Congratulations, you're having a baby girl."

Tears of joy slid down my pregnant face that had become round with my weight gain. But when I looked at the nurse, my smile slowly turned to concern. It was the way she kept pressing the probe against the side of my stomach and her expression that made me ask, "Is there a problem?"

The lines on her face didn't change. She gave my shoulder a squeeze. "Doctor Ahmad will be in soon to talk to both of you."

After placing the probe in its designated place, she pulled the hospital gown over my thighs and knees before she left the room.

"What do you think is going on?" I asked Cliff. Before my husband could give me an answer, the doctor walked into the room. After greeting me and Cliff, he moved close to the table where I laid and said, "Well, congratulations on having a girl." He took a breath. "There is no easy way to tell you this, but you are having a dwarf."

Cliff jumped up. "What's a dwarf?"

I knew Cliff knew what a dwarf was, but I understood his question. It was the only thing he could ask in this moment.

The doctor understood, too. He explained, "A dwarf is what is commonly referred to as a little person. Most of the time, dwarfism isn't diagnosed until birth or even after that, but from the images from the ultrasound, your daughter's skeletal images...we can tell."

As tears formed in my eyes, the doctor continued, "Your daughter will be born with a normal size torso, but she'll have small arms and legs.

She won't grow taller than four feet ten inches, but it's important for you to know that this will not affect her intelligence and she'll be able to live a healthy life.

"Now, I would be remiss if I didn't tell you the cons of dwarfism. There is a risk of malformed bones, joint disease, and nerve compression among other things." The doctor paused. "Do you have any questions for me?"

There were so many questions swirling in my mind, but I could ask not even one of them. When Cliff didn't say anything either, the doctor said, "I'm going to send you home with more information and my personal phone number so that you can call me if you need me or when questions arise."

I thanked the doctor and then, he left us alone. I dressed knowing what I was feeling and Cliff must have felt the same way because he didn't say a word. We were silent as we walked to the car and the ride home was just as solemn.

On the ride over, I had a difficult time deciphering the look on my husband's face, but it wasn't any easier on this drive home. He was stoic and I reached over to grab his hand, the way I always did.

Cliff

I was in shock for two reasons. First of all, I'd been sure that Melody was having a boy, and then to find out that our daughter will be a dwarf. What type of game was God playing with me? I didn't say a word as we drove and I was glad that Melody didn't speak either. As soon as I got home, I grabbed my laptop, sat in the chair across from the sofa, and did lots of research on dwarfism.

Out of my peripheral vision, I looked at Melody, sitting on the sofa, legs hanging over the arm of the sofa as she read the information Dr. Ahmad gave to her. Standing up, I left her in the living room alone. Melody, being pregnant, had put so much pressure on me and the only person I could talk to about it was Chrisette.

For the rest of the day, I didn't say another word to Melody. And for the first time in seven years, I went to bed forgetting to kiss my wife.

Melody

Cliff was more quiet than usual and I figured he was overwhelmed with the information that Dr. Ahmad gave us, because for the first time in our seven year marriage, he went to bed without kissing me. I laid next to him with my eyes open, rubbing my stomach. I was going to do everything that I could to help and love my baby, even before she was born. Cliff and I would be raising a little person, but she would have lots of love and love is all that matters.

Cliff

Chrisette met me at 57th Restaurant. It was in the back of a woody trail, in the outskirts of Atlanta. She looked absolutely gorgeous. She always dressed sexy. She was just plain seductive looking today in a burnt orange maxi dress with her back exposed.

After we hugged and sat in a booth, I talked and she listened and just her being there gave me comfort.

"It's going to be all right," she told me. "Children are a gift from God. You know that, right?"

Then, it was her turn to talk and I listened. I hung on to what she was saying while staring at her glossy golden lips.

We sat there for two hours that felt like minutes and I walked Chrisette to her car. I opened her door but before she climbed in, we shared a firework kiss that had me wanting more. The kind of kiss that left me surer than ever that I was ready to leave my wife.

Melody

A few days after our doctor's visit, Cliff and I decided to name the baby, Indigo. Well, I decided. Cliff had still been acting standoffish and I figured it was the news of our baby dwarfism. I knew that everyone handled stress in different ways. I was going to let Cliff do what he had to do, but I needed someone to talk to.

That's what I was thinking as I drove up the long driveway that led to my parents' home. I smiled knowing it smelled like Christmas, a combination of oranges and peppermint. The aroma had me giddy like a little girl. My parents and I were putting up the tree that my Dad cut down earlier that day. We'd never had an artificial tree and never would. I walked into the house, took a look around the foyer and thanked the Lord for my roots.

I took off my gloves, put them in the pocket of my coat and hung the coat on the rack, before yelling, "I'm home!"

"How are you, baby?" Mom asked me coming from the kitchen as I walked to the sunroom.

I walked into the room where my Dad was lounging, watching a basketball game. I gave him a kiss on the cheek, inhaling the aroma of one of the Padron Serie 1962 cigars I had given him a couple of months ago.

"You know I went to the doctor the other day."

I could tell that my mother was already holding her breath.

"We are having a girl!"

My mama jumped up and did the Holy Ghost dance while my dad just grinned. "Congratulations, Melody."

But then, I went into the other news. I explained to them that Indigo (they loved her name) was a dwarf and assured them that I was good with it.

"I'm having a healthy little girl and that's all that matters. All will be good in our world."

"If you're good, then, we're good, too," my mama said.

But before she stood up to hug me, I noticed a look pass between my parents.

What was that about? I wondered. I didn't ask; I figured they would tell me in their own time.

Melody

This was my favorite part of the year. I got to get woozy from the smell of pine from the Christmas tree while listening to The Temptations and Nat King Cold sing about chestnuts and giving love on Christmas day. We sat around and put the hooks in the ornaments. I wanted to let them know that the ornaments could be stored with the hooks in. But that would take some of the fun out of decorating, just like putting angel hair on the tree. Angel hair looked like what I imagined heaven to look like, but the cuts they left behind had always reminded me of the cuts I got from bathing after getting a whipping with a small but sturdy switch. Since I was pregnant, I couldn't place the Angel on top of the tree, so I held the ladder in place while Daddy did it. We sipped on egg nog and laughed about old Christmas stories.

Cliff

I was wearing a hole in the carpet by pacing back and forth. Yesterday, I'd finally found the courage to take the first step to ending my marriage -- I rented a townhouse. Now, I had to find the courage to tell Melody that I was leaving her. We would be going on our regular couples' Christmas trip in two days. I would wait to tell her I was moving out until after our trip.

Melody

We got up with the roosters this morning. Cliff and I held hands and prayed for traveling grace before we got on the road to make the sixteen hour drive to our cottage in Killington, Vermont. We had to leave earlier than our friends. We would be taking a lot of stops at rest areas in order for me to stretch my legs and use the restrooms. It started snowing five hours into our trip. I was excited and started singing, *"Santa Clause, Goes Straight To The Ghetto."* Then I reached for my phone, hit Facebook Live and started singing, *"I Saw Mommy Kissing Santa Claus."*

Cliff

I was laughing at Melody singing her heart out. It softened my heart. This was the Melody I fell in love with seven years ago. I was second guessing my decision to move out of our home.

The snow got worse. There was no way that we could travel any further. We stopped at the nearest hotel we could get to and unloaded our belongings. Melody was understanding but disappointed. I suggested that we put up our artificial tree since the snowstorm would have us trapped in the room for days. I put up the tree while Melody found the decorations.

Melody

I looked and looked for the lights for the tree before realizing that our friends, Rayna and Robert, were supposed to bring them.

"Ummm... Babe, we have no lights to decorate the tree." I pouted.

"I have the perfect solution."

We found our Christmas ribbons, cut them in half, sat beside each other and strung Froot Loop cereal on the ribbon to make the decorations. I started singing, *"Baby, it's cold outside, I've got to go away, baby, it's cold outside..."*. Cliff joined in the duet and at the end, we harmonized.

Cliff

It had been four days stuck in the hotel. Tomorrow should be clear to go back home, but for now, I just wanted to stare at my wife. She had always been angelic looking, but being pregnant added a glow to her. I was happy that I had not told her about my new place. I could never leave this woman.

Melody

It was Christmas Day and I was feeling it. I got out the shower, dried off, grabbed my brush, pretending it was my microphone, and started singing the 69 Boyz song, 12 Ghetto Days of Christmas. *"What you gonna' get her for Christmas..."* All of a sudden I felt warm water run down my leg. I screamed, "Babe, it's time." He grabbed my bag.

We got to the hospital just in time for Indigo's birth. Cliff held my hand and encouraged me to push. Indigo came into this world looking cherubic. Cliff and I looked at each other. I smiled and said, "Let's change her name to Josephine.

I looked at Cliff count Josephine's toes and fingers while I hummed, *"Have yourself a Merry Little Christmas."*

And now that I had my baby, I fully intended to do just that.

Dwon D. Moss is a Marine Corps Veteran, AALBC Best Selling Author, 2017 Black Pearls Literary Excellence Award Nominee, Writer, Story Teller, Entrepreneur, Sunday/Vacation Bible School Teacher and Motivational Speaker. She also has a column, All That Sass, in the Christian Magazine Real Life, Real Faith. Dwon is a guest host on the radio blog, Truth Heals Hurt, with Princess Gooden.

She has Co-Authored the Anthologies, The Ex-Chronicles, Single Mama Dating Drama and All I Want For Christmas, Published by Brown Girls Books. She is currently working on her Debut Novel.

Sister Grinch
By Venita Alderman Sadler

Beep. Beep. Beep.

"What the heck is going on?" I asked as my eyes opened.

Beep. Beep. Beep.

I was on the couch instead of my bed and my alarm clock was blaring upstairs. As I pushed off the sofa, I knocked over the empty wine bottle I'd devoured last night. Ignoring it, I grabbed my cell phone off the table and checked my messages. I didn't have any.

Ugh! So, Darnell's raggedy ass didn't even try to call me and make up.

I dashed up the stairs and turned off the alarm. As I sat on my bed, I replayed the argument we'd had last night.

"Why don't you want to get married?" he barked.

"I didn't say that. I said that I didn't want to have kids."

"It's the same thing. You get married, you have kids!"

"But, I don't even like kids," I responded.

He frowned. "Wait, what? You have nieces and a nephew."

"I don't like my nieces and nephew. I have to love them because my sister birthed them, but..." I stopped, thinking that was enough.

But Darnell stood in place, staring, before he whispered, "You serious about this?"

I nodded. "I am. I don't want kids."

"Even if I want them?"

I shrugged. "I'm sorry. It's my body and I say no."

The look on his face said that I'd shocked him. I didn't care. Darnell needed to know -- there would be no kids coming from this union.

After what felt like a couple of long minutes, he said, "I love you."

I knew he did and I knew he would see things my way.

"But if you don't want kids, then we don't need to do this."

I frowned. "Do what?"

"This. Us. It's over."

So he was gonna blackmail me? I shrugged. "Okay," I said, calling his bluff. He couldn't possibly want to break up just because of kids. But after he dressed, he grabbed his coat and walked out of my house.

The phone rang, startling me from my thoughts.

"Ashley, speaking," I announced.

"A simple hello would suffice," my sister, Latoya said.

With Darnell still on my mind, I said, "You answer your phone the way you want, and let me answer mine the way I like." Even though she couldn't see me, I rolled my neck with every word.

"Well dag, sis, what Grinch stole your Christmas?"

"Christmas isn't for another few days, so what do you want this early on a Saturday?"

"I wanted to talk to you about Mommy and Daddy's Christmas gift."

"What about it?" I snapped. "You and Maurice normally pick out something and I'm forced to go along. So, pick it out!"

"Wow. What's wrong with you?"

"Look, how much is my portion?"

"All righty then. I'll call you later with Maurice on three way and hopefully, you'll be in a better mood."

"Whatever!" I said, then hung up.

I knew my baby sister was shocked by my tone. I was always the cheery one, but I wasn't in the mood for her whining right now. Looking at my phone, I couldn't believe there wasn't a call, a text, a message -- nothing from Darnell.

Taking a breath, I decided to go out. Running errands would take my mind away from my boyfriend and by the time I got back, there'd be a call with his apology.

Wanting to get out as fast as I could, I showered, dressed, and was in the parking lot of Target before it was even eight. Yet, I still had to drive down every single aisle before I found a spot at least a mile away from the front door!

"This is ridiculous," I mumbled as I got out of the car. Yeah, it was the last Saturday before Christmas, but did everyone have to come out at the same time?

Inside the store, I peeled off my coat, hat, and scarf and threw it all into the basket before I rolled into the chaos of Christmas shopping.

Any other year, I would have been into this, soaking up the hustle and bustle and singing right along with *Joy to the World* coming from the overhead speakers.

I didn't feel any joy, though, as I pushed through the store, still thinking about last night. I'd spent three Christmases with Darnell, but now it felt like... I shook my head. No. No way. Darnell wasn't really going to break up with me.

I headed toward the Health and Beauty aisle, but then stopped when my phone vibrated. Fumbling through my purse, I tried to get to it as fast as I could. I frowned. Then, I pouted.

It was just a text from my brother.

With my head still down, I pushed my cart and read the text at the same time. Then, bam!

"Ooops, I'm sorry," I said, gaining back control of my cart. Looking up, I met the eyes of this fine chocolate piece of man-candy. "I'm sorry," I said again because I didn't know what else to say.

"Don't worry about it." He grinned, just to show me his dimples, I bet. "You can run into me anytime."

He had me locked in place, and he knew it. I couldn't stop myself when my eyes roamed downward, checking him out. And I zoned right onto his wedding band. My attitude came right back.

"What would your wife think of that?" I asked.

From behind him, a squeaky voice said, "She would tell you to watch where you're going." Then, this tiny wisp of a woman, stood by his side. Well, tiny may not have been the best word because she looked like she was about to give birth to triplets. I smirked at the heifer and moved my cart into the aisle. I was looking for deodorant, but came upon the pregnancy section first. I grabbed a pack of condoms, then turned around and said, "Hey cutie, use these next time." I tossed Mr. Chocolate Candy the box.

As he caught it, I said to her, "And you, bubble gut, I don't have a problem with smacking you into labor."

The looks on both of their faces satisfied me and I walked away. As I lingered on the next aisle, I heard her berating him about always flirting with some desperate tramp. I wanted to go back and tell her that I wasn't desperate -- I had a man. A butterscotch, Shemar Moore-fine man.

And then, I remembered.
I was depressed all over again.

***

All the way home, I kept checking my phone. Making sure that it was on and working. But once I was home and put away everything I'd bought, there was still nothing from Darnell.

But I did have that text from my brother.

I texted him back.

Sorry just getting back to you. How much do you need from me?

A few seconds later. . .

Where is my hello?

I rolled my eyes. *Hello...how much? Better?*

It took Maurice a moment to respond. *Much better. We decided to send them on a trip to the Dominican in May.*

Did I ask him all of that? *How. Much?*

I had to smile a little at that. Even my texts had an attitude.

$650 each. All-inclusive, plus a little spending money.

Maurice was just determined to tell me all that I didn't want to know. *Okay, I'll Paypal it.*

Another moment before...

That's all you going to say? Do you want the details: hotel, flight, views?

I wasn't surprised at his question because I usually was all up in the planning. But right now, I didn't care about anyone's issues when I had my own.

I'm sure you and Latoya got it covered. Love you. Ttyl.

It felt like only a second passed before...

You okay?

Yes. That's all I had for him.

Okay send the money to Latoya, because she charged it, and apologize to her.

When I didn't respond, Maurice sent another text.

TODAY.

I tossed the phone onto the bed, even more pissed. Latoya had told him that I snapped on her. She always told him everything. He was the oldest, but he wasn't my father and I didn't care what he thought.

Grabbing the phone once again, I checked the screen. Nothing!

Well if that was the way he wanted it... I guess Darnell and I were over for real.

"Fine!" I said and threw the phone onto the bed.

But truth be told, I was anything but fine.

***

It was almost six o'clock and I had barely moved. I tried cleaning to take my mind away from Darnell, but that was too boring. Then, I tried cooking, but I wasn't hungry. So, I laid down and stared at the phone. But there was no way that I could do that any longer. If I didn't do something, I was going to go crazy.

I wanted to be by myself, to sulk in this newness of singleness. But if I stayed alone, I was going to drown in sorrow. So, I forced myself to do something besides just stare at my cell phone screen. I tapped on a number.

"Helloo," Tia, my best friend since second grade, sang into the receiver.

"Hey, what do you have going on tonight?" I asked.

"Nothing, why what's up?"

"Misery wants company," I mumbled.

"Uh oh, let me order these guys some pizza and wings, then I'll be over."

I didn't know what guys she was talking about, but once I heard the cheering in the background, I figured that her husband, Jyaer, had some of his friends over.

"Give me twenty minutes," she said. "And I'm ordering a pizza and some wings for us since I know there'll be nothing left when I get home."

"Okay, see you in a bit," I said and hung up.

I decided to take a quick shower so that I wouldn't be sitting and waiting for Darnell. But then, just as I was relaxing for the first time all day, with the heat of the water beating on my back, I heard banging.

Turning off the water, I leaned my head out of the shower. Now I heard banging while someone leaned on the bell.

"What the...."

Clearly, it was an emergency, and after grabbing my robe, I took the stairs two at a time. Water was still dripping from my body, but I didn't care. Something bad was happening. I opened the door to a gust of cold air and a teenager holding two boxes in his hand.

"Here's your pizza!"

I blinked a couple of times. "Are you kidding me? Was it you banging and ringing my doorbell like somebody was chasing you?" I yelled.

"Listen *Linda*, I have to have this pizza in your hands within thirty minutes or it's free, and I been out here for almost five minutes. The clock's ticking."

I folded my arms. "First off, who is Linda, and I don't care about the clock you say is ticking," I snapped.

"Ma'am, please sign here if you want this pizza, it's cold out here."

I wanted to take the pen he had pointed in my direction and pop him in the mouth. Just as I reached out to do just that, headlights shined in my driveway and then, Tia jumped out of the car and headed to my door.

"Sorry I'm late, girl." She took the boxes and pen out the boy's hand and signed the slip. "And why are you at the door in a robe?"

I didn't answer her because I was too busy glaring at the teenager as she handed me the pizza boxes.

"Let me give you a tip, sweetheart," she said to the boy.

"Sweetheart?" I snapped. "Tip? This rodent doesn't deserve anything."

Tia looked at me with eyes so wide.

The teenager said, "Thank you, ma'am," to Tia, then to me, he added, "Your address is going on our Do Not Deliver list."

"And I'm adding you on my pest control list," I yelled as Tia shoved me into my own house.

She slammed the door shut and said, "Girl, what is going on with you? I've never in my life heard you say anything like that."

Her voice was filled with concern, as if she thought someone had taken over my body.

I wasn't ready to talk to her about it yet. "Let me go dry off and throw on something."

It took me just a few minutes and when I went back downstairs, Tia was curled up on the couch with a plate of pizza and chicken wings in front of her, laughing at the television. But when she glanced up at me, her smile went away and she signaled for me to sit down. She had my plate prepared and an opened bottle of wine sat in front of my food.

Tia turned the television off. "Ready to tell me what's going on?"

I took a breath. "Darnell broke up with me," I told her as I poured myself a glass of wine.

"Why?"

She sat in silence while I told her the entire argument. When I got to the end, I said, "The nerve of him, right?"

She paused a moment before she said, "No, this one is on you, girl."

That stunned me and hurt my feelings because Tia had been my girl from way back. "Oh, you Team Darnell now?"

"No, I'm Team Right and as your friend, it's my job to tell you when you're wrong. And today, you're wrong. He wants a full life with you, and you just dismissed him."

"He wasn't listening to me."

"You weren't listening to each other. But why don't you want kids? I never heard you say that before."

I shrugged. "I love my life. I mean, I barely want to marry Darnell."

Her eyes got big again. "I thought you loved him."

"I do. But I love my life. I love the freedom of doing what I want, when I want. I'm willing to sacrifice what I have to marry Darnell, but I don't want to add children to that mix."

"You'll be missing out on a lot without kids," she told me.

I shrugged. "And in today's times, marriages don't work out anyway."

"That's not true. Jyaer and I are just fine."

"You're the exception."

"What about your parents?"

"They're too old to divorce. But I'm sure they would if they could."

She shook her head. "You're just making excuses." She paused and said, "Though, I was surprised to find out Maurice and Olivia broke up and you didn't even tell me."

I frowned. "My brother, Maurice?"

Tia nodded. "Yeah. What other Maurice do you know who has a girlfriend named Olivia? They broke up, right?"

"Not that I know of. We were just texting and he didn't mention that."

"Well I'm not one to gossip, but I saw Olivia yesterday, downtown with this guy, laughing and carrying on. I just assumed...."

"That doesn't mean anything. Don't you have male friends?"

"Yeah, but I'm not strolling downtown in this cold weather arm-in-arm with them."

"Hmmm...." I hummed. Tia had a point there. Well, it looked like my brother was in the same position as I was. It wasn't going to be a Merry Christmas for either of us.

***

The next morning, the first thing I did was grab my phone and laptop and go downstairs. I turned on my tea pot and put two pieces of toast in the toaster before I opened my work email.

Even though it was Sunday, as the accounting department manager for a department store, I had to make sure all approvals for early check releases for tomorrow were completed. This was something we did for Christmas every year, and with the way I was feeling, this was going to be my only contribution to the joy of this season.

I completed that task, responded to emails, then sent a group email to my team letting them know that I would be working from home tomorrow and Christmas Eve. I was grateful for this kind of flexibility because I didn't feel like being around people right now. Especially not with all of their holiday cheer.

As I sipped my tea, I surfed the Internet, though my mind was on how horrible this Christmas was going to be. I thought about taking a trip somewhere, maybe to a cabin in the mountains -- something that Darnell and I had talked about doing after the new year. But now, I was contemplating taking that trip alone. It was just a dream, though. My parents would never allow me to spend Christmas away from them, even though all I wanted for Christmas was to be by myself.

With a sigh, I closed my laptop, and went back upstairs to soak in a hot bath. I enjoyed my lavender-scented bubble bath a little too much and by the time I got out, it was almost noon. I was supposed to be at my parents' house by one o'clock on Sundays, so I didn't have much time. I snatched a pair of jeans and pulled the first sweater I saw from the dresser. My purse and boots were already downstairs.

It was ten of one by the time I got in the car, but I still wasn't going to make it on time because I needed to stop and get flowers for my mother, something I did every Sunday. When I pulled up at my parents' house, it was a little after one-thirty.

I felt a feeling of foreboding as I walked up the driveway. I wanted to turn around and go home, but before I could do that, the front door opened and Maurice stepped out. My big brother pulled me into a hug.

"Be nice," he whispered in my ear as we stepped inside and he took my coat and purse.

He knew me too well. Turning around, the first face I saw was Latoya's.

"Finally decided to show up, huh?"

"Hi, Latoya," I said, even though I wanted to hit her with the flowers in my hand or better yet my purse because it was heavier.

She stood with her hand on her hip, I guess expecting more from me. I gave Maurice another glance and again, he mouthed, "Be nice."

So, I smirked and walked right past her.

Inside the family room, my dad sat with Latoya's husband, Claude. I waved to both of them, though I knew my father was surprised that I didn't stop to give him a hug. Inside the kitchen, when I saw Maurice's girlfriend, Olivia, I paused. So, she and Maurice hadn't broken up? Then what was she doing hanging out with other guys? Was she cheating on my brother?

"Hey Ashley," she greeted me.

I glared at her and went over to my mom who was standing at the stove.

"Hi, Mommy. Sorry I'm late," I said.

"Hey, baby, those flowers are so pretty. Put them in water for me," she said to me as she handed a dish to Olivia to take into the dining room.

Once Olivia left the kitchen, my mom said, "One o'clock means one o'clock, young lady, do you understand?"

"Yes," I responded as I put down her flowers and at the same time, wished that I had stayed at home. "Is there anything you need me to do?"

"No, everything is taken care of," she said.

That was my mother's way of dismissing me, so I went into the dining room, greeted my nieces and nephews and then, sat down at the table with my father, Claude, and Latoya who had already taken their seats.

When my mother came into the dining room, carrying another dish, she frowned. "Ashley, where's Darnell?"

Before I could answer, Latoya piped in, "He's probably late, just like his girlfriend."

That set me off. "Mind your business and worry about your man and those three roaches you got sitting over there."

"Did you just call my kids roaches?" Latoya shouted.

"Ashley!" I heard my mother say.

"That wasn't very nice, Ashley." Olivia shook her head.

"You got something to say to me?" I smirked. "You need to mind your business, too, Olivia. Or else I'll tell everyone how you're hanging out with another guy."

"Oh my," I heard Claude say.

"I cannot believe you called my kids roaches," Latoya yelled, sounding like she was going to cry. She told her kids to go into the other room.

While she did that, Maurice sat down next to Olivia. "What guy is she talking about?"

"I...I don't know," she said. "I don't know what your sister is talking about."

"I'm going to excuse myself," Claude said before my sister told him to sit his ass back down.

Then, Latoya said, "You need to apologize, Ashley."

I shrugged. "I don't have anything to apologize for. I'm not sorry. I was telling the truth. You do breed kids like roaches and Olivia is seeing someone else."

"Ashley!" my dad yelled.

"What, Daddy Dearest," I said with a smirk. That was something that I used to call my father when we were younger and he punished me. It was a name he hated.

My mother lowered herself into her chair and held her head as everyone shouted, demanding apologies from me. I did want to apologize to my mom -- but everyone else? Bump that!

"Enough," Maurice boomed, stopping all talking. "Ashley," Maurice glared at me. "Why are you trying to make everyone miserable?"

I pushed back my chair and stomped out of the room before I said something to Maurice. Me? Making everyone miserable? Did he notice the way Latoya had come for me? And Olivia? He needed to know the truth about that whore.

Maurice followed me into the family room. "What is going on?"

"Nothing. Everybody ganged up on me."

"No, they didn't. You called the kids roaches. And the stuff about Olivia, if you suspected something, you should have talked to me."

"I just found out," I said. "So, she is cheating on you?"

"No. You must have been talking about when she picked up one of my frat brothers who came into town to surprise me."

Dang!

"And this Daddy Dearest stuff, you need to stop that."

Before I could explain, my mom came into the room, her expression pain-stricken.

"Mommy-" I started, but she put her hand up to stop me.

"Ashley, I love you, but for right now, I think it would be best if you left."

"What?" I stood up straight.

Her stance nor her words changed. "Something is going on with you and until you get your act together and can come back as the loving Ashley that we know, then you're not welcome here."

"What?" I repeated as if that was all I could say.

"And that includes Christmas."

I couldn't believe my mother was saying this to me, but if that was what she wanted, then I was out. "Fine," I said and stomped toward the front door. I jerked open the closet, got my coat and purse, and marched out.

My brother came after me as I was getting into the car.

"Ashley, you know Mama didn't mean anything."

"She meant exactly what she said."

"No, she's just upset. You'll be over here for Christmas."

"No, I won't, but don't worry about it. I'm cool. All I want for Christmas is to be alone anyway." Then, I shut my door and pulled off, leaving Maurice standing there.

I guess I was gonna get my Christmas wish after all.

***

By the time I got home, my plans were made. I never liked intruding on anyone on a Sunday, but I called my director and informed him that I needed to take an emergency leave.

"Are you okay?" Mr. Mossdale asked.

"Yes, I'm fine. I still have plenty of vacation time left over."

"I'm not worried about that. I'm concerned about you."

"It's all good. Just something came up." I had to assure him a few more times before I was able to hang up and make my next call.

When Tia answered, I told her everything that happened at my parents' house.

"Wow, Ashley. I'm really worried. This is just not like you."

"Why does it have to be me? Everyone else was ganging up on me."

"I know, but still--"

"Look, I didn't call for a lecture."

"That's not what I'm doing."

"I called to let you know that I'm going away."

"When?"

"Now."

"Where?"

"To a place called Smokey Mountains. Darnell and I were going to go there, but this is as good a time as any."

"You can't go now. Christmas is Wednesday."

"I'm leaving as soon as I hang up from you."

"So, you'll be gone for Christmas?"

"You're a genius; you figured it out."

The way she went silent, I knew I'd hurt her feelings. And I didn't mean to. That's exactly why I needed to get away. I was hurting everyone.

I tried to soften it up. "So, do you want the information? I only called you so that someone would know where I was."

There was still so much reluctance in her tone, but she took the information, and then I hung up before she could lecture me some more. Less than an hour after I got home, I was back on the road -- to spend my Christmas alone.

***

I got to the mountains in a little under five hours and received a great surprise at check-in.

"One of the pipes burst in the cabin you reserved, so we're gonna put you in the one next door," the little old white-haired lady said to me. "Don't worry. It's an upgrade."

She led me to the cabin and it was an upgrade for real. Instead of the two-bedroom cabin I'd reserved, I now had a six-bedroom, four-bathroom space on three levels. There were fireplaces in every bedroom, in the living room, and the family area. And even though I liked the natural woodsy decor with bright colors, what I loved most was the pine fragrance in the air.

And then, there was the kitchen. Tomorrow I needed to go to the grocery store because the kitchen was gourmet style and I loved to cook for Darnell.

There he was again, forever in my thoughts.

Thinking of him took the smile off my face, but I stayed gracious to the lady who filled me in on the lodge's activities and then left me with a pamphlet of the resort. Once alone, I texted Tia and sent pictures. She texted me back the emoji with the mouth hanging open. That made me smile again, though I was still sad inside. All I wanted to do was take a shower and then go to sleep, and that's just what I did.

The heat of the sun warmed me before I even opened my eyes. I hadn't closed the curtains on the massive windows in the master bedroom last night. There was no need. The only thing that faced my window were the massive snow-capped mountains.

Glancing at the clock, I couldn't believe it was almost ten. I never slept this late, but it felt good today. Well, except for my growling stomach.

Showering and dressing as quickly as I could, I was down in the town within an hour, shopping at the small grocery store, roaming through the stores, and then stopping at a coffee shop for tea and a croissant. Back at the cabin, I settled outside on the balcony, sipping tea and enjoying the quiet of this space and the beauty of this view.

It was so peaceful, though I couldn't say that I felt peace. I was family-less, boyfriend-less, alone two days before Christmas. But wasn't this what I wanted?

I thought it was. I thought this was the way to get over my breakup with Darnell. The man who'd told me he'd love me through everything. But then, he didn't. I guess he wanted kids more than he wanted me.

The thought of that made me sigh. I just hoped that my Christmas wish would help me get me back to my old self.

I stayed on the balcony for hours, not going inside until my stomach growled again. I was about to make myself a sandwich, when my phone vibrated. I was sure it was Tia, but it wasn't.

WHAT ARE YOU DOING AT THE MOUNTAINS?

The all caps text from my brother made me sigh.

Hello.

TAKE THAT PHONE OFF DO NOT DISTURB AND ANSWER MY CALLS.

I texted back. *I'm okay, Maurice, and I love you. Ttyl.*

I'M NOT PLAYING.

I put the phone down, figuring if I didn't answer him, he'd stop texting me. But my phone vibrated again.

"Ugh!" I screamed before I picked up my phone. But this time, the text was from Tia.

Sorry, I had to tell Maurice. He came to my house.

I texted back. *It's cool, I know how he is. I'm turning this phone off. You have the cabin number in case of emergency. Do I need to define emergency?*

Her text back made me smile. *Lol, shut up and okay, but if I don't hear from you on Christmas, I'll give the number to Maurice.*

I laughed, but knew she wasn't kidding. I turned my phone off, tucked it inside my pocketbook, then pulled out a journal I'd purchased at the beginning of the year to write down all the things I was grateful for. That had been one of my New Year's resolutions and here I was at the end of the year, but I figured I'd get a head start on next year's resolutions.

Sitting in front of the living room's fireplace, I began to write: what I'd been feeling, how I missed my family already and missed Darnell the most. I wrote about how my Christmas wish to be alone wasn't the best wish I'd ever made, but since it was granted, I was going to make the most of it. I wrote until I was tired and then, I wrote until I fell asleep right there on the living room sofa.

I didn't wake up at all during the night, didn't open my eyes until the sun once again assaulted me in the morning. If nothing else, I was getting some good sleep with this good air up here in the mountains.

***

Just like yesterday, I showered and dressed quickly, only this time, I didn't go into town. Instead, I ventured into the woods on a hiking trail that the lady who checked me in told me was safe.

Hiking wasn't something I'd ever done before and it was beautiful -- the quietness and the stillness, the evidence of God all around me. I ran into other hikers, but most of the time it was just me and nature and my thoughts. I followed the trail until it came back around the lodge and I was shocked to realize I'd walked for more than two hours.

It wasn't until I was back in my cabin that I realized how exhausting the walk/climb had been. Maybe it was because of the altitude. Or maybe it was because of my attitude. For the rest of the day, I parked myself in front of the television, watching Christmas movies, laughing sometimes, and crying a lot. I sat there, watching TV and eating sandwiches until once again, nighttime came and I gave into the restfulness of mountain sleep.

It wasn't until I woke up the next morning, counted the days, and realized... It was Christmas. Pushing myself up from the sofa, I wrapped myself inside the blanket and then trudged to the window.

Like my other two days here, the sun shone brightly, like it was its job to greet all the guests.

I stood there for a moment before I said, "Merry Christmas," thinking about how this was what I wanted. Christmas alone, away from my family who wanted to be away from me, too.

Turning from the window, I looked through the cabin. What was I going to do? How was I going to handle Christmas alone when in truth, I wanted my family. And I wanted Darnell, too.

I jogged up the stairs to the bedroom, grabbed my laptop and opened my email. I wasn't going to be spending Christmas with anyone, but I owed a few apologies and I wanted to send a couple of I love yous, too.

I wasn't sure who to start with, but before I could begin, I heard a knock on the door. Jogging down the stairs, I figured it was the lady from check-in, probably wanting to make sure that I was okay and wanting to spread a little Christmas cheer.

. "Good morning," I said before I even pulled back the door, and then, my mouth opened wide.

"Good morning and Merry Christmas to you, too," said Latoya, with her hands on her hips.

"What...are you doing here?" I stammered.

"Don't be asking no crazy questions." She walked past me. "It was a long drive and I hope you have plenty of food up here."

I stood frozen, even as my niece and nephew and Claude followed behind her, all saying, "Good morning and Merry Christmas."

Next came Maurice and Olivia, who both hugged me and told me (without words) that all was forgiven. By the time my mom and dad came through the door, my eyes were filled with tears. But it wasn't until the person who brought up the rear -- it wasn't until Darnell followed my parents, that I began to sob.

"What are you doing here?" I cried.

"I came for you. I love you, Ashley. And I'm sorry."

"No, I'm the one who's sorry. I love you, too. And if you want them, I'll have a dozen kids."

He laughed. "We'll have to talk about that."

"Well, before you talk about any kids," my dad said from inside, "isn't there something else you have to do?"

"Oh, yeah." Then, right there on the porch, Darnell got down on one knee and pulled a box from his inside coat pocket.

And before he even asked me, I knew for sure that I had all that I ever wanted for Christmas.

Venita is an Award Winning, National Best-Selling Co-Author of The Ex-Chronicles (Online Secrets). Venita's short story "Daddy's Girl" is featured in the Turning Trials into Triumphs anthology and she has a journal titled "A Bitter to Better Journey." Venita is currently working on her trilogy titled "A Family of Secrets." Stay in touch at www.VenitaAldermanSadler.com or on Amazon, Goodreads, Facebook and Instagram (Venita Alderman Sadler) and on Twitter (VenitaASadler).

Check out the other amazing anthologies from Brown Girls Books

www.BrownGirlsBooks.com

www.ingramcontent.com/pod-product-compliance
Lightning Source LLC
Chambersburg PA
CBHW031335170626
46807CB00002B/709